1ST EDITION

A MEMBER OF THE CLUB

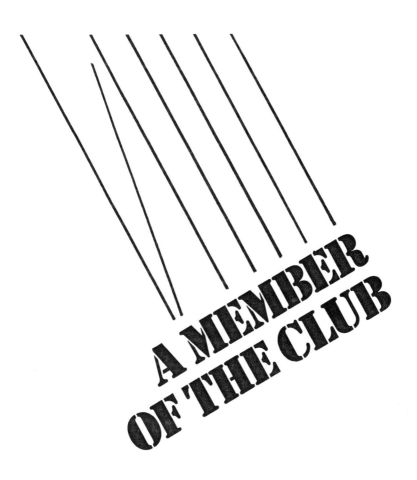

A MEMBER OF THE CLUB

a novel by

Peter Niesewand

IC Thomas Congdon Books   E.P. Dutton   New York

First American edition published 1979 by E.P.
Dutton, a Division of Elsevier-Dutton Publishing
Co., Inc., New York

First published in England 1979 by Martin Secker
& Warburg Limited

For information contact: E.P. Dutton, 2 Park
Avenue, New York, N.Y. 10016

Library of Congress Catalog Card Number: 79-51652

ISBN: 0-525-15495-7

10 9 8 7 6 5 4 3 2 1

When they arrived at the arena, the place was seething with the lust for cruelty. They found seats as best they could and Alypius shut his eyes tightly, determined to have nothing to do with these atrocities. If only he had closed his ears as well! For an incident in the fight drew a great roar from the crowd, and this thrilled him so deeply that he could not contain his curiosity . . . So he opened his eyes. When he saw the blood, it was as though he had drunk a deep draught of savage passion.

St Augustine's *Confessions*

ONE

It was their third day of marching, and Jan Rousseau could feel his senses sharpening. His hearing had become acute, as it never was in town, listening beyond the sound of boots on the hard-baked earth, and the bushes and grass swishing to one side as they pushed through, or the intermittent low buzz of a fly's wings around his head before it landed to drink the sweat, separating these sounds out and concentrating on the silence of the bush by day, listening for distant human voices, or the movements of animals. At night, as he and the other three tried to sleep, taking turns to sit guard for four-hour stretches, the sounds changed. All around were the insect noises, sharp and loud in the darkness and carrying far, the whine of mosquitoes circling, then breaking off abruptly as they landed to feed – too light even to feel until the itch began around their bite; and, occasionally, the far-off trumpeting of an elephant. Jan lay in his sleeping bag with his boots and socks off and stared at the stars. With the harshness of the sun gone, the air had a cold edge to it. Sleep, when it came, was shallow and brief. His ears listened constantly beyond the insistent chirping of the crickets and the lazy, infuriating whine of the mosquitoes, for other noises.

A column of men, whether villagers returning from a beer-drink, or terrorists moving to an objective, would probably make some sound, even if they were not talking. One man might cough, and the noise would echo through the darkness like a rifle shot. Another could stumble in the darkness and curse. Perhaps there would just be the rustling of a bush. Or a man might light a cigarette, and even that brief grating of match against box would carry two, even three hundred yards at night. In sleep, Jan Rousseau was listening.

The days in the bush had made his eyes alert too, attracted by the slightest unusual movement, scanning the ground for clues about who had passed that way recently.

He paused from time to time to examine broken grasses, and then inspected the surrounding dust for footprints or spoor. He picked up animal droppings, mostly from buck, and crumbled them in his fingers to test for warmth, smelt them for freshness, examined the area to see in which direction the animal had gone, and decided whether it alone had been responsible for snapping the dry grass stalks. His eyes watched particularly for signs of man. He found one or two scuff-marks in the dust made by the bare feet of tribesmen. There were several small kraals scattered over the area, and he paid little attention to these. What he wanted to find were bootprints with distinctive crisscross patterns, for the men who made these marks were his quarry.

Jan Rousseau smoked when he was at home; in the bush on a mission such as this, neither he nor his men were allowed such city luxuries. Just as cigarettes blunted a man's sense of taste, so they also affected his ability to pick up smells of the bush: smoke from a woodfire, for instance, or a cigarette, which carried faintly on the wind. As Rousseau and his men moved nearer their objective, through thorn scrub and dried grasses, their bushcraft became more important. Their orders were to avoid making contact with anyone. Although the area was sparsely populated, it was not an easy task. The map supplied by the army forward HQ had the known bantu kraals marked, but there was no guarantee that it was comprehensive, and there was always the chance of coming across hunters or a group collecting firewood.

The day was oppressive, although on the horizon clouds gathered. Jan and his comrades moved on, fit men, used to exercise: walking easily at first despite the heavy packs on their backs and the R1* rifles slung across their shoulders, but tiring as the temperature rose and the loads began to cramp their muscles. About two miles further on, the thorn bushes thickened and the ground rose sharply into a rocky kopje. They would rest there.

Behind him, one of his men cleared his throat and said quietly, "Gott. Jesus. It's bloody hot."

Rousseau turned and pointed to the small hill. "Half an hour, then we'll have a break."

"Shit, Jannie. Can't we have a break now, man?"

* The R1 rifle is the South African-manufactured equivalent of the Belgian FN.

"Half an hour. I've got to take bearings from the top of the kopje."

They moved on, the sweat running from their bodies. Jan Rousseau felt it trickle down from his hair, and he wiped heavily at it with his fist before it ran into his eyes. Like the others, he wore no shirt under his lightweight camouflage jacket, yet the jacket itself was wet with perspiration. His tight shorts were also becoming soaked and he could feel chafing around the insides of his thighs. He looked back at the others again, and saw that they were beginning to hunch over as the sun climbed towards midday.

"Try to keep a decent lookout, for Christ's sake," he said softly. "You look like your bloody mothers carrying a sack of coal up some stairs."

"Fuck."

"Come on, Viljoen. Maybe your girlfriend's going to be waiting on top of that kopje."

"Fuck that too. I couldn't do anything about it. I'm too shagged."

"That's a sad story. Let's move."

They walked in silence, the kopje not seeming to get any closer. Jan Rousseau felt not just tiredness now, but that his energy was being sapped. He would have to remember to take another salt tablet when they rested, and they must also look for more water soon. His own bottle was less than quarter full, and he knew the others would be in a similar, or worse, position.

Even before he was sure he had heard or seen anything, some instinct made him freeze, and he knew without turning that the others were motionless, too. They scanned the bush ahead. Jan felt his nostrils flare like an animal's as he tried to pick up a strange scent. There was nothing. Their ears strained for a sound but none came.

Behind him Viljoen said softly, "See anything, Jannie?"

Rousseau shook his head.

"Well let's get to that kopje, then," Viljoen said.

"No, wait. There's something there. I don't know what it is. Get cover. Keep down."

Almost doubled over, they ran for some rocks and dropped behind them. Jan Rousseau fumbled in the webbing of his belt to

3

open the binocular case, raised himself on his elbows and edged to the side of his rock. He checked the position of the sun to make sure it would not reflect off the lenses and give away their presence. Slowly he inspected the scrub and grass ahead from left to right, then back again. Nothing. The earth was baking as he lay upon it, and he felt the sun beating down on his back and his bare, tanned legs. He lowered the glasses, rested them on a stone, and listened.

A faint sound. Someone was out there, hidden from sight in the bush. He couldn't be sure of the direction. He glanced across at the others. They had heard it, too. It came again: a man's voice, and a laugh. With his hand, Rousseau motioned to the others to keep flat. He took the glasses and scanned the bush.

Two black figures were picking their way through the scrub. He focused on them. One was an old man; the other, perhaps his son. They were moving across the path of his squad, not towards them. Jan turned on his side and held up two fingers to indicate the number ahead, and motioned the direction they were taking. Then he studied them again. The young man was twenty to thirty, shabbily dressed. It didn't look as if he was armed. The old man was carrying something – difficult to see – but it looked like a stick and not a rifle. Rousseau watched them out of sight and waited ten minutes. Jesus, it was hot. At last he inspected the area again with his glasses and stood slowly up. The others followed. He motioned them forward, and they resumed their march to the kopje. After five minutes, Rousseau spotted the footprints of the tribesmen in the dust and squatted down to inspect them. Both bantu had been wearing shoes, but there were no patterns on the soles. The squad moved on, more cautiously now because they could be near a kraal. There was no way of knowing where the tribesmen had come from or what they were doing. The twenty minutes lying in the hot dust had served as a rest from the weight of their packs: that, and the possible presence of others nearby, gave them a second wind.

Rousseau knew that all of them, even Viljoen, were listening and watching as they walked, and their backs were no longer bent under the rations and equipment in their rucksacks to a point which reduced the efficiency of their lookout.

As they neared the kopje, Rousseau led them in a skirting

movement to the north which kept them in the cover of thorn scrub and gave them a closer look at the small hill in case anyone was up there. It also brought them to a point where the climb would be easier, yet would still be sheltered by rocks and bushes. As soon as they went up the kopje, they risked being exposed to view. When he was satisfied, Rousseau doubled over and ran the fifty yards to the point where the land rose, and began the climb. Behind him he could hear Viljoen. They dropped behind some rocks and waited. After a minute, the other two joined them.

"We'll keep to the cover of that line of rocks, OK?" Rousseau said. The others nodded.

There was no need to run now, and anyway the climb was a stiff one. The men were panting when Rousseau finally chose a point near the summit, shaded by a rock and some bushes, and unhitched his pack. They slumped, exhausted, and let their muscles relax. Several minutes passed and no one moved.

At last, Jan Rousseau rolled over onto his side and fumbled in the pouches of his webbing for the map of the area. He got to his feet and walked the remaining short distance to the summit where, still being careful to stay close to cover, he opened the map out on a rock and looked round. From the kopje, the land stretched flat towards the horizon: grass baked dry and brown, with green clumps of thorn trees, although even those looked dry and brittle. On the horizon there were some more kopjes, and as he lifted his binoculars he could see a rim of green in the distance. That must be the river. They could make it there by nightfall, but from this point on they would have to be even more careful for they were approaching their objective.

Rousseau studied the map and consulted his compass. They had made good progress. The day after tomorrow they would split up and complete their appointed tasks. Afterwards, they would march back to base.

He worked out a map reference for their position and converted it into the day's code. Then he climbed down, his boots kicking a small shower of stones, to where the men lay talking quietly.

"Come on, boetie,*" he said to Viljoen. "Get the radio set up."

Viljoen got to his feet reluctantly.

* Brother.

"Gott, I could do with a smoke," he complained.

"Next week," Rousseau said. "You can do what you like next week."

Viljoen unclipped the manpack transceiver and set it on a rock with the aerial clear of trees. He switched it on and consulted his notes for the frequency. When he was ready, he said: "OK, Jannie. You can be disc-jockey."

Rousseau put on the headset and picked up the microphone. He depressed the transmit button and the hum of the transceiver died as the energy of the batteries was diverted into pushing out the signal.

"Four-two. Signals, over."

The transceiver hummed again as they waited for a response, but none came.

He said again: "Four-two. Signals, over."

Still nothing. Viljoen said, "Try another position, Jannie."

Rousseau picked up the transceiver and carried it two hundred yards to a small clearing nearer the summit.

He tried again: "Four-two. Four-two. Signals, I say again, signals, over."

He listened through the static, and a voice came back: "Four-two, signals two, over."

Rousseau thought, oh shit, that's not very good. He raised an arm and beckoned Viljoen across.

"Four-two, OK," he said into the microphone. "Wait."

Viljoen asked: "Still nothing?"

"No, boetie, I've got them, but they're only hearing me strength two."

"It's not their lucky day. How do you hear them?"

"Strength five. Is there anything we can do?"

"We could put up a di-pole aerial if you want. Have you got a lot to say?"

"No, just our position."

"Then let them suffer."

Rousseau shrugged. He depressed the transmit button. "Four-two, message, over."

"Four-two, send, over."

"Four-two, Voortrekker eight-zero-zero-four; extra two-one-nine-zero. Roger so far, over?"

There was a pause, then the voice said: "Four-two, say again, over."

Rousseau repeated the message slowly.

"Four-two, OK, over," came the reply.

So far, so good, thought Rousseau. Now they just need to know we haven't picked up anything yet.

"Four-two, no contact, repeat, no contact, over," he said.

"Four-two, Roger, over and out."

He switched off the transceiver and looked across at Viljoen. "That's it," he said. "We'll have another half-hour rest and then get moving."

Viljoen nodded and walked back to rejoin the others. Jan Rousseau stayed where he was, in the shade of a Msasa tree, and leaned back against a rock. They were near now, and sitting by himself he could feel the fleeting shadow of apprehension in his chest: the shallower breathing, a heartbeat which was starting to become noticeable, the things inside that he'd fought against all his life.

He looked out over the land of Northern Natal and into Mozambique. The border would be near that river, the narrow green rim on the horizon. Beyond that would be the camps and villages suspected of giving the terrorists food and shelter. It was difficult to tell which village was guilty and which innocent, but soon there would be no doubt. They would seek out these places and go up to them late at night, fitting on trees, digging into the ground, hiding among rocks, the tiny specialist pieces of electronic equipment which the South African Defence Forces were now using: the battlefield sensors which detect infra-red heat emissions given out by engines, or by people as they walk near; the tiny chemical "sniffers" which identify the presence of explosives; the sensors which respond to ground vibrations caused by vehicles.

Each device was equipped with its own low-power transmitter, and the information they relayed would be picked up by local surveillance centres on the South African side of the border and fed into the computers. Then the government would know where terrorists were, and in approximately what numbers, without having to commit thousands of troops to patrolling wide areas of the country.

The computer-controlled defence system, deep inside solid rock a thousand miles away at Silvermine, and proof against nuclear attack, would watch for them. What the sensors felt, and smelt, would decide which village would be punished, which destroyed. Jan Rousseau and his men carried the means to accomplish this in their webbing packs. Up and down the border with Mozambique, along the Eastern Transvaal, in the Kruger National Park, around the Swaziland border, and east of them in Natal, other similar squads were moving into selected areas. Finding the enemy was always the biggest problem in a guerrilla war, and now they had machines which would help them do it.

But first the sensors had to be in position and working properly, and the men had to get back undetected. The border with Mozambique was still officially open, and thousands of tons of South African cargo continued to be shipped out through the Mozambique port of Maputo. But everyone knew this situation wouldn't last.

Already more guerrillas were starting to filter through, better armed, better trained. Their Cuban advisers had got the whites out of Rhodesia and now they were turning their full attention onto South Africa. Rousseau and his men knew that their country was next on the list.

Time to move. Rousseau stood up and lifted the transceiver by its webbing straps. He hunched his back to sling it over his shoulders, and as he did his eye was fleetingly caught by a mark in the sand. It had been in shade before, but the movement of the sun had exposed it plainly to view. Rousseau dumped the manpack transceiver instantly and went across to crouch by the mark. Half of it was indistinct, smeared by the boots of either himself or Viljoen, but the criss-cross pattern was unmistakable. Rousseau cursed himself for not having seen it before: for letting his guard drop just because they were having a break. There must be dozens of similar marks all around them, although they'd probably obliterated many through carelessness. He felt foolish and ashamed. He had radioed back that they had made no contact, when he was practically sitting on terrorists' footprints.

The question was: how fresh were they? Rousseau studied the direction the man had walked and followed it. The terrorist had obviously been taking trouble to stay on rocks or stones as much as possible – which was more than he and his own men had done, Rousseau reflected bitterly – to cut down on the evidence left behind. Men spending even a few minutes in a confined area left literally hundreds of footprints, not to mention broken grass and sticks marking where they sat and walked.

For several yards there was no further sign of the man, and then suddenly there was a strong and clear bootprint where he had apparently overbalanced from a small rock and landed heavily in the dust. A short distance after that the kopje fell away into a sheer drop of fifty or sixty feet, and at that lookout point Rousseau found a burnt match. He picked it up and studied it. It had been burnt down almost its entire length. Either the terrorist smoked a pipe, which was unlikely because of the strong smell this gave out, or he had been lighting cigarettes for others as well as himself. Rousseau scratched in the sand with his fingers, and then widened his search to include the dry grassy area to the side, but he could find neither cigarettes nor pipe ash. The terrorists had probably stubbed them out on their boots and flicked the butts over the side.

Rousseau retraced the footprints back to the clearing where his transceiver lay, and down to where his men rested in the shade.

A lot of grass had been crushed, but there was no way of telling whether it had been done by the guerrillas or his own men. Occasionally there was the impression of the edge of a boot which was not Defence Force issue.

Viljoen asked: "Wat makeer, Jannie? What's wrong?"

"Fucking terrorist bootprints. They're all around."

The others scrambled to their feet.

"Shit, Jannie, where did you find them?"

"I was almost sitting on one of the bastards up there," Rousseau said bitterly. "OK, very carefully now, fan out and see what you can find. We've probably destroyed most of them around here. Boetie, go back the way we came; Cronje, to the east; and Venter, keep going down that path there. Get under cover as much as you can. Move."

Rousseau climbed onto a rock and surveyed the kopje. The terrorists had obviously tried to keep off sandy areas which would leave footprints, and this meant their paths would be confined to small rocks, which could act as stepping-stones, or dry grass areas. How would they do it?

Rousseau moved forward, stepping from stone to stone, and found himself going in a sweep round the side of the kopje. When he could go no further there was a clump of grass to jump onto, but he lowered himself carefully into the dirt and inspected the grass. The centre had been crushed by the weight of a man, or men, and some of the dry grass on the outside was broken or bent.

From that point on there was nothing immediate to step onto, and Rousseau found another bootprint. Then there were some small stones which could have been used, and beyond that virtually a dead end. Rocks on three sides, and the kopje beginning to slope down. Rousseau climbed halfway up between two of the rocks and glanced over, but could see nothing. He started to retrace his steps, but a sixth sense made him pause. He moved back to the rocks for a second look.

This time he hauled himself onto the top for a closer examination: nothing, except a steep and difficult climb down. Then he tried the western side, a much more difficult climb, one foot balancing on a small ledge while his hands pushed against two rocks, and he hauled his body up until he could get a firmer foothold.

It was easy from then on, and he dropped down into a narrow rocky clearing with boulders on either side. Through gaps he could see that the kopje dropped away sharply.

Rousseau pushed forward, and suddenly he saw the bootprints, dozens of them scuffed in the sand, with no attempt at disguise now in this hidden place. He squatted down to study the markings.

There had not been one man, but several. There were different boot sizes and some of the impressions were lighter and others heavier, varying with the weights of the terrorists. Had they slept there? It was not impossible, but it was too narrow to make a natural choice. So what had they been doing?

Rousseau moved on, his legs spread apart, one foot on each stony side of the passageway so as not to disturb the bootprints, until he reached the end, blocked off by a huge rock. To one side was a pile of small rocks and stones, and as soon as he saw it Rousseau knew what lay beneath.

He picked up the stones carefully and laid them to one side. Underneath the earth was freshly dug, and he scooped it away with his hands.

The dirt which covered the black plastic bags of arms and explosives was only two inches thick, and within a minute he was hauling out the cache. It was hard, hot work. He unwrapped twelve anti-personnel mines from their heavy-duty plastic covering and examined the communist markings on them, and twenty Kalashnikov rifles. Beneath these were the boxes of ammunition. He bent his legs and squatted down to take hold of the heavy cases, then tensed his body and hauled them to the surface: seven or eight thousand rounds in all.

Jan Rousseau was sweating heavily. Christ, if only he knew how long it had been since the terrorists had hidden the arms, and where they were now.

He retraced his steps along the passage, making sure he did not disturb the criss-cross bootprints, and climbed back over the rocks. The others were back at the clearing where they had rested.

"What did you find?" Rousseau asked.

"Nothing," Viljoen said. "If they came up the same path as us, there's nothing to show for it."

Cronje said: "Not a bloody thing down there, either."

"Venter?"

The fourth man shook his head. "Nothing."

"OK. There's an arms cache hidden in the rocks round there."

"Shit, bloke. How did you find that?" Viljoen asked. "That's bloody fantastic."

"Their footprints are all around it," Rousseau said. "And they left a pile of rocks to mark the spot."

"What have they got?"

"Kalashs. Mines. Ammo. The usual."

Venter said: "What are we going to do? We're not supposed to be here."

"We're going to leave it – re-bury it and cover our tracks."

"Fantastic," Viljoen said laconically. "They'll use one of the Kalashs to shoot your ouma*, and you'll get your balls blown off stepping on one of the mines."

"No I won't," Rousseau said. "We're going to leave a surprise

* Grandmother.

for these bastards. I need two sensors: one a sniffer, the other infra-red. Cronje, fix me up a pound of gelignite with a remote-control detonator."

He turned to Viljoen: "Boetie, get the sensors. Venter, cut four small branches and then start going over everywhere you've walked and brush out your footprints. We don't want anyone to know we've been here."

The men got to work. Viljoen unstrapped his webbing pouches and sorted out the sensors. They were grey and brown metal objects, no bigger than a matchbox, and from each protruded a small wire aerial.

Rousseau led Viljoen to the rocks which blocked the entrance to the hidden corridor.

"What we want to do, Boetie, is to leave a sniffer somewhere round here so it can tell the computer if more weapons are being brought up. If they're going to store more stuff here, we don't want to stop them taking it in: just bringing it out."

Viljoen glanced at the rocks around. "That's easy enough," he said. "Where are the weapons?"

"Behind that lot." Rousseau gestured to the rocks on the western side.

"Christ, they carried it up there?"

"There must have been at least three of them doing it. Probably more."

Viljoen looked round again, then made his decision.

"Jannie, come over here and give me a piggyback."

Rousseau squatted down in the dust, and the other man straddled his shoulders. "OK, go," Viljoen said, and Rousseau pushed himself upright, staggering slightly to keep his balance.

"Closer to the rock," Viljoen said.

Rousseau stood with his face and body almost brushing against the rocky side, while Viljoen set the sensor into a small recess. It took less than a minute.

"Ja, OK," he said. "That's it."

Rousseau lowered him onto the ground and flexed the cramping muscles in his shoulders and neck.

"You need to lose some weight, boetie."

"You need more exercise, Jannie, that's your trouble. You're getting fat."

Rousseau punched him on his thick forearm. "Let's get the gelly before we go in. Cronje should have it ready by now."

Rousseau walked a few paces back until he could see the man still bending over the small package of explosive. When he was ready Cronje stood up and carried it across, wrapped in yellow plastic.

"Thanks," Rousseau said. "You've kept the remote-control code number?"

"Ja. Of course." Cronje looked at him with faint hostility.

"Good bloke. Now can you get a branch from Venter and brush out your footprints?"

Cronje nodded and turned away. Rousseau wondered what was eating him, but shrugged. There were too many things to do now to worry about that.

Rousseau and Viljoen clambered over the rocks and into the clearing, then, legs apart, shuffled along the stony sides of the passageway until they came to the arms cache. Viljoen whistled. "Not bad," he said. "It'll make quite a bang."

Rousseau nodded. "I want the infra-red sensor somewhere here so it can tell the computer when the terrorists get back and how many there are. The sniffer will say whether they're bringing in arms or not. If they are, we can let them store them. If they're taking stuff out, then the computer can detonate the gelly and the whole lot will go up."

"I'd like to see it. It'll be better than Guy Fawkes."

"So where do you want to put the sensor?" Rousseau asked.

Viljoen looked around. The boulder at the end of the narrow passage had grass growing at its base, and he went to inspect it, parting the dry strands carefully and feeling behind for crevices. He found a small one and pushed the infra-red box inside it. A centimetre or two projected out of the end, but the grass covered it completely.

"Fine," Rousseau said. "Now we've got to plant the gelly where it will set off everything else."

"What about at the bottom of the hole?"

"Will the detonator be able to pick up a strong enough signal to blow?"

"You bet it will."

"OK. Let's get everything packed back in."

Rousseau laid the gelignite with its remote-control detonator in the hole, and the two men replaced the ammunition boxes, Kalashnikovs and mines on top of it, and covered the cache with soil and stones.

When they had finished, Rousseau inspected their work. A terrorist would not be able to tell that anyone else had been there.

They went back to join the others. While the job of covering their tracks was completed, Rousseau got out his codebook and composed a message to the surveillance centre telling them what he had done, and giving them the individual code numbers for the sensors and the remote-control device being operated at that map reference.

Communications from his manpack transceiver were slightly better than before, but Rousseau had to repeat the message three times before it was acknowledged. From the local surveillance centre, the information was fed into the Troposcatter communications system – a powerful over-the-horizon signal focused into a pencil beam and feeding into the underground complex at Silvermine, near the Simonstown naval base.

From that moment, computers monitored the small kopje near the Mozambique border, and held the power of life and death for a group of unknown men.

Rousseau and his squad hitched their packs back on and climbed down. They had been at the kopje for three hours, and now they were running behind schedule. They had to be at the river by nightfall.

TWO

John Courtney straightened his red-and-blue striped tie in the mirror as the lift took him up to the board-room. He was to give the presentation-to-client of the new baby milk campaign, and he was unaccustomedly nervous. If they could land the Nu-Kreem account, it would be one of the biggest on the agency's books. They certainly needed it.

Politically, things had been going badly in South Africa, and whenever things went badly, businessmen cut back. One of the first casualties was advertising.

Van Niekerk and Tessler was among the biggest of the home-grown advertising agencies and, in common with the others, they had been affected by the recession. There was talk of sacking staff. Nu-Kreem would help put them back on solid ground again.

The campaign was to launch a new baby milk product designed primarily for the bantu market. John Courtney reflected that baby products aimed at whites always did well, regardless of the state of the economy, because whatever else they might cut back on few white parents were prepared to stint their offspring. But this lucrative market in baby milk was already held by established products, and in any case the main selling point of the Nu-Kreem version was that it was cheaper.

If it had been a car or a box of soapflakes, rather than something to feed a child, a lower price might have attracted white customers, but few European parents would want to save a few cents on a pack of baby milk. The reverse was true, in fact. If Nu-Kreem wanted to break into the white market, and if these had been boom times, John Courtney would have recommended making the price five or six cents more expensive than any other milk, to give them a chance. Snob appeal, and the idea that cost equalled quality, could have carried it through. But the bantu market was the one to concentrate on now.

The lift stopped on the thirtieth floor. John Courtney picked up his brief-case, glanced for the last time in the lift mirror, and stepped out.

The air-conditioning in the corridor was cooler, and the carpeting thicker, than in the rest of the building. In the background, Muzak soothed. He walked through the foyer, lush with potted plants and ferns, and grinned at the blonde receptionist.

"Morning, Mr Courtney," she said, the thickness of her accent contrasting with the delicacy of her features.

"Hello, Sarie," he said. "Is Ron in yet?"

"Yes, he's ready for you. The two nanny-girls look really sweet."

"Oh," Courtney said. "Good."

He walked further down the corridor, knocked briefly on the door of Room 3067 and went in. Ron Prentice, one of the senior account executives, looked up from a pile of huge cardboard sheets, pasted and painted with ideas for the campaign.

"Morning, John. You haven't seen these final paste-ups yet, have you?"

"No. Are they any good?"

"Look fine to me."

Courtney flipped through the charts with their bold Letraset captions, the comic strips of black nurses and smiling babies, and the layouts for newspaper advertisements.

"They're good," he said finally. "What about the nurses?"

"They're next door, in the messengers' room," Ron Prentice said. "I wasn't going to have them sitting around my office, thanks very much."

"What do they look like?"

"They look like kaffir nannies in Red Cross uniforms. What do you think they look like? At least they don't smell."

Courtney felt a surge of irritation. "They're not kaffirs, Ron. They're bantus."

Prentice shrugged. "Call them what you like. Bantu nannies. They're still not going to sit in my office. I'll send them down to yours."

"I'll go and have a look." Courtney walked back into the corridor and put his head through the door of the small room – little more than a cubicle – where the two black messengers who serviced that floor and made the tea were stationed. Two young black women in smart white and red nurses' uniforms were sitting on hard wooden chairs. When they saw him, both rose to their feet. The hands of one twisted nervously in front of her. Both kept their gaze somewhere round Courtney's knees.

"Good morning," Courtney said. "Let's have a look at you. Good. Now turn around. That's fine. Very good. Do you know what you have to do?"

The women shook their heads. "No, master."

"Well, we're giving a presentation-to-client. You know what

that is? Well, it just means I'm going to talk to a lot of people and show them some things, and then the lights are going to go out. When they do, the two of you will be standing behind some curtains. I'll show you where. There'll be two tins there. You pick those up and hold them in front of you like this." Courtney demonstrated, holding the imaginary tin at waist level, a hand top and bottom. "Don't be scared. Smile and look pleased, because what you're holding is very good for bantu babies. Do you understand?"

The women nodded.

"OK, fine," Courtney said. "Now there isn't another door into the board-room, and we're keeping both of you as a surprise, so I'm going to take you in now and show you where you must wait behind the curtain. You must stay there and not move. And don't talk. You can take the chairs from this room. We're not due to start for another half an hour at least, and then it will be about twenty minutes before you come out. Do you understand?"

They both nodded again.

"Right. Take those chairs and come with me." Courtney led the way down the corridor to the oak-panelled board-room with its modern overhead lighting. A white barman was setting out drinks and glasses along a table on one side, and two slide projectors were being positioned near the wall beside the door. Courtney escorted the women to the far side of the room where a screen had been erected in front of a velvet curtain. He pulled the curtain back to reveal a space eighteen inches in width.

"Put your chairs in here," Courtney said. "If you want to go to the lavatory, go now. There must be a bantu lavatory somewhere in the building. Do you want to go?"

The women shook their heads.

"Right," he said. "Remember, when the lights go out we'll be showing some slides. The two of you come out and go to this point here." He walked the five or six steps from the curtain to the spot where he would show off the women in their nurses' uniforms. "You," he said pointing at the one, "come over here. And you," summoning the other with his hand, "stand here. Remember to hold your tins the way I told you. Someone will bring them to you in a few minutes. Now another thing: don't handle the tins before you have to. I don't want to see them dirty by the time you get out. If your hands sweat, they'll leave marks. And for God's sake don't be nervous. You're supposed to be nurses. Smile. Look confident. OK?"

The women nodded: "Yes, baas."

"Good," Courtney said. "Then arrange your chairs and sit there. Don't move until the lights go out."

The women sat silently on the wooden chairs, and Courtney let the heavy velvet curtain fall to cover them. He looked at his watch. Twenty minutes to go.

He thought, God, I need a cup of coffee. Courtney walked back to Ron Prentice's office.

Prentice looked up. "What did you think they looked like, then?"

"They looked like nurses. That's what we're paying for them to look like. Have you got any coffee on the go?"

"The messengers are both out. You can ask Sarie if she wouldn't mind making you a cup."

Courtney passed a hand over his forehead in irritation. What he really needed was a drink. It was just after 11 a.m.

"We need to get those paste-ups into the board-room pretty soon so we can arrange them in order," Courtney said.

"The messengers should be back in a few minutes."

"Oh hell, I don't want to wait for that. I'll carry them through myself. Come and give me a hand."

The two men carried the cardboard sheets through to the board-room and stood them against a wall. Prentice returned to his office, and Courtney went across to the barman.

"Could you get me a Bloody Mary right away, please?"

"Yes, sir."

While it was being mixed, he sorted out the paste-ups and put them on an easel in order of use, and then he sat down on one of the velvet armchairs beside the main board-room table with his drink. He felt suddenly depressed. He'd had a preliminary meeting with the Nu-Kreem people, but he knew none of them well. Van Niekerk and Tessler were only one of the agencies bidding for the account, and the competition was strong. What could he say to them to swing it? What would the others have been saying?

Having the nurses was a good idea. Courtney glanced across to the velvet curtain, but could see no movement. He wondered if they were still there. Shit, he'd wring their necks if they'd gone. He got up, walked quickly across and pulled the curtain aside accusingly, and the two women, sitting silently, stared back at him. He felt a twinge of embarrassment.

"You all right there?" he asked, giving a quick smile.

"Yes, baas."

"Good. We'll be ready to start in about ten minutes."

Courtney went back to his chair and finished his Bloody Mary. It wouldn't be good for the clients to see him drinking that early in the morning. He handed his glass back to the barman.

"Would you like another, sir?"

"No thanks. That was fine."

Other members of the agency began drifting into the board-room: the creative directors of the various sections, a couple more account executives, and finally both Sydney Van Niekerk and André Tessler, which showed how much store the agency set on landing the account. They shook Courtney's hand and wished him luck.

"I hope you've done your homework, John," Tessler said. "I hear that the boys at the other agencies were given a rough time during their presentations."

Courtney raised his eyebrows. "Oh? What happened?"

"No details, I'm afraid. Apparently there were some hard questions from the Nu-Kreem boys. But we're the last scheduled presentation for the account, which is good for us. We're the last impression they'll take away before deciding."

"I hope it'll be a good one," Courtney said.

"We all hope it will be good. Your ideas for the campaign are fantastic. We all think so. Now we have to get them across."

Tessler turned as the door opened and the contingent from Nu-Kreem filed in. There were eight of them: starting with the Managing Director and ending with the Marketing Manager. Everyone shook hands.

When they were settled round the table, André Tessler gave a short speech of welcome then handed over to John Courtney.

Courtney walked over to the easel, which was covered with a green velvet cloth, and turned to face his audience. The Nu-Kreem Managing Director lit a large cigar and sat back in his chair, his face impassive. The Marketing Manager had already started making notes. Courtney smiled at them and hoped his voice wouldn't falter.

"Gentlemen," he said, "we know we're only one of a number of agencies competing for this account, and that the competition is very strong. But here at Van Niekerk and Tessler we feel we've got something special to offer you. As you know, this is a purely South African company. The directors are South African, and every member of the creative staff is South African. Of course, most of us have had experience overseas – you can see this from the high quality of our campaigns – but the point is, we're all local. *We know the bantu!* We're not immigrants, or a branch office of some overseas agency. Now *you* want to sell to the bantu and *we* can show you how to do it best. Everyone involved in this campaign knows what he's doing – and I can tell you we're all very enthusiastic about it.

"Of course we've carried out market-research. But behind everything in the campaign I'm going to outline to you now is something else as well: instinct, and local knowledge.

"Now I'm not saying that other agencies don't have South Africans working on proposals for your campaign, but what I am saying is that at Van Niekerk and Tessler every single person connected with it – every artist and every copywriter – is as South African as you are yourselves, gentlemen."

Courtney turned and pulled the green cloth from the easel, crumpled it into a ball and tossed it onto a chair. The white cardboard sheet had written across it on the top in bold, black letters: THE YEAR 2000. Everyone stared at it.

Beneath the heading, narrow white cardboard strips were slotted into position to cover other messages.

Courtney said: "The bantu population of South Africa now stands at thirty-five million, according to the latest census. More than half these people are under the age of sixteen. The bantu birth-rate is the highest of all population groups in this country."

Courtney pulled a cardboard strip from its slot. Beneath it was written: BANTU BIRTH RATE – 2.86%.

Courtney said: "It's 2.86 per cent, whereas the white growth-rate is only 2.04 per cent. Those are the latest official figures, but with the current uncertainty and the rise in white emigration, we'll probably find that figure for whites is down in the next statistics.

"What does this mean to the Nu-Kreem Corporation and its

new baby milk powder? It means a massive new and largely un-tapped market. Bantu women are receptive to the idea of pow-dered milk for their piccanins, rather than breast milk. More about that later.

"Where is this market, and how can we get to it? Well, of course, a lot of it is in the bantu homelands, and that can be reached with radio commercials, advertising in black magazines, and special promotions. But there's a significant and growing proportion of the black consumer market right at hand."

Courtney moved towards the easel again, and slid out a second cardboard strip.

The message said: 20,000,000 BLACKS IN WHITE AREAS.

"By the year two thousand, it is estimated that twenty million bantu will be living in townships surrounding the white areas. That may seem a long way away now, but the point I'm trying to make is that although the township market is very big already, it will grow to be phenomenal. Many of the men will be wage-earners. There must be a million or so babies in that figure. Their parents will be an easily reachable audience, and the Nu-Kreem product will be established as being significantly cheaper than other established brands.

"Now because it is cheaper we have to avoid giving the im-pression that it is in any way inferior to other products, so our campaign concentrates on the advantages that this milk will give to a bantu baby."

Courtney lifted the first cardboard sheet off the easel and rested it against the wall. The new sheet was the blow-up of a cartoon strip: ELIAS MAKES THE GRADE.

"The bantu we've chosen for this cartoon strip, designed for both newspapers and magazines, is a piccanin called Elias. This example shows the baby Elias being breast-fed by his mother. I hope you can see from back there that the piccanin is obviously discontented – perhaps not getting enough milk – and the mother looks worried."

The Nu-Kreem Managing Director fumbled for his glasses and peered across the table.

Courtney went on: "The next picture shows Elias crying through the night. The mother is holding her head in her hands and she's also crying, and the father is there in the background, trying to sleep and obviously very angry. The clock shows it's three in the morning.

"The third picture has the mother and father taking Elias to the clinic. You can see the clinic doctor has got the child's clothes off, and he's a pretty skinny and unhappy piccanin.

"And here's the product. The doctor hands it to Elias' mother, saying 'Your breast milk is no good. You must use this. It is better.' And this is a good point, gentlemen, to introduce you to what we propose you call the new baby milk powder."

Courtney stepped behind the easel and picked up a white and blue tin with a picture of a fat, happy black baby on it, and the product's name in red.

He held it up: "It's called BEST MILK. You'll see the link at once: BEST Milk – Breast Milk. It's short and memorable. And we use the slogan which you'll see at the end of this cartoon: BEST Feed Your Baby.

"In the rest of the cartoon you can see that Elias sleeps through the night, puts on weight, does well at school and then goes on to university – here he is getting his degree – and finally there we show him, happy and smiling, working as a clerk in a township Post Office."

Courtney removed the cardboard sheet and revealed another cartoon behind it. "In this version, we still start off with Elias crying all night and the clinic doctor telling his mother her breast milk is no good, but Elias goes on to become a body-builder, wins the Black Mr South Africa competition, and marries this bantu beauty queen."

Courtney let the audience study it for a few moments, and then unveiled the third cartoon. Here, Elias was shown growing up to be a great athlete, and winning a gold medal at the South African Games.

Then Courtney said: "Lights please, Steve," and the board-room was plunged into darkness. The slide-projector was switched on and the legend "BEST Feed Your Baby" was flashed onto the screen. Just outside the beam of light, Courtney could see the dim shapes of the two black women groping their way out from behind the velvet curtain to the places he had allocated them.

The next slide showed a fat and contented black baby being

held by its smiling mother. The caption read: "My own milk was no good, so the doctor told me to use BEST Milk. Now my baby will grow up to be a champion!" In the bottom right-hand corner was the red, blue and white pack, and the slogan "BEST Feed Your Baby". There were other slides in similar vein.

Courtney said: "Obviously, we propose spending most of the Best Milk budget on newspapers and magazines, and on radio ads as well, but we think that a big effort ought to be made in direct promotion, both out in the bantu homelands, and in the satellite townships. Lights, please."

There was a pause before the lights came on, and Courtney held out his right arm to indicate the two black women dressed as nurses. Fixed smiles on their faces, they stared back at the group of white men, who puffed cigarettes and cigars and looked at them incuriously.

"Saleswomen such as these," Courtney said, "would be given a basic grounding in child welfare, put into uniforms to maximise black consumer confidence, and then sent out into bantu areas. We propose that they take with them a large number of free samples. I have here a basic kit of what we have in mind."

Courtney opened a red, blue and white cardboard box and pulled out a cheap plastic feeding bottle and teat, a bottle brush and a small mock-up pack of Best Milk.

"This sample kit costs less than five cents, ordered in the sort of bulk we propose. The saleswomen would give them away, with instructions on how they should be used. This pack of Best Milk is enough to last a child for six days. By that time he should be weaned over to the product, and the mother's own milk supply will be drying up, so she'll go and buy some more."

The Nu-Kreem Managing Director made a waving motion with his cigar, and Courtney thought: here it comes.

"Mr Courtney," the Managing Director said, "that sounds very interesting. But what the other advertising agencies warned us of again and again was the danger – the danger to life, one of them called it – of over-selling a product like ours to un-sophisticated people. Baby milk powder can be misused. A baby can be given too much, and that's bad. Or it can be given too little, and starve. And what about hygiene?"

"These are all valid points," Courtney agreed. "Of course, sir, we don't want to put babies onto Best Milk when their mothers are happily breast feeding them. But there are many mothers, bantu as well as white, who don't want to breast feed. There are other mothers who want to, but can't. Certainly hygiene is a problem, and certainly babies can die of malnutrition if their mothers try to make a pack of milk powder go further by cutting back the amount they put into a bottle. But the job of the saleswomen will be to educate the people when they give out the free samples: they will be trained to show mothers how to clean the bottles, and how much of the powder to use."

"What if their advice isn't understood, or the people ignore it?" the Managing Director asked.

"Well, sir," Courtney said. "We can only try our best. It would be the same problem if you were the manufacturer of a fast new sports car. It can do two hundred kilometres an hour, but with petrol rationing in South Africa the top speed limit is seventy kilometres. You're providing the motorist with the means of breaking the law. You don't want him to break it, of course, but you're showing him how. And then he misuses the car, kills himself and perhaps others. It's sad, but it's not your fault."

The Managing Director nodded.

"Well, that concludes the presentation," Courtney said. "Are there any other questions?"

THREE

It was midnight before Jan Rousseau and his men were ready to move from their camp. They were twelve miles inside Mozambique territory. Rousseau opened a small tin of matt black cream and they took turns smearing each other's faces with it. They checked their maps.

Two miles ahead of them should be the village of Chari. Army intelligence believed it had a basic population of four hundred men, women and children, but the name came up in interrogations of captured guerrillas as a final jumping-off point before they infiltrated into Northern Natal. It had been designated as hostile.

North-west of their position were other, smaller villages which needed monitoring. Anything east of Chari was being taken care of by other squads on this same night.

Rousseau and his men studied the maps for the last time.

"Cronje, you come with me and we'll do Chari," Rousseau said. "Viljoen, take these two villages to the north-west and drop a couple of sniffers in this area here, just along the ridge." He indicated with his finger on the map. "Venter, you've got the long walk tonight. Leave Viljoen at the ridge and go further north to this village, Akaki, which is just by the river here. Treat it as hostile, which means sniffer, infra-red and vehicle sensor spread around.

"Also move down-river three or four miles and drop sniffers along there. Back here by five a.m. – no later. Any questions?"

There were none.

Rousseau said: "Remember what the Captain told us about keeping out of everyone's way. If one of us gets caught, the whole operation's in danger. So don't let them see you, but if they do then don't get caught. Now let's move."

They hitched on their packs and picked their way quietly through the thick scrub cover in which they had spent most of the day, before splitting up: Rousseau and Cronje heading north for Chari, Viljoen and Venter going north-west towards the ridge.

Rousseau gave Viljoen the thumbs-up sign, and watched briefly as he and Venter moved off. There was a new moon, and the night was dark. The men were lost in the blackness within a few seconds.

With Cronje two paces behind, Rousseau made his way slowly towards Chari, boots treading cautiously, hands and arms out fending off bushes. Behind him, Cronje cleared his throat softly. The night was shrill with crickets. They walked for an hour, skirting thick clumps of thorn trees, careful not to dislodge stones. When the land began sloping away downhill, Rousseau put out his arm and felt Cronje's body brush against it in the dark. The two men stood silently and looked into the blackness.

Rousseau's hand went down to his webbing and unfastened the slim night-sight. It would magnify the dim light of the stars and the reflection from the sliver of moon to give a clear picture of the land: an effect similar to seeing a daylight scene through a blue filter. He lifted the night-sight to his eye and spent several minutes studying the area.

They were nearer the village than he had realised. The first group of huts was only a hundred yards ahead and on their right. The main cluster was five or six hundred yards further on. A small fire was still burning somewhere in the village. The glow was hidden by a mud and thatch hut, but the night-sight showed smoke drifting up. There were two Msasa trees near the main part of the village. If they could get up one of them, it would be a perfect site for a sniffer. Just to the right of the trees was a well-worn dirt track which branched off a quarter-mile along. Rousseau guessed that one branch went off to the river, and the other snaked southwards. He could see a number of small paths into the village, but the track by the trees seemed to be the main one.

Rousseau squatted down and signalled Cronje to come close. He put his mouth to the other's ear and spoke very quietly.

"The first huts are a hundred yards down on our right. The main village is beyond that – six hundred yards or so. There's a fire down there. No sign of movement. It looks like the main path goes close to some Msasas. We must try and get a sniffer planted up one of the trees."

Cronje nodded. Rousseau handed him the night-sight and waited until he had the lie of the land. Then he pushed it back into his webbing and stood up.

"Let's go," Rousseau whispered. Silently they moved forward, walking even more slowly now. One slide of stones caused by an ill-judged step could alert anyone sitting at the fire, or wake one of the village dogs. There were always village dogs, and their yapping would rouse everyone.

Twenty yards before they reached the main cluster of huts, Rousseau turned away from the trees, to the left, and began to circle the village. After a few steps, he paused and took out his

26

night-sight again. Ahead he saw a clump of rocks. He handed the night-sight to Cronje.

"First sniffer in there," he whispered.

Cronje nodded, and the two men edged towards the rocks. He studied them again with the night-sight and chose a crevice partly covered by grass to plant the small bug.

They went on. Their circling movement took just over an hour, but in that time they planted a further sniffer and two infra-red sensors.

This left them with the main path and the Msasa trees to cover. There was no sign of movement from the village, and no sound. Curiously, the crickets had gone silent. Rousseau stood motionless and strained to hear another sound, but there was none.

Looking at the main path through the night-sight, it became obvious that occasionally it was used as a road. Some tyre tracks could be seen. Rousseau could not make out bootprints.

He went close to Cronje again. "How many sensors left?" he whispered.

"Three. One of each."

Rousseau nodded. He himself had none. "OK. Vehicle sensor near this path."

Rousseau selected a spot with the help of the night-sight, and the two men picked up sharp stones and scraped away at the hard earth in the middle of a clump of grass. They buried the small box and patted the dirt down on top of it.

They moved closer to the village and dug a second small hole at the base of a rock for the infra-red, which would tell the computer how many people were around.

"Right," said Rousseau softly. "Now the sniffer up the tree."

They went across to inspect the Msasas, growing just where the path entered the village. One of the trees was too flimsy to take the weight of either of them. The slightest pull bent the branches immediately. They tried the other one, and it seemed much more sturdy.

Cronje took hold of a branch, and Rousseau cupped both hands, interlocked his fingers, and held them under Cronje's boot to give him a lift up.

The young soldier pulled himself into the tree, and the

branches shook with a slight rustling. Rousseau looked up, but it was difficult to see Cronje now as he fastened the sensor into place, screwing it into a branch with a small, sharp, gimlet-like tool. The branches rustled with the effort of him pushing.

The cough the men heard sounded as if it came from two feet away.

Rousseau dropped in his tracks beside the path. Cronje froze in the tree. They listened.

With his head on the hard ground, Rousseau could hear the vibration of the boots as they came nearer, and a mumbling of voices. He lifted his head slightly to peer into the darkness, but he could see nothing. Slowly and cautiously, his hand moved down to his webbing belt and pulled out the night-sight.

They were about twenty yards away, a band of thirty men carrying rifles: looked like Kalashnikovs. Rousseau felt the hairs prickle on the back of his head and his heartbeat was loud in his ears. He was lying close to the road: too close. He wriggled back slightly. They were almost on him. He slipped the strap of his R1 rifle off his shoulder and inched it down. It seemed impossible that he would not be seen.

The first guerrilla passed on the far side of the path, and Rousseau pressed his body into the earth. Then the others came. Rousseau watched them, his head on one side, seeing boots and legs and the butts of rifles.

In the village, a dog started barking, and then another, their excited yapping mingling with the tread of the boots on the hard-baked earth.

Then Cronje lost his footing.

In the tree, his boot – braced against a branch – slipped suddenly, and he lunged for another branch to save himself falling. The Msasa shook with his weight. All but ten of the terrorists had gone past, and they stopped in their tracks to stare up into the darkness.

Cronje looked down at them, feeling suddenly quite cool. He had been discovered but Rousseau had not. Neither of them could be captured.

The guerrillas were talking, calling and pointing, but they could not yet identify him in the darkness of the tree, and he saw that some were unslinging their Kalashs.

Cronje took his R1 in his right hand and jumped, landing and rolling like the paratrooper he was trained to be, firing as he got to his feet, even before the terrorists had slammed home the bolts on their rifles. Cronje loosed a burst into the group, the explosions deafening in the darkness, and before the first two began toppling forward, he took off into the night, weaving to escape the returning fire.

Men poured out of the huts: guerrillas – many more than the group who had returned – ran out in pursuit of Cronje. Their shots merged into a continuous burst.

Rousseau wriggled further backwards, away from the path, then doubled over and began running. He could hear people coming towards him and he threw himself onto the ground again. Shit, he'd forgotten the huts further back. Bare feet pounded hollowly on the earth as they ran past, and soon they were gone.

The shooting stopped, and he could hear shouts of triumph. Rousseau raised his head and looked back at the village. They had got Cronje, either killed or a prisoner.

He pulled out his night-sight and watched. Three minutes later he saw them bringing Cronje, arms twisted behind his back, into the village. It looked as if he had been hit in the shoulder: his camouflage jacket was ripped and it was soaked in blood.

On the ground were the bodies of two terrorists, and his captors shouted angrily and twisted his arms as they led him past, pulling at his bullet-shattered shoulder.

Rousseau could see Cronje's face contort and could hear his shout of pain. In six or seven seconds, Cronje would be inside the village. He now had nothing on him to indicate his mission. The only information they could get would be from interrogation. They must get nothing.

Rousseau clipped the night-sight onto his adapted R1 and squinted through it.

He aimed slightly to the right of Cronje's backbone, and squeezed the trigger. The recoil hit into Rousseau's shoulder and the explosion echoed across the land. Rousseau looked again through the night-sight.

The terrorists were running for cover, throwing themselves down and opening fire at random into the darkness.

Cronje was on the ground. Rousseau could see with a sickening feeling that he was still moving, squirming, trying to roll over, but suddenly he stopped and lay still.

Rousseau got to his feet and began to run.

FOUR

John Courtney folded the *Rand Daily Mail* so he could read the main sports page, and propped it against the economy-size box of Post Toasties on his breakfast table. It was his habit to read the paper backwards, saving the bad news for last, although these days politics overlapped into the sports columns so often it made no difference.

This morning was an example. The lead sports story was the continued refusal of the International Olympic Committee to allow South Africa to take part in the next Games, despite the easing of the colour-bar in local sport, and the rest of the page was taken up with the angry reaction of South African officials who accused the world body of double standards.

Courtney yawned and looked out over the balcony of his flat where he was breakfasting in the sun, to glance at the modern buildings of Johannesburg sloping away down the hill. The day was going to be hot. He loosened his patterned tie, undid the top three buttons of his purple shirt and leaned back for a few seconds. Although it was only seven-thirty, the sun was already burning and the sky was cloudless.

There was a discreet movement beside him, but Courtney paid no attention. His bantu servant, Stephen, in the rough white linen uniform and red fez which came with the job, placed two halves of a ripe honeydew melon on a china plate in front of him and then withdrew. Courtney's eyes did not focus on him.

"Stephen!"

30

The black man stopped and turned around, tray in hand. "Yes, baas John?"

"Is the madam up yet?"

"No, baas John."

"Bloody hell."

Stephen waited a few seconds until it became clear he had been dismissed, then went through to the kitchen.

Courtney turned back to the paper and refolded it to look at the front page. The splash story was the row over the death of a young South African commando, Andries Cronje, killed by terrorists in Mozambique. Cronje had been nineteen. There was a picture of his mother. She was holding a photograph of her dead son, and she had been crying.

The Mozambique Government was furious about the incident and was taking it up at the UN, charging that Pretoria had staged an armed incursion into their country.

The South African Minister of Defence, Piet de Wet, replied that Cronje and other commandos had gone across the border in hot pursuit of a terrorist gang responsible for atrocities and explosions in the Natal area, and that two terrorists had been killed in an exchange of fire. De Wet defended South Africa's "hot pursuit" policy, and pointed out it would not be necessary if Mozambique stopped giving active support to guerrillas.

Courtney sighed. South Africa had been under an international arms embargo for years, and it looked as if full economic sanctions were not far off. It would make life difficult for Van Niekerk and Tessler. A lot more advertising budgets would be cut back if things went on like this.

Courtney ate his melon. It wouldn't only be advertising that was cut. It would be everything. He wondered if South Africa would survive in the long run. He wished he knew. People were leaving in increasing numbers, and businessmen were already getting their money out.

Courtney heard the telephone ring inside his flat and he waited while Stephen went to answer it. After a moment the servant reappeared with the phone in his hand, and plugged it into the extension socket on the balcony.

"It's a call for you, baas John."

"Who is it, Stephen?"

"I don't know, baas."

"I've told you before, you must always ask who's calling."

"I did, baas John, but the other baas wouldn't tell me."

Courtney sighed. "OK. Forget it."

He picked up the phone. "John Courtney here."

"Morning, John. It's Ron Prentice."

"Oh hello, Ron. What's up?"

"Good news. We've got the Nu-Kreem account."

A broad smile broke over Courtney's face. "We have? Fantastic! That's really great. When did you hear?"

"Tessler just phoned me. The Nu-Kreem Marketing Director called him at home this morning, but for some reason Tessler didn't have your home number. So he called me and I said I'd pass it on."

"Great! When do they want to start?"

"Right away. They've asked for a creative meeting this afternoon to discuss the details of the campaign. Can you make it?"

"I don't have my diary here, but I think I'm OK. Anyway, I can cancel whatever else is on. Thanks for calling, Ron."

"My pleasure. I like bringing good news."

"See you in the office."

Courtney hung up, still beaming, and walked quickly through the flat to the bedroom. Moira Logan was sitting in front of the dressing-table mirror, putting heated rollers in her hair. She wore a flower-patterned housecoat of pink and light blue, and fluffy blue slippers.

"I got it!" Courtney announced triumphantly from the doorway.

Moira Logan did not glance round from the mirror, but he could see from side view that her face had an inquiring, ready-to-be-pleased expression.

"Got what?"

"The Nu-Kreem account," he said. "I've got it!"

She pinned in the last curler, turned round and held out her arms. "Darling, that's marvellous! I'm so pleased for you." She hugged him.

"They've set up a meeting for this afternoon."

"That's wonderful. Who was it called?"

"Ron Prentice. Tessler phoned and told him."

"Tessler phoned Ron Prentice?" Moira asked, a note of caution and disapproval in her voice. "Why didn't he phone you? It's your campaign."

"He didn't have my home number."

"Well, I think he could have found out what it was and called you himself."

"Ron Prentice offered to tell me," Courtney said lamely.

"Trust Ron Prentice to take the glory." She turned back to unwind the heated rollers from her hair.

"He's not taking the glory, Moira. He's passing on a message."

"Well, Tessler should have done it himself."

"But he didn't. Ron did."

"Trust that company. I think you ought to say something to Tessler."

"Like what?" Courtney asked tetchily. " 'Mr Tessler, the girl I'm living with thinks you should have phoned me yourself'?"

"I don't know why you can't see it," she said. "It's very rude."

Courtney felt the edge taken off both his victory and his enthusiasm, and he sat on the unmade bed in silence. Moira unrolled the last curler and glanced at him in the mirror. There was a long silence.

"I'm sorry," she said at last. "Now I've spoiled it for you. I didn't mean to. It doesn't matter. I just thought it was rude of Tessler." She began to brush her hair and there was another pause. When he didn't reply, she said again: "I am sorry." And then: "I'll make it up to you tonight."

She smiled at him briefly in the mirror.

Courtney got up and stood behind her, his hands on her shoulders, kneading her soft flesh. He looked at their reflections. Moira was small-boned and slim, with fine features and a mouth just a fraction too small. But she was an attractive girl. When they went out together, men looked at her all the time. He could feel her collar-bone under his fingers, and he moved to stroke her blonde hair. Courtney, at just on six feet, was seven inches taller than the girl. He was good-looking but overweight. His hair was dark brown, and his face had a rumpled and creased look. One of his girlfriends before Moira called it a bedroom face. His eyes were brown and usually friendly and humorous, but now they had no expression.

"I must go," he said and moved away. Moira reached out and grabbed his arm.

"No don't," she said. "Stay here."

"I must. I'll be late. There's a lot to do."

She held onto him and pulled him towards her. "You mustn't sulk," she said.

"I'm not sulking."

"I just thought Tessler was rude, after all the work you'd put in. He shouldn't have phoned Ron Prentice."

"Let's not go through it again," Courtney said. He tried to move away but she held on. "It doesn't matter," he said, quietly and emphatically.

"Give me a kiss." She tilted her face up.

Courtney stooped and brushed his lips against her cheek.

"No, a proper kiss," she said.

He sat on the edge of the bed, leaned forward and kissed her mouth. It tasted of toothpaste. Her firm pink tongue flicked out and ran over his lips, along his teeth and on to touch his own tongue. He pulled her towards him.

She stroked her hands down his chest and thighs, and rubbed them over the front of his trousers. She could feel him growing hard. He unfastened her housecoat and moved down so that he could suck her nipples.

In Courtney's ear, she whispered: "What about Stephen?"

"Bugger Stephen." His voice was furry.

"Is the door closed?"

She knew it wasn't. Courtney looked up. "Hang on," he said. He swung his legs off the bed and went across to close and lock it. He took off his tie and shirt, kicked away his shoes and undid the belt on his trousers. Moira lay across the bed, naked in her open housecoat, watching him.

"We're going to have to be very quiet," she said.

"Like a mouse," said Courtney.

He was sweating when he finished, and he lay damp and heavy on top of her, listening to his heart thump. She didn't like sweaty men, but he didn't care. He was still inside her, and he didn't plan moving yet.

She stayed quite still as she had throughout. Several minutes passed, and Courtney felt himself dozing into sleep.

34

Moira said in a small voice: "What's the time?"

Courtney looked at his watch. "Oh Christ. It's eight-fifteen."

"You'll be late."

He sighed and kissed her neck. "That was nice," he said. Moira did not reply.

He rolled off and lay beside her. She got up quickly and tied the housecoat around her, then went into the bathroom. He could hear water splashing in the basin. He'd better have a shower, he thought.

He waited until she came out, then went through and stepped into a jet of lukewarm water. Afterwards he towelled himself vigorously.

Moira had dressed quickly and gone out of the bedroom. He could hear her giving orders to Stephen. He pulled on his trousers and shirt and was putting on his tie when the door opened and she came back in.

"There's a registered letter for you, John," she said. "I signed for it."

"Oh?" He took it from her. "Government," he said, looking at the envelope. "Department of Defence. Bloody hell."

He tore it open and read the letter inside.

"Jesus Christ," Courtney said in disbelief. "I don't believe it. I've been called up!"

FIVE

Jan Rousseau sat uncomfortably in the green leather chair, waiting for the Colonel. He was alone in the office. One wall was dominated by an aerial survey map of the border area with Mozambique, with red, green, blue and yellow pins stuck in at various points. There was no key to explain their significance.

The Colonel's desk was large and wooden, and bare of papers.

Behind it was the Commando crest, and photographs of passing-out parades and parachutists, framed in brown wood. The square of green carpet on the floor ran to within two feet of the wall.

By the door there was a large set of cupboards, many with padlocks, and a squat heavy metal Chubb safe was positioned to one side. The fourth wall was used for bookshelves: army manuals, cream and black files with the South African coat of arms on the spines and writing in a thick black felt-tipped pen to identify the subjects, a neat pile of army magazines, and a rack of reference books.

Outside the burglar-barred window was a tree, and beyond that a concrete path, bounded by neat flower-beds, which led to the parade-ground. The sky was overcast; the day humid. Three squads of recruits practised squarebashing; three sergeant-majors stood rigidly to attention at the side near their squad. Even at that distance, Rousseau could see their mouths move as they roared commands, shouted obscenities, but he could hear nothing except for the "tchunk" sound of the electric clock on the wall as the minute-hand flicked stiffly over to the next mark. Every sixty seconds there was a "tchunk", and Rousseau found himself waiting for the noise.

Otherwise, all was silence.

Rousseau waited twenty interminable minutes, but when the door opened it took him by surprise. He jumped to his feet and saluted the Colonel and Captain walking in, together with a civilian. The officers returned the salute. The civilian nodded a greeting.

"At ease, Rousseau," the Colonel said, "Sit down." He indicated the civilian. "This is Mr du Preez from Defence Force headquarters. He wants to hear what you've got to say." He settled himself at his desk, du Preez at his right arm, then produced a bunch of keys and unlocked a drawer. From it he took a file.

Captain Fourie sat in a chair by the side of the desk, a tough man, big and muscular, wearing a commando beret. The hair which showed under it was short, almost shaved. Captain Fourie waited for the Colonel to speak, hitting his swagger stick gently and silently into the palm of his hand. Mr du Preez watched the young soldier carefully.

At last Colonel Winter looked across and said: "Well, Rousseau, we've all read your report. Now tell us again. What happened?"

Jan Rousseau said: "I killed Cronje, sir."

"*You* did?"

"Yes, sir. I shot him. In the back."

The men exchanged glances.

"Was it a mistake?" Mr du Preez asked quietly.

"No, sir. I aimed to kill him," Rousseau said. "He had been captured. He was already wounded – shot in the shoulder."

"Not by you?" Colonel Winter asked.

"No, sir. By the terrorists."

"Why did you shoot him?" – du Preez again.

"So they couldn't torture him, sir. We'd planted all our sensors. There was nothing they could find on him to show what we'd been up to. They could only get the information out of him by torture."

Captain Fourie said: "What makes you think he'd have told them anything?"

"If the pain was bad enough, sir, he might have done. They'd shot him in the shoulder – I saw the wound through my night-sight. I was seventy or eighty yards away, and it was bad. As they tried to take him into the village they twisted his arm – the injured one – and I could hear him scream. I didn't want to take the chance."

Du Preez asked: "Why didn't you just tell us you shot him by mistake?'

"It wouldn't be true, sir. It's on my conscience. I feel terrible about it."

The Colonel looked over his head at the cupboards beyond. "I expect you do," he said. "Start from the beginning, Rousseau. What happened?"

Rousseau told his story in detail. Occasionally du Preez broke in with a question, or took him back over a particular part. When he had finished, the Colonel and du Preez consulted briefly in whispers, then the Colonel asked: "By jumping down from that tree and getting the terrorists' attention away from your position, Cronje was taking a chance, wasn't he? You could almost say he was committing suicide."

"What do you mean, sir?"

"He must have known his chances of escape were very small, and he was determined to go out fighting."

"Yes, sir," Rousseau said. "He opened fire as soon as he hit the ground."

The Colonel glanced across at the Captain then leaned towards du Preez again, who spoke to him in a whisper for two or three minutes. Rousseau could not make out more than a mumble. He waited apprehensively. At last the Colonel nodded and replied: "I think you're quite right. And we must also consider morale." The Colonel turned back to the soldier.

"Well, Rousseau," he said. "I'm not going to minimise the seriousness of your action. To kill a comrade-in-arms – there are circumstances in which it would be a capital offence. You would be hanged, or shot."

Staring at the carpet, Rousseau said softly: "Yes, sir."

"On the other hand, we're not saying that this is one of those occasions. Do the other men in your squad know what you did?"

"No, sir. I couldn't tell them. I just said he'd been shot."

"Well, don't tell them. I order you now not to say a word of this matter to any other person. Do you understand?"

Rousseau looked up bewildered. "I'm sorry, sir," he said. "I don't follow you."

"What I mean is this: the matter – the killing of Cronje – is now an official secret," Colonel Winter said. "It comes under the Official Secrets Act, in just the same way as the planting of the sensors in Mozambique. I don't have to tell you the serious penalties there are for breaches of the Official Secrets Act."

"No, sir. But what about me? I killed him."

"Mr du Preez and I think – and don't you agree, Captain? – that in the circumstances it was justifiable. A patriotic act. Cronje would have expected you to do it. Certainly the government would have expected it."

On the sidelines, Captain Fourie nodded.

The Colonel rummaged in his desk drawer for a booklet.

"Here we are," he said. "Standing Orders for Unconventional Warfare Operations. The section headed 'When soldiers are to fire' ... let's see: '(a) It is your duty to shoot if it is the only way to (1) Defend yourself, your comrades, families, police and all peaceable persons against serious attack.' I think we're all agreed that Cronje was under serious attack. In fact, he was in danger of being tortured brutally, and you could be said to have defended him from that. Whatever the final cost. And here we are again, Subsection Two says it's your duty to shoot if it's the only way 'to protect government property and equipment against serious damage'. There's no question that if the terrorists had got hold of those sensors because of what Cronje told them under torture, they'd have done them serious damage. Destroyed them, probably. Certainly put them out of action. So there you have it, Rousseau. Without looking any further into the Regulations, you did your duty. And so did Cronje. A gallant soldier. He is being recommended for a posthumous decoration."

"Yes, sir."

"That's all."

Rousseau stood up and saluted, feeling a strange mixture of relief and disappointment. "Yes, sir. Thank you, sir."

Colonel Winter looked at him shrewdly. "One more thing, Rousseau. Don't brood about it. You did what you had to. No blame can be attached to you. The South African nation can be grateful for the success of the mission. With the exception of poor Cronje, every other squad did its job and got back without being spotted. We've already had the first computer reports from Silvermine, and the sensors are working as they should. So, well done."

"Yes, sir."

"Remember, not a word about Cronje. Not to anyone. As far as people are concerned, he was shot and killed by terrorists. Now I imagine you're going to be keen to get back into action against those bastards."

Rousseau nodded. "Ja, I am, sir."

"Good man. I'll see you're posted back into the border area before long. I'm going there myself. We're having a lot of trouble in the Eastern Transvaal with bantu tribesmen. There's quite a bit of co-operation with the terrorists that we've got to stamp out. You can help us do it."

"I will, sir."

"Meanwhile, you probably want a bit of time off." Colonel

Winter turned to Captain Fourie. "Do you suppose you could fix Rousseau here with a five-day pass?"

Fourie grinned at Rousseau. "I'm sure it can be organised, sir," he said.

SIX

John Courtney waited impatiently in the restaurant bar, morosely drinking a Scotch. Was this going to be a celebration or a wake? André Tessler, whose brother, it turned out, was a Private Secretary in the Department of Defence, had given no hint over the phone when he had called from Pretoria and suggested lunch. Tessler had been to see the Department unofficially to put the case for the exemption of Courtney from one year's continuous territorial reserve duty.

Christ, Courtney thought, draining his glass. Twelve months in the army at the age of thirty-two. He'd done his national training when he was eighteen, and territorial camps for ten years after that. He knew that some reservists were now being called back for three-months' training, and that was bad enough. But one whole year. Three hundred and sixty-five days. They had to be joking.

He called out loudly: "Barman!" and pointed at his glass for a refill.

Courtney looked moodily round the room. It could have been an extension of Van Niekerk and Tessler, except that the carpet was a slightly different colour, and tiny light-bulbs had been recessed into the dark painted ceiling to give the impression of stars. But the sun filter curtains were exactly the same green, yellow and orange stripes, and those bloody jungly plants were everywhere. And the Muzak, of course. Christ. The Scotch wasn't improving his temper.

Tessler came into the bar in a rush, pushing the horn-rimmed glasses further back on his nose, giving Courtney's hand a limp shake, refusing a drink.

"I'll have one at the table," he said. "Let's go through and eat. I'm sorry to be late but the traffic on the Johannesburg road was terrible."

Courtney finished his whisky in a gulp. They went through to the dining-room and the Head Waiter hurried up, leather-covered menus in hand, smiling a welcome.

"Mr Tessler! Good to see you again, sir. Your table is this way, please."

"Hello, Luigi," Tessler said. "How are you keeping? Busy as usual, I see."

"It comes and goes, Mr Tessler." He pulled out a chair at a corner table and Tessler took it. Courtney sat opposite. They scanned the menus in silence, and when they were ready to order, Luigi was again immediately at hand.

Courtney watched him go. "Well?" he asked Tessler. "What's the score?"

"Not good, John. I don't think we're going to be able to keep you out."

"Oh shit, André. I can't go in for a year. What about the Nu-Kreem account? It's my baby, no one else's."

"I know that, John. I told them the agency's problems and I said we might even have to lay off other employees if you were called up."

"And?" Courtney said.

"I saw five senior men at the Department. I can't mention their names because my brother fixed it unofficially, but they were very good men, very senior. They gave me a very fair hearing."

"Then they said no."

"They said no. They've put you in a special category. They're pulling in reservists up to the age of thirty-five for three-month camps, but they're just ordinary soldiers. They want you longer for a particular duty. Naturally they wouldn't tell me what it was, but you're not going to be doing squarebashing. Or at least, not much."

"Christ. I wonder what 'special category' means."

"Your guess is as good as mine. But they're obviously after you because you're a fine advertising man. There were lots of questions about that – and strangely enough, about the Nu-Kreem campaign. Someone had told them about it. They were pretty well briefed. They wanted to know what else you had planned, how you dealt with bantu consumers, that sort of thing. I gave you a glowing reference, of course, but towards the end I was starting to feel a bit sorry I had. I wanted to show how much we needed you, but I think I just proved how much they did."

"Oh hell. Where in God's name is the wine?"

Tessler lifted a hand and summoned Luigi. The bottle was opened and being poured within two minutes.

"I'm sorry I couldn't get you off, John," Tessler said. "We haven't come to the end of the road if you want to fight it. We can apply to the Exemption Board for a deferment. But I don't think there's much point. After the meeting I had a quiet word with my brother, and he told me one or two things which I must say came as a bit of a shock." Tessler took a sip of his wine. "Cheers," he said to Courtney.

"Cheers."

"Between you and me," Tessler went on, "we're really up against it now. The government expects sanctions on South Africa within the next month or so. This means the financial crisis is going to get much worse. Bad news for the agency. And then there's the security situation."

"What'd he say about that?" Courtney asked.

"It's not good, John. Terrorists are coming in from Mozambique, along most of the borders with Transvaal and Natal. They've got bloody good equipment now. The government expects the attacks to get much worse. A lot of the tribesmen in the border areas are co-operating with the communists, and this means they give them food and shelter – and, of course, they aren't giving information to us. Worst of all, no one knows what the Cubans are planning. It could be that they're getting ready to join the fight themselves."

"Against South Africa?" Courtney asked incredulously.

"Could be," Tessler said. "The Department has reports that hundreds of Russian tanks are being landed in Beira – more than the Mozambique army could ever want. Don't repeat this, or I'll be for the high jump. And also a lot more Cuban soldiers are arriving there, too. I tell you, John, they're worried. From what they've told me, so am I."

SEVEN

Northern Transvaal. It was sweltering inside the camouflaged briefing tent, pitched at a forward camp east of the town of Chicundu, and Jan Rousseau chose a chair in line with the only slight draught of air coming in.

They were sixty miles from the Mozambique border. The briefing officer was a member of BOSS, the Bureau for State Security, who had been operating in the area.

The briefing officer waited until they had settled down, and then began.

"Kêrels,* the problem, very simply, is this." He pointed at the map with his stick. "Along this whole border, and to a lesser extent in Northern Natal, our intelligence is drying up. In the past, most of the information has come from the chiefs and headmen and the ordinary bantu. As you know, the government is very generous in the way it rewards information. And of course, we're very severe with people who deliberately withhold information. But there's been a decline – a very big decline – in the intelligence we've received over the last three months. Now this could mean there isn't anything to tell us, and that no terrorists are coming across."

His audience laughed, and the briefing officer smiled wryly at them. "Ja, we all know this isn't true," he said. "We'd be glad if it was, but it isn't. So it means our informants just aren't coming across with the goods. Perhaps they're scared. We know the

* Chaps.

43

terrorists torture and kill those bantu who don't help them, or who are known to help us. We should never forget that the threat from the communists is a very powerful one. Of course, while the government understands the problem of those blacks who have been intimidated into silence, it doesn't sympathise with them. It can't. The whole nation is at risk. We can't allow the lily-livers of some bantu to imperil the safety of everyone, white *and* bantu. If they're afraid of the communists, then they must be more frightened of us. More frightened!" He smacked the stick into the palm of his hand for emphasis. "They have information; we want it, and we must get it." He cleared his throat and consulted his notes.

"There are also those bantu who have gone over to the side of the terrorists, and who are harbouring them," he said. "There are people in this area who know exactly where arms have been hidden. They must be weeded out, these people. They must be brought to justice. We'll be able to get them if we get the informants' network operating again. You may ask, does this mean we now have to treat the bantu like ... like ..." he looked blank. "Er ... oh God, what's the word?" The briefing officer stared at his notes again.

"Like kaffirs?" someone suggested, and the tent erupted into a roar of laughter.

The briefing officer grinned. "Ja, I know what we all think about that," he said. "No, what I wanted to say was, do we have to treat them like enemies? The answer is no. I'm not saying that we should trust them, far from it. But we must maintain good relations whenever we can. What do I mean by this? I mean use your common sense. For example, you're in an APC,* you're going along a dirt road and there's a herd of cattle in front of you. Don't run them down. Cattle are very important to a bantu. They have a social significance a white man doesn't understand. A mombi† isn't just a beast to them. It's wealth and it's social standing. So leave them alone. Don't shoot at them. And if you're on patrol and you feel like some fresh meat, don't just go and bayonet a mombi. You'll be storing up grief for all of us if you do. Is that clear?"

* Armoured personnel carrier.
† Cow.

44

The briefing officer looked around. "Second point," he went on. "If you go to search a kraal and you see a pot of beer, don't kick it over. They might be using it for some ceremonial purpose, and your action will damage good relations.

"Thirdly, be careful who you hit. There are occasions when it will be your duty to assault certain bantu – for example, if you want information. But try not to bash someone if you're not sure who he is. If he's the headman's son or someone like that, get advice before you go ahead. You can turn a friendly village against you by giving the wrong black man a clout.

"Leave their women alone, for God's sake. Any soldier found to have slept with a bantu girl, with or without her consent, will have us coming down on him like the wrath of God. I don't have to remind you that the Immorality Act forbids sexual intercourse between the races. If you have relations with a black girl, when we get to hear about it – and we will – you won't know what's hit you.

"Lastly, don't forget your manners. Manners are very important to the bantu, and they're different to ours. For example, if you go up to some black men remember to greet them straight away. The bantu expects his superior to greet him first. You'll find more about tribal customs in your briefing sheet. Read it. Any questions?"

A hand went up in the middle of the tent. "Interrogation, sir," a young soldier asked. "How far can we go?"

"As far as you need to," the briefing officer said. "If you believe a person, man or woman, has information on terrorists or their sympathisers, it's your duty to get that information. There are different ways of going about it. Most of you have seen what goes on already. You'll all evolve a technique you'll feel comfortable with, and which will do its work. We cannot be squeamish, gentlemen. The stakes are too high."

Another hand went up. "If a bantu dies under interrogation, sir, what's our position?" a sergeant asked.

"You're a bloody fool if he dies without first telling you what you want to know," the briefing officer said with a thin smile. "The idea is to keep him alive and talking. But legally, you're clear. If you genuinely believe the prisoner has an important piece of information, you're acting lawfully, whatever you do. It doesn't matter if it later turns out he didn't actually know anything, or he'd been telling the truth all along. It's only necessary for you to have a genuine belief at the time of the interrogation and you're indemnified. Any other questions?" He paused. "No? Then dismiss."

There was a scraping of chairs and a murmur of conversation as the men dispersed. Jan Rousseau stayed where he was until the tent was almost clear. Three seats along another man waited, making notes in a pad on his lap.

Rousseau glanced at him with amusement. "Think you're going to have trouble remembering all that, Sergeant?"

John Courtney looked up suddenly and grinned back. "It may be old to you, Sergeant, but it's all new to me. I'd never have believed some of it. I'm writing it down for when I think I must have been dreaming."

"Where are you from?" Rousseau asked.

"Joburg. I've just been called up for reserve duty. Got here this morning."

"Poor bloke. Still, only ninety days to go. I'm in for life."

"It's more than that," Courtney said. "Three hundred and sixty-five days for me. I've been called up for a year."

Rousseau whistled sympathetically. "Jesus, a year," he said. "That's new. I thought it was only three months for civvie reserves."

"It is for most people. I'm supposed to be in a special category, whatever that means."

Recognition dawned on Rousseau's face. "Oh Christ, I know," he said. "You're the advertising bloke. You're attached to my battalion."

"Oh," said Courtney. "Good. What am I going to be doing?"

"The Colonel will brief you," Rousseau said, "but you're supposed to win the hearts and minds of the people for us. I suppose you'll be getting your pips soon. They always commission psych-ac men. They'll probably make you a lieutenant."

"What's psych-ac mean?" Courtney asked.

"Psychological action," Rousseau said. "They're very hot on it now."

"Ja, well, it will make a change from what that officer was telling us this morning."

46

"Oh no," Rousseau said. "That's psych-ac, too. In this war you win the hearts and minds of the bantu by not fucking their women, not kicking over their beer pots, and putting the boot in everywhere else."

"That's a pretty crude way of going about it, isn't it?"

"It's a crude war," Rousseau replied. "Basically they have information. We want it. They won't give it. So how should we get it?" Courtney shrugged. "I'll tell you how," Rousseau said. "We strip a kaffir naked. We put electrodes onto his balls. We turn on the current. Then, when he's stopped screaming and shouting, sometimes he talks and sometimes he doesn't. If he talks, the interrogation doesn't take long and it's effective. Ten marks out of ten. If he doesn't talk, we move onto other things. As the man was saying this morning, everyone has their own techniques. It doesn't matter what, so long as it's effective."

"Christ," said Courtney in an awed voice. "I don't think I could do that to anyone, not even a bantu."

"Who said anything about you?" Rousseau asked. "Get someone else to do it. I haven't put an electrode onto any bugger's balls. Not yet, anyway. I've watched others do it, though, and if I haven't felt like watching I've taken a walk and come back in an hour when it's all over. It's all for the best in the long run."

"I don't think I could even order anyone to be tortured like that," Courtney said.

"Oh hell," said Rousseau, clicking his tongue on the roof of his mouth disapprovingly. "You don't order them to be tortured, bloke. You order them to be questioned. There's nothing wrong with that, is there?"

"No, I suppose not."

"Then when they're brought back, they're ready to make a statement. That's how it happens."

"And that's what I've got to do for the next year?"

Rousseau laughed and shook his head.

"No," he said. "You're going to be too senior for that. You'll probably sit in an office and think up other ways of making people talk."

"What? Interrogation methods?"

Rousseau stood up. "No, bloke, nothing like that. You're the sophisticated end of the operation. It doesn't take a giant brain to work out techniques like holding people under water until they nearly drown. Anyone can do that. You're going to have to find subtle ways of getting the bantu on our side and talking. I wish you joy. Now come on, I'll show you where the Colonel's office is. He'll want to give you a full briefing himself."

Rousseau led Courtney out of the tent and along a dirt path following a line of trees. Tents were pitched in the shade, their outlines broken by camouflage netting, and soldiers sat or lay about reading, talking, playing cards, waiting for their next duty to begin. The path led to a whitewashed brick building with a silver tin roof, formerly a farm store-house, which the Defence Forces had requisitioned and partitioned into offices. A pole had been erected a few yards from the front entrance, and a South African flag hung limply from it.

Rousseau pushed open the door and went in. A sergeant sat on duty at a desk in a small entrance area, and beside him a corporal operated a small field-telephone switchboard.

"Morning, Sergeant," Rousseau said. "This is Sergeant Courtney. He's going to be doing psych-ac. I think the Colonel wants to see him."

"Oh ja, he's expected. Come this way, Sergeant."

Rousseau held out his hand, and Courtney shook it warmly. "Thanks for your help," Courtney said.

"It was nothing," Rousseau replied. "And don't worry. It's going to be easy. Once you get started, you won't even notice the short cuts you take. You'll become like the rest of us."

Courtney grinned sheepishly. "Maybe," he said. "Perhaps I'll see you later."

"Ja, sure."

Courtney was led to a small whitewashed office where Colonel Winter sat at his desk, reading through intelligence reports. The Sergeant rapped loudly on the door as they stood in the entrance.

"Sergeant Courtney's arrived, sir," he said.

Courtney saluted and waited uncertainly. Colonel Winter looked up frowning, then he said: "Oh yes. At ease, Courtney. Come and take a seat over here."

"Thank you, sir."

Winter smiled at him. "You're just in time. We need a man like you working with us in the field."

48

"Yes, sir."

"You're big in advertising, I understand."

Courtney wondered whether to be modest, but decided against it. "Yes, sir," he said.

Winter's smile turned to a grin and he laughed shortly. "Ja, I like a man who knows his worth," he said. "Do you know what psych-ac is?"

"Psychological action, sir."

"Correct. That's what you're going to be doing. Do you know what it means?"

Courtney hesitated. "Well, I was listening in to a briefing this morning. About interrogation."

"Oh ja." Colonel Winter sounded indifferent. "Well that bit needn't worry you very much. Interrogation's not a psych-ac job – at least, not directly. Your job is to help us regain the support of bantu in this area. It looks as if we've lost it. The informer network has dried up almost completely. You've got to get it restored."

Courtney nodded. "That won't be easy, sir."

"Oh there are all sorts of ways," the Colonel said. "Here's something for you to read." He opened a drawer of his desk and pulled out a buff-coloured booklet. "This is supposed to be pretty good. The Directorate of Operations in Pretoria put it out – *Guide to Psychological Action*. It's restricted to senior officers. Oh, by the way, you've got the rank of Captain. I've got your commission and your pips here. Congratulations."

Courtney sat for a moment, overwhelmed. A captain! Christ. "Thank you, sir," he said at last.

Winter pushed the booklet and a bulky brown manila envelope over the desk. "Speak to Sergeant Reynolds on your way out. He'll fix you up with other items of officer's equipment."

"Yes, sir."

"Meanwhile, let me give you a welcoming pep talk. A lot of the things you see and do here will be new to you. You might not like some of them, but I assure you they're all necessary. All of them." He paused for emphasis. "I suppose you were told at the briefing this morning about the reasons for the sudden lack of co-operation from the bantu?"

"Yes, sir. Intimidation, and some have joined the communists."

49

"That's right, but it goes deeper than that. A lot of the young bantu have gone over the border for terrorist training. There are some villages you can go to near here where you won't see a boy between the ages of twelve and thirty. Other villages are giving food and shelter to terrorists. We're pretty sure that some of the people who've been into Mozambique for training have already come back to their kraals and are living there normally. But of course they'll have arms hidden away somewhere, and they must have some sort of plan of action."

Courtney asked: "What sort of thing are we doing at the moment to regain support?"

"Whatever we can. We thump them if we catch them, of course – make examples of offenders. If we kill a terrorist, we usually make the people come and look at the bodies."

"Isn't there a danger of creating martyrs?"

"Ja, there is, so we have to be careful how it's done. Your advice will be important on things like that. You see, the bantu believe that some of the terrorists are invincible. They cover themselves with piss and tell the tribesmen that bullets will bounce off them, that sort of thing. It sounds fantastic, but there you are. Some bantu will believe anything. So we show them the corpses to let them see the terrorists are liars. We've also got to do our best to enlist the support of spirit mediums. You know who they are?"

"Sort of witchdoctors," Courtney said.

"More than that. The ancestral spirits are supposed to speak through them, so whatever spirit mediums say, the tribesmen believe because they think they've got a hot line to heaven. If the spirit mediums say 'tell the government if you see a terrorist', then we're laughing."

"But they're not saying that at the moment," Courtney said, "or we'd be getting information."

"Exactly. So the problem is, how to win them round. We could pull them in for interrogation and make them feel very sorry for themselves, but that would probably be counter-productive. We've found that rewards sometimes work with people like that."

"Rewards or bribes?"

"At the moment, bribes mainly," Winter said. "But not just

bribes by themselves. They must be backed by a show of force and determination. The bantu has got to be convinced we're going to win, so he can help us without fear of ending up on the wrong side. We've got to show a continuing presence in this area. This means ceremonies, military music, displays to make them think twice about opposing us – police dogs, helicopter drills, low-flying jets, that sort of thing. Then there's the dirty tricks department." He smiled. "That's you, Captain."

Courtney smiled back apprehensively. "Sounds ominous," he said. "What do I have to do, sir?"

"Well, basically we're already doing all these things I've been talking about, and it hasn't made a cent's worth of difference. We'll carry on with them, of course, but we need something more subtle as well. That *Guide to Psychological Action* will give you some idea. For example, we want to plant rumours to discredit the terrorists. You're going to have to decide what. It's obviously got to be something that could be true, and it shouldn't be trace-able to us. We've got a few undercover agents around who'll start the ball rolling: a few, but not many. Still, if a rumour is well chosen and put out at exactly the right time, it'll spread like a bush fire."

"I think I could do that all right, sir," Courtney said.

"I'm sure you could. You may find it difficult to start with. Some promising rumours just fall flat without any reason. But don't be discouraged. Learn from your mistakes. You're here for a year. There's time to practise."

"Ja, of course, sir."

"Oh, and one last thing," Colonel Winter said. "Communist influence is pretty insidious. It's present in a lot of things in our own European culture – music, theatre, books, television, that sort of thing – attempts to undermine our way of life, sap the moral fibre of our youth. We're lucky in South Africa. The government protects us from the worst excesses through cen-sorship. But some still filters through. We're not only watching the bantu for signs of communist influence, we've got to make sure our own house is in order. I want a report from you, every month, on the psychological situation of our own troops here. I'll send it on to headquarters for processing. It's part of your job to watch for signs of communist influence among the men and even

– God forbid – among the officers. If you suspect anything, let us know in the report. If you have proof, come straight to me, day or night. Any questions, Captain?"

Courtney shook his head numbly. "No, sir."

"Then get yourself settled in. Good luck. If you have any problems, I'm here to help. An office has been allocated for you in this building. Sergeant Reynolds will show you where it is."

Courtney stood up and saluted. "Thank you, sir. I'll do my best."

Colonel Winter smiled. "It'll be a bit strange at first, but I think you'll enjoy it. It's certainly a challenge for a young man."

EIGHT

John Courtney, with his new captain's pips on his epaulettes and a Defence-Force-issue swagger stick, left his tent for a walk round the camp, feeling self-conscious. It was bloody hot in the Northern Transvaal – much hotter than Johannesburg. He felt the sweat from his armpits soaking through his shirt. The men's tents were pitched about fifty yards from the officers', and a few dozen soldiers sat around in the marginally reduced heat of the shade. A couple of privates walking in his direction saluted him. It felt really strange.

Courtney heard a whistle, and a voice from under a tree said: "Jesus Christ. A captain! Not bad."

He looked around. Jan Rousseau was whittling at a piece of stick with his army knife, and grinning at him. Despite himself, Courtney grinned back.

Rousseau got up and came across. He made a parade-ground halt, knee raised to hip height, and right foot driven sharply into the ground. Then, still grinning, he saluted. "Morning, Captain!"

"Fuck off, Sergeant," said Courtney, embarrassed.

"Whatever you say, sir. But if you like I could show you around. I think we're going to be working together quite a bit."

"Oh, why is that?"

"The Colonel said so."

"I see," Courtney said. "Yes, I'd like to see around. What's your name?"

"Jan Rousseau, sir."

"I'm John Courtney." They began walking along the dirt path.

"You're in advertising in civvie street. Who with?"

"Van Niekerk and Tessler. You probably haven't heard of them."

"No, I haven't," Rousseau said. "You married?"

"No. You?"

Rousseau shook his head.

Courtney said: "You're a bit young for it anyway. How old are you?"

"Twenty-one."

"Much too young."

Rousseau looked at him. "And you? Thirty-eight, thirty-nine?"

"For God's sake," Courtney said. "I'm thirty-two. Although sometimes I feel like fifty. I felt fifty when I got the letter calling me up for a year."

"It won't be so bad," said Rousseau. "You'll be surprised how quickly the time goes." He pointed to a large open-sided tent with wooden tables and benches set out in it. "That's the men's mess tent. The officers eat over there." He indicated a smaller tent nearby with tables and fold-up chairs. "The cookhouse is behind. You can probably smell it. The grub's awful but there's a lot of it."

They walked on and Rousseau said: "There's no air-strip here. The nearest one's ten miles away. But the choppers land just there, in the middle of that clearing."

Rousseau turned·off onto a track leading down a steep slope through some trees. It came out at a group of farm outbuildings. Soldiers with R1 rifles sat around on walls and stones, and two or three leaned against a wall. They straightened up as Courtney approached and saluted him. He returned the greeting. "At ease," he said. Out of the corner of his eye, he saw Rousseau grin at him, but he ignored it.

"What's this?" Courtney asked, pointing at the buildings with his stick.

"This is where we keep the prisoners," Rousseau said. "There's a twenty-four-hour armed guard. Want to look inside?"

Rousseau led the way into the main building and said to a private: "Who've you got in today?"

"Two bantu women in that room, Sergeant," the Private said. "And we've got a man in the other. But he's not here at the moment."

Rousseau nodded. "OK, let's see the women."

The Private unlocked a padlock on one of the doors and pushed it open. Rousseau and Courtney peered inside, and the smell hit them at once. Two women, scarves around their heads, simple dresses, bare feet, sitting on the floor, stared back at them, the fear on their faces unmistakable. One of the women held a baby tightly in her arms. It was asleep. The room was bare of furniture. An enamel bucket in the corner reeked of urine and faeces. The stench poured out into the passageway.

Courtney felt nausea rising and backed off, trying not to choke.

"Private!" he said, when he got clear of the door and into fresh air.

"Yes, sir."

"Get that room cleaned up right away! Get that bloody filthy bucket emptied now!"

The Private shrugged. "But they slopped out this morning, sir."

"I don't care," Courtney said. "Get it done again!"

"Ja, OK, sir."

Courtney walked quickly out of the building, Rousseau behind him.

"You all right?" Rousseau asked.

It was still a conscious effort to control his stomach. "Only just," Courtney said.

"You get used to the smell. They probably don't even notice it in there," Rousseau said. Courtney did not reply.

They walked past the outbuildings, and took another path for

54

several hundred yards. The trees were dense to one side, and the ground on the other sloped gently away to a fallow field. Courtney began to feel better.

A small, solitary, white building faced them.

"Well," said Rousseau pointing. "That's where it all happens."

"Where what happens?"

"Interrogation. Do you want to go and have a look, sir?"

Courtney paused. Did he? Did he really want to know what went on? He felt many things: apprehension first, then curiosity, and an indefinable sense of excitement, which appalled him even as he recognised it begin. "Why not?" he said with a shrug. "In for a penny, in for a pound."

They moved nearer the building. "You'll find there's not much inside, but it does the job," Rousseau said. "It's got water and electricity, which are what count, and it's private. It's far enough away from everyone else not to cause a nuisance. People can make as much noise as they like and they won't disturb anybody."

They were right up to the building, and they could hear no sound. There was no guard outside.

Courtney said, feeling more confident: "There's no one in there now."

"Ja, there bloody well better be," Rousseau said. "They've taken a bantu from the guardhouse back there, and if he isn't here, I'd like to know where he is."

The door was locked. Rousseau knocked sharply on it.

A voice shouted from inside: "Who's that?"

"Sergeant Rousseau with Captain Courtney. Open up."

They could hear a key turn and the door swung open. A young, stocky sergeant with a spiky blond moustache stood holding an Rı rifle. In the gloom behind him, Courtney could see another soldier.

"Oh sorry, sir," the Sergeant said. "I'm just carrying out an interrogation."

"Ja, Sergeant. Do you mind if we look around? I'm the psych-ac officer," Courtney said.

"Ja, of course, sir." The man stood aside. Courtney and Rousseau went in. The cement floor was soaked with water. There were two plain wooden chairs in the room and a wooden table. There was a cupboard in the corner, padlocked. Two windows were set high in the wall. From the ceiling hung an electric wire with a bare light bulb attached. There was a small sink with a cold tap. Attached to the tap was a length of hosepipe.

A bantu man lay in a pool of water on the floor, and he was making soft sounds of choking.

The Sergeant said: "Do you want me to carry on, sir?"

Courtney felt his stomach leap, and that bloody surge of excitement again. "What's the score?" he asked, as levelly as he could.

"This man has been meeting terrorists near his village."

Rousseau asked: "Which village is it?"

"Lapatu. About ten miles south-south-east."

Rousseau nodded. They waited for Courtney's answer.

"Carry on, Sergeant," he said, and avoided Rousseau's eye.

The soldier closed and locked the door to the brick room, and it became quite dark. Courtney could only just make out the figure of the suspect, but he could plainly hear him start to sob.

"How long have you been interrogating him, Sergeant?" Courtney asked.

"Not long, sir. About an hour."

"Got anything useful yet?"

"Ja, he admits he's seen terrorists and that he went with another man. But he says he can't remember who it was."

Courtney nodded. His eyes were becoming accustomed to the gloom. He sat on the edge of the table. It was higher than the chair, and it gave him a better view.

The Sergeant and the Private went to stand over the man on the floor.

"Phineas!" the Sergeant roared. "You lying shithead! Who went with you to see the terrorists?"

"No one, baas. No one went with me." The voice was imploring.

"Well, who else did you find there? Answer, kaffir!"

"I did not know him, baas. I did not know him!"

"Ja, you did! Who was he? Answer or I'll kill you!"

"Please, baas! I don't know! Please!"

The Sergeant turned to the Private. "Hennie, turn it on." The

Private went across to the tap and gave it two turns. Water gushed out the end of the hose, splashing over the black man, who pulled his knees up and tried to turn his face away from the water, whimpering.

The Sergeant gave him a kick in the backside with his boot, so hard that Courtney could hear the leather make contact with bone, and the man cried out and straightened his body instinctively, rolling over away from the wall. The second kick of the boot sank into his stomach, just below the ribcage, and the wind was knocked out of him in a long grunt.

The Sergeant knelt in the wet on the floor, and the Private by him. Together they held a towel tightly over the man's face and gushed water onto it. The man's body twitched and writhed, but they held him down quite easily. The water poured onto the towel and ran over the floor to drain out of a gap at the bottom of the door.

Courtney heard Rousseau say: "This is the water treatment. It's quite effective. It gives a person the feeling he's drowning. Quite often he is." Rousseau's voice was normal, conversational.

Courtney, who could feel the pressure of blood pumping in his head, round behind his eyes, looked at him blankly. Then he said: "Oh, I see." And his voice sounded normal, too.

At last the Sergeant said: "OK, that's enough," and the Private turned off the tap. The sodden towel was pulled off the man's face and his breath came in long, drawn-in wheezes as he fought for air.

"Right, kaffir," said the Sergeant. "Do you want some more?"

Through the wheezes, the voice, barely audible: "No ... no ... no."

"Then will you speak?"

The head nodded. The Sergeant turned to Courtney: "I think we're in business, sir."

They waited for ten or twelve minutes before the man was coherent, and even then it wasn't easy to hear him.

"Who was there when you went to see the terrorists?"

"Ndlovu."

"Who?"

"Ndlovu."

"Ja? Who's Ndlovu? Where does he live?"

"Lapatu."

"The same village as you?"

"Ja ... ja, my baas."

"When did you and Ndlovu see the terrorists?"

"I don't remember ... three weeks ... after the big rains when the river flooded."

"Where did you meet?"

"At the kopje behind the kraal. We met there."

"Who else was there?"

"No one. No one, baas. Me and Ndlovu."

"How many terrorists?" the Sergeant demanded.

"Ten. Ten or twelve. I did not count."

"What did they want?"

"Food," the man said, still fighting for breath. "They wanted to eat."

"What did you bring them?"

"Mealie meal and chickens."

"And then?" the Sergeant asked.

"We left them there and we went back to the village."

"Who else in the village knew you were seeing the terrorists? Did your headman know?"

"Baas?"

"Did your headman know, you stupid kaffir?" the Sergeant shouted.

The man looked bewildered. "Baas," he said. "Ndlovu is the headman."

The Sergeant straightened up. "Ja, you hear that, sir?" he said. "The fucking headman's in on it. That means the whole village is."

Courtney said: "I've seen enough," He stood up, his face drained of colour. "Thank you, Sergeant."

"No trouble, sir." He went to unlock the door. "It turned out to be useful, didn't it?"

"What? Oh ... oh, ja. Very interesting."

The door opened and Courtney and Rousseau stepped out into the sunlight. Courtney felt dizzy as if he had been drugged, then he knew he was going to be sick.

He moved away from Rousseau. "Leave me alone," he said, and he began to run for the clump of trees. Courtney dropped on his hands and knees in the shade and began to heave. His stomach and chest ached with the effort. When he was finished, he slumped exhausted against a tree. Gradually he opened his eyes. Rousseau was watching him, about five yards away. Courtney didn't care.

Rousseau came and sat beside him. He pulled the water bottle out of his webbing belt and unscrewed the top. He put a hand round the back of Courtney's head and tilted it forward until his lips touched the rim of the bottle.

"Don't worry, bloke," Rousseau said gently. "It's always hard the first time. It was the same with me. But you'll find it's downhill all the way from here."

The water in the bottle was warm, but it washed the acid from Courtney's mouth, and tasted good.

NINE

The army Land Rover drove into Lapatu in mid-afternoon and pulled up in a cloud of dust. Everyone in the village stopped to watch, not drawing closer, most just standing outside their mud and grass huts, or waiting half-hidden in the gloom of doorways.

Four soldiers carrying rifles jumped out and walked quickly towards a group of black men who were sitting smoking, squatting on their haunches. The pace at which the white soldiers moved told the villagers they were there on business.

The front soldier said: "Where is the headman? Where's Ndlovu?"

The tribesmen stayed silent, staring at the dust.

"Verstaan jy? Do you understand? Where's that bastard Ndlovu?"

A voice from behind them said calmly and with dignity: "I am Ndlovu. What do you want with me?"

They wheeled around. The headman was standing by a hut. A small dusty boy with a running nose held onto the leg of his khaki trousers.

"Kom!" the soldier said. "Come with us!"

The headman half turned his head and called quietly into the hut. A woman ran out at once, seized the boy by the hand and pulled him back inside. The child began to cry.

Two soldiers grasped the headman's arms and ran him to the Land Rover. Ndlovu half climbed, was half pushed, into the back.

The wheels span as the Land Rover accelerated away. The headman sat passively, gazing at his dry brown village, set in that dry brown landscape, not knowing if he would ever see it again. The people watched him go. Inside a hut, some women began to wail and lament, as if he were already dead.

The Land Rover bumped over the rough paths back to the main camp, with Ndlovu hanging onto the sides for support. It stopped at the group of outbuildings which the camp used as a guardhouse. Ndlovu was bundled out and locked into a small, bare, airless room. He sat on the floor against the wall and waited.

A quarter of a mile away, Colonel Winter, John Courtney and Jan Rousseau met to decide his fate.

Winter had his back turned, staring frowning out of his office window into the bush. "There's no reason to treat the headman differently from any other suspect," the Colonel said. "If our information is correct, and it probably is, it means the whole village is poisoned. Once the headman's in with the terrorists, you can be sure everyone else is. I don't think we're going to win them back to our side. All we can do is make an example of them. Don't you agree, Captain?"

"Well, sir," Courtney said. "I watched part of the interrogation of the other bantu from the village."

"Oh ja?" the Colonel kept his back to them.

"I've thought about it since then, and the thing I keep coming back to is this – yes, the man admitted Ndlovu was involved with the terrorists, but did he do it because it was true, or because Ndlovu's was the first name he could think of, and he wanted the interrogation to stop?"

The Colonel swung round. "Isn't the answer to that straightforward? We interrogate Ndlovu and find out."

"With respect, sir, I wonder if it is. If someone was to take me down to that room, kick me in the ribs and half drown me for long enough, I'd probably admit I was involved with terrorists too," Courtney said.

"I take it you don't approve of some of our techniques," the Colonel said dryly. "But I can tell you they work."

"It isn't that," Courtney replied hastily. "I'm just wondering if in this case – at this time – it's the most efficient way of getting the information we need."

"Ja? Well, what would you suggest?" Winter asked.

"Obviously I think we ought to talk to Ndlovu. But let's question him rather than interrogate him, if you know what I mean. Let's assume for the sake of argument that the information we got this morning is wrong – something a man said simply so he'd be left alone – and that Lapatu isn't a hostile village. I'm not necessarily arguing that it's friendly, but there's a chance it may be neutral. If we treat the headman unfairly, we risk alienating two or three hundred people. We ought to question him in a routine way, then send him back and keep watch. If they are making contact with terrorists, it should be possible to find that out. When we do, we can make an example of the village if you like. But by holding our fire now, it may give us a chance to get to grips with the terrorists involved."

Colonel Winter shook his head emphatically. "Nee. Have you any idea of the manpower we need to keep watch on a village like Lapatu, Captain? Well it's huge, and the bantu would know about it in twenty-four hours."

Rousseau said: "Permission to speak, sir."

"What is it, Sergeant?"

"We could use sensors, sir – put sniffers in the area. They'd tell us if there were any arms about."

Winter looked thoughtful. "That's not a bad idea," he said. "It might be worth a try." He turned to Courtney again: "All right," he said, "you can use Lapatu as your first exercise, Captain. Sergeant Rousseau will be in charge of any interrogations necessary. You can use the velvet glove now, and Rousseau will go back to our old trusted remedies if necessary later. Leave us, Sergeant."

"Yes, sir." Rousseau saluted and walked out of the office.

"Right, Captain," said Winter, settling himself at his desk. "Let me make myself clear. We're taking a chance on this. Those terrorists could be planning anything. They might have an attack scheduled for tomorrow. If we leaned on Ndlovu now he might tell us about it, and we could save lives. But we're not going to. We're going to hang on, play it your way. Now I don't care how you do it, but I want to come out in front on this one. I want to see a clear advantage in it. If the village comes out on our side, fine. But if the village is guilty, then the whole village is going to be punished. Ja, and you, Captain, are going to be the man to organise the punishment. I don't know what you're going to do, but you're going to have to work it so it'll be an unmistakable lesson to all bantu in this area. Do you understand, Captain? It's *your* baby."

Courtney felt his heart sink. "Yes, sir."

"Right. You'd better go and get on with it. You don't want to keep the kaffir waiting, do you?"

"Sir." Courtney saluted.

Outside in the hot sun, Jan Rousseau fell into step and looked quizzically at Courtney. "Another pep talk, sir?" he asked.

"Ja, I'm afraid so, Jan. If it turns out that the village is hostile, I've got to make an example of the people. Christ. What am I supposed to do? Push them into a hut and throw in hand-grenades?"

"Jesus," said Rousseau. "I'm glad it's not me. Puts interrogation in a different light, doesn't it?"

Courtney shook his head numbly. "How did I get myself into this?" he asked. "I'm sorry I opened my mouth."

"The privilege of rank," said Rousseau. "Come on. Let's get to work. Cross the other bridge when you come to it."

"Ja, you're right. Now what are these sensors you were talking about?"

"Oh hell," Rousseau said. "They're great little boxes. Battlefield sensors: more or less our secret weapon. Highly classified. They're about this big." He indicated with his fingers. "About the same as a matchbox. We use four different types. One detects sound, ground vibrations caused by vehicles or infantry, that sort of thing. The other is infra-red. It picks up the heat that people, or engines, give out."

62

Courtney asked: "How do you tell which is a vehicle and which is a man? Or an animal, come to that?"

"Well, you don't, but a computer can. It sorts out false alarms from the real thing. It can give you a pretty good idea of how many people are around too. The third sort – the one we're going to be using for this job – is a chemical sniffer. It can pick up explosives – anything from gelignite or rockets down to a few clips of ammo. There's one other type of sensor we've got, but we don't use it much. It sets up an invisible light beam across an area. If someone walks across it, they interrupt the beam. It's a kind of optical tripwire. The computer can also set off explosives by remote control."

Courtney was impressed. "Fantastic," he said. "Where did we get them? I thought there was supposed to be an arms embargo."

Rousseau said cheerfully: "Christ, we're not short of arms. Embargoes are like rules: they're a challenge. People like to break them. We got our first sensors a few years back – bought them off the Americans. They used them quite a bit in Vietnam, and when that war ended there was a lot of surplus stock. The West Germans make some too. We've got some of the most up-to-date ones now."

"What about the computer?" Courtney asked. "How do we get one of those?"

"There's a whole bank of them already working down at Silvermine. That's just near the naval station at Simonstown. What happens is that the sensors have small transmitters. Our communications people pick up the signals and feed them into Silvermine for analysis. They'll let us know from there if anything happens."

"That sounds pretty efficient," said Courtney. "How long will it take to get them installed around Lapatu?"

"Not long. We've got some in stock here. We can do it tonight."

The men climbed down the slope to the group of outbuildings where Ndlovu was being held, and the soldiers on guard duty came to attention and saluted Courtney.

"I want to see the headman," Courtney said.

"Yes, sir. I'll bring him to the interrogation room."

Courtney looked at Rousseau. "Do we have to use that place?" he asked.

Rousseau shrugged. "There's nowhere else. You know what conditions are like in there." He inclined his head towards the outbuilding cells.

"OK," said Courtney. Then to the soldier: "Ja, bring him to the interrogation room. We'll wait there."

"You'll need the key, sir," the soldier said. He disappeared inside and came back with a bunch on a chain. He selected an ordinary household door key. "It's that one to get in." He held up a second key – a Yale. "That's for the equipment cupboard if you want to help his memory along."

Courtney felt his stomach leap again. Jesus, he wished they'd stop.

"That's fine," he said, taking the keys. "Just bring him up."

He and Rousseau walked off to the interrogation room. The floor was still wet, and it smelled damp and musty. Courtney turned on the light. They sat on the hard, upright wooden chairs and waited.

There was a flurry of movement at the door and a voice shouted: "Get inside there, kaffir! Now we'll teach you a lesson!"

Ndlovu was pushed inside, almost sprawling onto the wet concrete, but recovering his balance in time. He glanced quickly around the room, apprehension obvious in his eyes.

The soldier said: "Ndlovu, sir."

"Thank you, Corporal," Courtney replied. "You can leave him here. We'll bring him back in due course."

"Ja, sir." The soldier saluted and turned to go.

"Leave the door open will you."

"Sir."

Ndlovu stood in front of the wooden desk.

Courtney asked: "You are the headman at Lapatu village?"

"Ja, baas." His voice was quiet and it did not tremble.

"Do you know a man called Phineas from the same village?"

"Ja, baas."

"Where is Phineas now?"

Ndlovu shook his head. "Some soldiers took him."

"Ja," said Courtney. "They brought him here so we could ask

him questions. He told us that he was helping the terrorists."
There was no expression on Ndlovu's face. "He told us he gave
them food at a kopje near the village. Do you know what else he
told us?"

"No, baas."

"He said that you too were helping the terrorists. You,
Ndlovu, the headman."

"Nee, baas!"

"You were with him at the kopje, giving the terrorists food."

"Nee! No! No, baas!"

"Ja. How many terrorists did you see there?"

"I was not there!"

"Why should Phineas lie and tell us you were there if you were
not?"

Ndlovu made no reply.

Courtney demanded: "Why should he lie, Ndlovu?"

Ndlovu looked him in the eye and said simply: "I do not know
why. I was not present when he said this thing. I do not know
what was happening to him when he said it."

Rousseau broke in: "What is happening to you, Ndlovu, you
cheeky kaffir?"

"Baas?"

"What are we doing to you now?" Rousseau asked.

"Nothing," Ndlovu said.

"So why should we do anything to Phineas? We asked him
and he told us. He said you were with the terrorists."

"I was not with the terrorists."

Courtney said: "Have you ever seen any terrorists?"

"Nee, baas!"

"Haven't any ever come to your village and asked for help?"

"None have come."

"What would you do if they came?"

"Baas?"

"Well answer me!" Courtney said. "What would you do?"

"I would tell the soldiers," Ndlovu replied, his gaze focused
somewhere on the table.

"You know there are big rewards for bantu who give information about the terrorists?" Courtney continued.

"Ja, baas."

"OK," said Courtney. "That's it. Let's take you back."

Courtney and Rousseau led Ndlovu out of the interrogation room, locking the door behind them. They brought him back to the farm outbuildings and handed him over to the Corporal in charge.

"That was quick, sir," the Corporal said in surprise.

"Ja, it was. Keep him here overnight. We're returning him to his village tomorrow."

"Yes, sir."

Courtney and Rousseau went to the communications stores and selected the sensors they would need to monitor the area in and around the village, including the kopje where the meeting with the terrorists supposedly took place. There was fairly frequent military traffic near Lapatu, so before night fell Rousseau took a Land Rover and was able to plant sensors in the adjacent bush and up the kopje without appearing too obvious. He returned to the camp and waited until after midnight before driving back to within half a mile of the village. He walked cautiously towards the huts and concealed the remaining sensors around the perimeter.

Rousseau slept late, but woke around midday. Courtney was waiting for him. After lunch they collected Ndlovu from the outbuildings and loaded him in a Land Rover. They also took with them two hand-grenades and some extra clips of ammunition.

No one had told Ndlovu where he was going, or what was being done with him, and, as they drove into Lapatu, Courtney could see on his face puzzlement and concern. They stopped in the middle of the village, and around them people stood silently, watching.

"Right," said Courtney. "Hop out, Ndlovu."

The headman climbed out, wondering what the soldiers planned doing. Courtney said: "Tell the people that if they see a terrorist, they must let us know straight away, or there'll be a lot of trouble. Ja, I mean it. A lot of trouble."

Ndlovu stared at them dumbly. Was that all? Was he free?

The Land Rover accelerated away. Ndlovu and the villagers watched it go, none of them moving. When it was out of sight the men crowded round, and the women began to dance and chant in triumph.

Back at camp, Courtney and Rousseau walked straight to the signals office.

"Message for you, sir," said the Sergeant at the desk. "We've decoded it."

"Thanks." Courtney read it quickly, then grinned broadly and beckoned Rousseau across. The message was short and direct. It gave the codename for Lapatu village itself – Zebra – and after it a date-time group: 041413. It said: "Arms, explosives, Rate One. Out 041417. Ends."

"Bugger me," said Courtney in admiration. "It really works!"

"Of course it works," said Rousseau. "I fixed them myself, didn't I?"

"What's Rate One mean?"

"Well, the quantity of arms and explosives is rated on a scale from one to ten. It doesn't deal in fractions. So a single rifle bullet is rated at one, and so are a couple of grenades and some ammo clips."

"Oh I get it," Courtney said.

"Now there's one other thing we've got to do."

"What's that?"

"Get orders out to Defence Force personnel to keep well clear of that whole area," Rousseau said. "We don't want any false alarms. Let's go see the Colonel."

TEN

The computer watched over Lapatu for three days and nights with nothing to report. All Defence Force personnel gave the area a wide berth. Ndlovu and the tribesmen discussed the strange ways of the soldiers and could reach no conclusion about why he had been freed. There was no news of Phineas. He remained a prisoner. His relatives went to the camp to ask if they could see him, but were turned away. Soldiers swore at them and said they did not know anyone called Phineas.

John Courtney sat in his office and drafted pamphlets for distribution to the villages in the area. He really needed an artist to help him, he thought. They must have called one up. He drew a rough sketch of a weeping bantu woman sitting by a cooking pot. Under it he wrote: "This woman is crying because she has VD. She got it because she was raped by a communist terrorist. The terrorists carry VD and other diseases. Now she has infected her husband, and her husband has given VD to his other wives. When her child is born it will be blind."

Under it, in big block letters, he wrote: "DO NOT HELP THE DISEASED TERRORISTS. TELL THE WHITE SOLDIERS. THEY WILL RID YOU OF THEM."

A second pamphlet showed a crude drawing of a fat terrorist, bristling with weapons. Courtney wrote: "This is a mad dog communist terrorist. See the rifles and weapons he carries. He may say he has come to free you, but soon he will turn his guns on you and your children. Do not listen to the lies of the communist. He wants to steal your cattle. He wants to steal your land. He wants to steal your wives. He wants to kill your sons. TELL THE WHITE SOLDIERS. THEY WILL RID YOU OF THIS COMMUNIST ENEMY."

Colonel Winter was pleased with the pamphlets, and dispatched them to Pretoria with a suggestion that they be printed up as soon as possible.

It was midnight on the fourth night, and Courtney had just dropped off to sleep under the mosquito net in his tent when he was shaken awake by a signalman.

"Sir! Wake up! There's an urgent message for you!"

Courtney sat up in his camp bed, his mind still groggy with sleep. "What? What's up?"

"An urgent message, sir, from Silvermine. It's being decoded now."

Courtney was fully alert in an instant. "Christ, it's happening," he said. "Go and wake Sergeant Rousseau and get him over to the signals office right away."

"Yes, sir."

Courtney pulled on his camouflage pants and jacket, and buckled his webbing belt. He took his beret off the steel chest of drawers, then put on his boots and began to run. There was a slight chill in the night air, and the sky was bright with stars. Light spilled out of the windows of the signals office. Courtney went in.

"We're just finishing decoding, sir," the duty Sergeant said. "Be ready in a minute."

Courtney heard the sound of boots running towards the office. Jan Rousseau pulled on his camouflage jacket as he ran.

"OK, that's it, sir," the Sergeant said, pulling the in-clear message off his pad and handing it to Courtney.

"Have a look, Jan," Courtney said. The two men studied the piece of paper. "What's Mountie?" Courtney asked.

"That's the codename for the kopje," Rousseau answered. "What's the time now? – Twelve past midnight. Ja, so this all started about twenty minutes ago. Okay. 'Mountie 082351. Arms, explosives Rate Three. Out 082354.' Shit, that didn't take them long. Now where did they go ... Christmas 082356. Where's Christmas? Christ, let's look at the map." Rousseau unfolded it on a table and put the message over it. "Right," he said to Courtney, "here's the kopje. They got there at 2351 and stayed a couple of minutes. Then they moved off to where ... Jesus, where did I plant Christmas? Ah, here we are. They're moving away from the village again. Christmas at 2356, and out of it at 2358. They're walking in that direction." He motioned with his hand. "We don't have any more sensors in that area. Bugger it."

The signals Sergeant called across, holding up another coded telex message. "There's more in, sir."

Rousseau raised his eyebrows. "They've either doubled back, or there are others."

Courtney asked: "What are we going to do?"

Rousseau said: "Well, if you'd like to give me the order, sir, I'll rustle up a squad of men and we'll see if we can catch some commies."

"Right. Do it. Have someone wake the Colonel and tell him."

"Ja, sir."

Rousseau left at a run, and Courtney watched the signals Sergeant going through the painstaking business of decoding.

Rousseau was back before the second message was ready, and Courtney could already hear running boots and talking, men forming up outside the signals room, and Land Rovers being started, their engines revving loud in the night.

Rousseau took the second message and plotted the terrorists' movements. "Magazine at 0003 ... that's over here. It's the same lot. They obviously swung round in a flanking movement. Wonder why they did that? Oh, ja, here's why. Look at this. Arms and explosives are put at Rate Four. The first message gave them as Rate Three, which is quite a well-armed band. Now it's gone up a notch. Either they've been joined by other terrorists, or they picked up extra equipment round the area here. I reckon they've got more blokes. I don't see that they'd have had time to get extra stuff out of hiding. So out of Magazine at 0005, and what next? Into Crossroad at eight minutes past, and out at eleven ... that's it there ... and jackpot! We've got them. Zebra at fourteen minutes past. There's not an out time for that. They've stopped in the village."

A hand fell on Courtney's shoulder. He straightened up and saluted. "Morning, Colonel," he said. "Sorry to get you up."

"What's up, Captain?"

"We've got terrorists, sir, in Lapatu."

"You surprise me, Captain," Colonel Winter said dryly. "What are they rated at?"

Rousseau said: "Computer rating started at three, sir, but it's gone up to four. Looks like they picked up some friends."

"That's quite high," Winter said. "OK, Rousseau, you're in charge of the attack. Have you got everything you need?"

"Ja."

"Then move."

As Rousseau ran out, Courtney said quickly: "Can I go along, sir?"

"It's outside your line of territory, Captain. You're not trained for it."

"No, sir."

Colonel Winter thought for a moment. "Actually it might do you a bit of good," he said. "Ja, why not. Keep your head down and don't for Christ's sake get in the way."

"No, sir."

Courtney ran for the door and flagged down Rousseau's Land Rover as it moved off. "I'm coming with you," he said.

Rousseau grinned. "Hop in, sir."

The Land Rover led a convoy of three bumping over the dirt track out of the camp towards Lapatu. Courtney looked at his watch: twenty-five minutes to one.

"How long will it take us to get there?" he asked.

"Half an hour if we're lucky," Rousseau said. "The last mile we have to do with lights out. Thank God there's a full moon. Then we're going to have to cover about half a mile on foot. We'll park behind the kopje."

They drove on in silence for several minutes, the Land Rover bucking and bumping over the track, headlights starkly illuminating the bushes and trees.

The radio in the back of the Land Rover crackled.

"One-zero signals, over."

Rousseau picked up the microphone. "One-zero, OK, over."

"One-zero, OK. Message, over."

"One-zero, send, over."

"One-zero," control said, "Zebra out 090032. Roger so far, over?"

Rousseau groaned. "Jesus, they've left the village." He pressed the SEND button. "Roger, over."

"One-zero. Crossroad 090035. Rate Four. Out 090038. Over."

"One-zero, Roger, out."

Courtney asked: "What now?"

"Bloody hell," Rousseau said. "Now we try and track them. There isn't a lot we can do at night. Unless we get lucky, we're going to have to wait until dawn."

A few minutes later came the confirmation. The terrorists were moving back the way they'd come, past the sensors and out of range. Rousseau took the Land Rovers in a sweep to the north to try and cut them off, and parked in the cover of a clump of trees. The soldiers fanned out, moving cautiously through the bush, straining for any unusual sound or the slightest movement. There was nothing. After an hour, Rousseau called off the hunt.

"We'll start again at first light," he said. "Let's go back to camp and get some rest."

Courtney stayed at the base when the others left just after five to begin tracking. The sky was lightening and the silhouettes of trees and hills were just emerging from the blackness. The tracker squad picked up the criss-cross bootmarks of between ten and fifteen terrorists, and followed them for four miles. Then they reached the main tarred road, and stopped. It was the end of the line. Rousseau radioed for instructions.

Colonel Winter ordered him to pick up Ndlovu and bring him back to camp. Then he summoned Courtney to his office.

"Well, Captain," he said. "Are you satisfied now? Is the village hostile or isn't it?"

"I don't think we know for certain yet, sir," Courtney replied. "But ja, I agree it's probably hostile."

"What more proof do you want, Captain?" Colonel Winter's voice had an angry edge to it.

"We have to ask the villagers, sir. If they deny that the terrorists were there, then that's the proof. It's just possible they arrived out of the blue last night and there hasn't been enough time for the bantu to let us know about it."

Winter snorted. "Well," he said, "you'll have a chance to ask the headman. I've told Sergeant Rousseau to pull him in again for questioning."

"Yes, sir."

"And remember what I told you earlier, Captain. You can have one more try with Ndlovu, and if you get nowhere, then it's over to Sergeant Rousseau for interrogation. Is that clear?"

"Yes, sir."

"There's also the matter of punishing the bantu in the village. I'll be waiting to hear your proposals. I want something that'll be a lesson to everyone in this area, but at the same time try and avoid the obvious pitfalls, like turning them into martyrs."

"Yes, sir," Courtney said.

"Let's get the initiative again, Captain. You may go."

Courtney went out into the morning sun and squinted up at the cloudless sky. A fly settled on his forehead and he swatted at it. Didn't it ever rain in this rotten, miserable hole? Damn Ndlovu and his bloody village. Courtney had done his best. If the man lied now, there was nothing anyone could do to help him.

Courtney went to the Officers' mess tent for breakfast, and then sat in his office waiting for Rousseau's return.

It was eleven o'clock when Jan Rousseau walked in. "Sit, Jan," said Courtney, pointing to a chair. "How did it go?"

"Bloody awful. We followed the tracks to the main road, and that was that. There were ten or fifteen of them."

"Did you pick up Ndlovu?"

"Ja. He's down in the prison block."

"Look, the Colonel's given me one last crack at him. We don't know that the village is hostile until we ask someone whether they saw any terrorists last night. If Ndlovu was there, and he denies seeing anyone, then that's it. I'll hand him over to you. You can put electrodes on his balls for all I care."

Rousseau grinned. "Gee, thanks a ton," he said.

"You haven't eaten?"

"No. I'll have a bite now if that's all right."

"Sure," Courtney said. "I'll wait till you're ready, then we'll go and see what Ndlovu has to say for himself."

Rousseau went off to get breakfast, and Courtney sat in his office, doodling on a piece of paper on which he'd written: "See the communist terrorist beating the innocent sons of the soil. The terrorist will torture and murder to get your cattle, your land and your wives . . ." Bloody hell.

What could he do about Lapatu? There wasn't much he could do about Ndlovu. Unless the headman really was on the white side, he would find himself in for a very rough ride. Jan Rousseau was a nice guy, but Courtney had no doubt about his toughness. Christ, he was a commando after all, and he hadn't got there by being gentle. And what about the village? What would the Colonel consider a suitable punishment? Take the men out and shoot them, maybe? It would be legal all right, but if word leaked out and got into the press there'd be a massive international outcry and they'd have a village of martyrs. No, it couldn't be anything as crude as that. Bring all the men and women in for interrogation perhaps? Give them a spot of water torture and let the courts put them in prison for life? That was possible, and it would certainly be a lesson for other bantu in the area.

But there was the question of proving exactly who had, and

who had not, co-operated with the terrorists. And the court would have to be told how the army knew terrorists were in the village – which meant giving details of the sensors. The Colonel probably wouldn't want that either. How about killing their cattle and wrecking their crops and leaving them to starve? Oh hell, they'd be martyrs again. But there must be something. Courtney thought: we ought to hold a Creative Meeting of Defence Force personnel in this area, this remote branch of Van Niekerk and Tessler, to see who can come up with the best method of punishing a village of two or three hundred men, women and children, without either turning it into a symbol of black revolution, or being caught in the act by the rest of the world.

He got up to see how Rousseau was getting along. He walked across to the mess tent and sat on the other side of the table. Rousseau finished a mug of tea and looked across at him inquiringly.

"Ready?" he said. Courtney nodded. They walked along to the farm buildings and Courtney called to the Corporal on duty in the main building, his voice sounding rougher than he meant it to: "OK, let's have the keys to the interrogation room. Get Ndlovu there, at the double!"

"Yes, sir!" The Corporal fetched the keys and Courtney and Rousseau went to prepare. As they walked towards the room, they could hear the combination whine and clatter of a jet helicopter coming in low. It passed over the trees just in front of them and hovered before dropping onto the landing zone.

"That's an Alouette," Rousseau said. "French."

"What's it doing?"

"There's a big hunt on for the terrorists. It's probably part of it."

Courtney unlocked the interrogation room door and stepped inside. The concrete floor was dry now, and there was no smell.

"Can you throw me the keys, sir?" Rousseau asked.

Courtney did so. The Sergeant went across to the cupboard and unfastened the padlock. He looked inside and scratched his head. "There aren't too many alternatives," he said.

Courtney came forward to look. On one shelf was a hosepipe, a towel, and a length of rope. On another, a pair of large crocodile clips attached to an electric flex, with the other end fastened to a

74

small hand-operated generator. If you cranked the handle, it produced current. There was a hood without eyeholes, a rubber cosh, and long strips of material which could be used as gags. On the bottom shelf were several sets of handcuffs, and more lengths of rope. That was all.

Ndlovu came sprawling into the room, kicked in the small of his back by the duty Corporal, and fell on his face on the concrete. The Corporal said: "Ndlovu, sir," and left. Courtney turned to Rousseau: "Lock the door."

Courtney found his breathing had become quite shallow and he could feel his heart pumping. The room darkened into gloom. Ndlovu picked himself off the floor, a rivulet of blood running down his cheek where the skin had split open. He stood before the two soldiers.

Courtney said quietly: "Ndlovu, where were you last night?"

"At my hut, my baas."

"Where is your hut?"

"At my village. At Lapatu."

Courtney paused, then continued: "Think carefully before you answer now. Did you go away from the village at any time last night?"

Ndlovu shook his head emphatically. "No, my baas. I was there all the time."

"What happened last night?" Courtney asked.

"Nothing, master. Nothing happened."

"Did anyone come and visit you?"

There was a fleeting look of surprise on Ndlovu's face, then he said: "No one."

"Are you sure?"

"No one came."

Rousseau cut in: "Some terrorists came to your village last night."

"Nee, no, my baas! No terrorists!"

"Tell the truth, you bastard!" Rousseau shouted, the veins standing out on his thick bull neck. "You had terrorists there, didn't you?"

"No. No one. No one came."

Silence fell. Rousseau looked at Courtney. "Well, Captain," he said. "Is he mine?"

75

Courtney nodded. "Yes," he said. "He's yours."

"Do you want to go?" Rousseau asked.

Courtney thought for a moment then shook his head. "No, I reckon I'm in this now. I'll stay."

"Will you help, or shall I call someone else in?"

Courtney's mouth was quite dry. He felt his lips sticking together and his tongue was tacky when it touched his palate.

"I'll do what I can." Courtney turned back to Ndlovu. "I have tried to save you from this, but now there is nothing that can be done until you tell the truth. Do you understand?"

Ndlovu said defiantly: "I saw no one, my baas."

Rousseau went to the cupboard and fetched out handcuffs and the electrodes.

"Strip, kaffir!" he said. "Get your fucking clothes off!"

ELEVEN

Courtney sat on the hard wooden chair, physically exhausted and emotionally drained. Even Jan Rousseau was showing signs of strain. Ndlovu lay naked and handcuffed on the cold cement, teeth clenched, making a low agonised growling sound in the back of his throat, a sound which came in waves with his gasps for breath. Except for yelling obscenities at them, he had said nothing. He would not answer questions now, not even to deny accusations. If he wasn't swearing, or screaming, or crying out, he was making this terrible anguished panting. Courtney's arm ached from cranking the generator, and his mouth tasted bitter with the wretchedness and futility of it.

The crocodile clips were still attached to Ndlovu's body, biting deep into his nipples, moved there after being fastened to his genitals.

Rousseau looked across at Courtney. "You all right?"

"Ja. Just about. And you?"

Rousseau nodded. They stared at each other.

"What now?" Courtney asked.

"I don't know about him," Rousseau said, indicating Ndlovu, "but I need a break. We'll start again this afternoon. One thing about this sort of interrogation: it gets easier all the time for the guys who do it, and it gets harder all the time if it's being done to you. We'll break him, even if it takes a week."

"I'm not sure *I* can take a week," Courtney said.

"Ja, sure you can," Rousseau replied. Then he said, seriously: "You've changed a lot in the last four or five days, bloke. You've come a long way already. You're a paid-up member of the club now."

"I think I might resign."

"You can't resign," Rousseau said simply. "It's like losing your virginity. Once you're in, that's it for life."

"Thanks a lot."

Rousseau clapped an arm across his shoulders. "That's your initiation over with, Captain. I'll clear up and we can go and have lunch."

Rousseau stopped beside Ndlovu and jerked the crocodile clips off his nipples. The headman sucked in his breath sharply. Rousseau unfastened the handcuffs, wound up the flex neatly, picked up the generator and packed them all back in the cupboard. He snapped the padlock shut and went to unlock the door. Light, and air, flooded in.

"Jesus, that's better," Courtney said. He hadn't realised how fetid the room had become.

Rousseau went across to stand by Ndlovu. "Right, kaffir!" he shouted. "On your feet! There'll be more this afternoon unless you start talking. Think about it. Come on! On your feet!"

Ndlovu made an effort to rise, but his knees buckled.

"Come on! Up! Up!" Rousseau yelled. Ndlovu lay where he was, not moving.

Courtney asked: "Are you sure he's all right?"

"Him? Ja, he's fine. A bit shaken up and sore. He's not going to die. The current we gave him is painful, that's all."

"What'll we do?" Courtney said.

"Leave him there," Rousseau replied dismissively "We'll send the Corporal up to get him."

They left Ndlovu lying on the floor of the interrogation room and walked back towards the cell outbuildings. They handed the keys over and left instructions to collect Ndlovu, then set off back to the main camp.

The Alouette helicopter was in the air again, circling in a tight turn, and the men watched it.

"I wouldn't mind going up in one of those," Courtney said. "It looks great."

"It's a good ride," Rousseau agreed. "It can be pretty exciting. You'd like it."

"I must try and arrange it some day."

"Hey, bloke, I've got an idea," said Rousseau suddenly. "How about today? Let's mix business with pleasure."

"Oh? How?"

"Well, I'll bet. Ndlovu's never been up in a chopper. It'll give him a chance to see his village."

Courtney looked at Rousseau blankly. "What do you mean?"

"You'll see. Let's go talk to the pilot."

They walked to the landing zone and waited as the Alouette hovered and settled, its blades stirring up a whirlwind of dust. "Wait here," said Rousseau and, keeping his head down, ran over to the helicopter. Courtney could see him in conversation with the officer at the controls. They spoke for three or four minutes, then Rousseau came running back, ducking under the blades, which still revolved slowly.

"Right," he said, "that's fixed. Round about three o'clock, and he'll take us on a tour of the district."

"What about Ndlovu?"

"Oh, he's coming too."

Courtney looked at Rousseau reprovingly. "Now come on, Jan, what have you got in mind?"

Rousseau laughed. "Wait and see, sir."

Courtney found he could, after all, eat lunch. The tiredness had left him, but he still felt a core of depression. Just after three, Rousseau came to collect him and they went to get Ndlovu from the cell block. While the Corporal was bringing him out, Rousseau took the keys and disappeared up towards the interrogation

78

room. He returned with four pairs of handcuffs and some coils of rope.

Ndlovu was pulled out of his cell. When he saw Courtney and Rousseau he gave a frightened start, but then swore under his breath and fell silent. He was still having difficulty walking and seemed to be in pain.

Rousseau locked one pair of handcuffs onto each of his wrists and one pair onto each of his ankles, so that the spare ends jingled as he walked. They led him to the landing zone.

The Alouette was parked, its blades still. The pilot sat in the open doorway reading a newspaper.

"Hi there," Jan Rousseau greeted him. "Ready to go?"

The pilot nodded. "Ja."

He jumped out and ducked under the helicopter's fuselage. "OK," he said, "lay him down parallel with the landing struts."

Rousseau pushed Ndlovu underneath the Alouette. "Lie down, you bastard. No. Not on your back, on your face."

He tied a rope to one empty handcuff, and gave the other end to the pilot to fasten round a strut. Rousseau dug Ndlovu in the ribs with his boot. "You'd better pray we're good at knots."

Soon, the headman was spreadeagled on the ground, a rope from each limb attached to the extremities of the sled under-carriage.

"OK," said the pilot. "Let's get going."

Courtney and Rousseau climbed into the helicopter and buck-led their seat belts.

"Jan," said Courtney. "What are we going to do?"

"What do you think? We're taking Ndlovu for a ride," Rousseau said.

The jet engine began to whine and, after a few seconds, the main rotor turned slowly, picking up speed. Dust rose around the helicopter and completely enveloped Ndlovu, then the noise increased and they lifted off. The dust whirled up, hitting Ndlovu in the face and forcing itself into his lungs, while he dangled helplessly feeling a terrible pain in his joints, which twisted under the weight of his trunk. The steel handcuffs tore into his wrists and ankles. He tried to turn his head to the side to escape the dust, but it made no difference.

The helicopter hung fifteen feet above the ground for about a minute, and then shot straight up into the sky. Inside, Courtney felt his stomach churn with the sensation, and there was painful pressure on his eardrums. Ndlovu began to scream in pain and terror.

The pilot took the Alouette up to two thousand feet and started swinging it round in tight circles. Each movement, every alteration in his centre of gravity, ripped at Ndlovu's joints. Then the Alouette dropped like a stone, and the headman's pain eased as the weight lessened, but his panic increased as he plummeted. Suddenly, up again, and the jerk caused explosions of agony over his body.

Inside, Rousseau shouted to Courtney above the noise of the engines: "Great ride, isn't it?"

Courtney nodded, grinning.

The pilot took the Alouette down to tree-top level and began the flight towards Lapatu village. The branches and leaves brushed against Ndlovu, tearing his skin and clothes. The earth unwound below his terrified eyes, a changing panorama of brown dust, whipping up as they passed, flashes of green accompanied by the blows to his face and body from the branches as they scraped by, then brown dust, and a river quickly passing underneath. Then there was brown again, and huts, a cluster of huts, with people looking up, staring. Which people? Which huts? In his pain, Ndlovu recognised nothing, and even when the pilot hovered over the village he still did not comprehend where he was because the dust came up again into his face and eyes and blinded him. Those on the ground recognised the headman though, and watched, silent and appalled. At last the helicopter turned for home.

Ndlovu fainted on the way back, overcome with pain. He revived just as the pilot was dropping for touch-down at the landing zone, and he was enveloped by another storm of dust.

The breath was driven from his body as he hit the ground and the sled undercarriage settled on each side of him.

The whine and chatter of the engine died away, and he was aware of men standing round, untying the ropes. He felt himself being lifted and dragged, and then dropped suddenly on some dry grass.

Courtney and Rousseau stood watching.

Courtney knelt beside the man and said seriously: "You see what you have brought on yourself, Ndlovu? All this will stop if you tell the truth. Who was at your village last night?"

The headman summoned up his last reserves of strength. They saw his lips move. Courtney brought his head close to Ndlovu's mouth.

"Ja, what did you say?" Courtney asked. "Who was at your village?"

The lips moved again.

Rousseau asked: "What did he say, sir?"

Courtney stood up embarrassed. "He told me to fuck off."

Rousseau burst out laughing. "Christ, he's a hard bugger," he said. "You can't help admiring him."

They half-carried, half-dragged Ndlovu back to the cell block. Afterwards, Courtney went to his tent and lay down on his camp bed. He tried to analyse his feelings. He didn't feel sick any more. But he did feel curiously empty.

TWELVE

They gave Ndlovu the water treatment the next day, and he endured. At one point Rousseau had to give him artificial respiration to get him gasping again. Still the headman said nothing. They carried him to his cell and left him crumpled on the bare cement floor. Then they went back to Courtney's office, and Rousseau took up smoking again.

"Well, Jan," Courtney said. "Still think you're going to break him?"

Rousseau exhaled slowly and shook his head. "I just don't know. He's a hard bastard. Maybe not."

"What are we going to do?"

"Keep trying, I suppose. I might use the cosh tomorrow, see if I can soften him up that way. What else can I do?"

Courtney sat deep in thought, and at once a plan formed in his mind, taking shape quickly, meeting the objections he tested it with. Yes, it could work. At least it would stop the interrogation and make the contest a bit more sporting. If they weren't going to get a confession out of Ndlovu they wouldn't be able to get a conviction in a court, so they were stymied in that direction. But there was a way to neutralise the village. Bloody hell, yes. Courtney felt a surge of excitement. He grinned at Rousseau.

"Jan," Courtney said, "I've got it. Now you might think it's a bit mad at first, but hear it through and use your imagination."

Rousseau listened carefully, and by the end he was laughing. "You're a bad bugger," he said. "Remind me never to buy anything you advertise. Think you can sell it to the Colonel?"

"Let's go and see. Will you back me?"

"Ja, why not? It sounds all right."

The men went through to Colonel Winter's office and Courtney knocked on the door.

"What is it?"

"Morning, Colonel," Courtney said, saluting. "Can Sergeant Rousseau and I have a word with you?"

"You'd better come in. What's on your mind?"

"The headman Ndlovu, sir. And what we should do about Lapatu."

"Oh yes." Winter looked interested. "The plan you've been promising me."

Courtney couldn't stop himself grinning. "I think I've worked out a good one. It may sound a bit off-beat at first, but I think it's got a good chance of being effective. First of all, Ndlovu. He's not talking, sir. We've tried everything."

Winter looked across at Rousseau: "You've been interrogating him thoroughly, Sergeant?"

"Yes, sir," Rousseau said. "Captain Courtney and I have been working on him together."

"Captain Courtney has?" Winter looked thoughtful. "Bit out of your province, isn't it, Captain?"

"In a way, sir, I suppose it is. But I thought I was involved in this problem, and I ought to be completely involved. The way Ndlovu has reacted to interrogation is very important, I think. It really dictates the line we should follow now."

"Very well," said Winter. Then to Rousseau: "The interrogation has been thorough?"

"Very thorough, sir, ja. Electrodes, water. We even took him on a helicopter ride to see his village," Rousseau said.

"Oh it was you two, was it?" Colonel Winter replied. "I watched some of it out of my window. What did Ndlovu have to say after that?"

Courtney said: "He told me to fuck off, sir."

Winter looked thoughtful. "He did, did he? Has he said anything else?"

"No, sir," answered Courtney. "He refuses to talk at all now. He just swears at us."

"So," the Colonel said, a trace of amusement in his eyes. "A hard nut. What's your plan then, Captain?"

"As I mentioned earlier, sir, it may seem a bit off-beat at first," Courtney said, "but if you listen to it in its totality, I think you'll find the logic fair enough. Basically, I think we should stop interrogating Ndlovu and begin treating him well – food, medical attention, the lot. Secondly, I don't think we should punish the village. I think we should reward it. Throw a party there – beer, Cokes, buns, sweets, everything."

Colonel Winter stared at Courtney as if he had gone mad. Courtney's voice faltered for an instant under the hostile gaze, but he gathered his composure and ploughed on, as if he were giving a presentation to a doubtful advertising client, keeping his voice clear and positive.

"I also think we ought to get hold of a flagpole," Courtney continued, "and plant it in the middle of the village. We run up the South African flag, and we tell the tribesmen that we'll kill anyone who takes it down. That bit should be the only threat in the whole campaign. So there's the picture. Lapatu was a hostile village which helped the terrorists, gave them food, and probably all sorts of other assistance. They felt free to come and go without danger of being informed on. Then one day the headman gets picked up and tortured. There's no point pretending he wasn't – we hung him over the village for everyone to see. Suddenly things change. The headman is released and allowed back home. He's not in bad physical shape. I don't know what we've done to his sex life, but that's his problem. He looks all right.

Then the village starts flying the South African flag. The army arrives and gives them a party, brings presents for the kids. Word about that will be around in no time. Now imagine you're a terrorist, sir. What would you make of it?"

Winter considered the proposition, then put one hand over his eyes and began to laugh. "Jee-sus Christ!" he said.

Courtney pressed his advantage. "Ja, you see their problem? The only explanation is that the headman talked, and Lapatu has gone over to our side. At best, the terrorists can't trust the people any more so the village is neutralised. What's more likely is they're going to come to Lapatu for an explanation. Ndlovu and his friends could find themselves being interrogated by the communists – which would make a change. Now we've got the sensors, so we'll know when the terrorists move in. It gives us a chance for another crack at them."

Winter grinned amiably at Courtney. "I can see why you're big in advertising, Captain. Well, Sergeant Rousseau, what do you think?"

"I like parties, sir," Rousseau said. "I think it's fantastic."

"So do I," said Winter. "Right, Captain, you're on. What do you need?"

"A flagpole, sir. That's the centrepiece of the whole plan, and a South African flag of course. A nice big one."

"We've got a couple of spare flags here. And there's got to be a pole in Chicundu we can requisition," the Colonel said. "It might take a couple of days."

"Oh that's all right, sir. I don't think we should move in until next week anyway. We've got to give Ndlovu time to recover, and we've got to get everything prepared. I'd also like a military band."

"That's easy. How about a display of police dogs, or a flypast?"

"Not the police dogs, sir. Nothing too aggressive. This is a party for the converted. A flypast might be nice, though: it'll help attract attention, especially if the planes can loop-the-loop and that sort of thing. Trail coloured smoke if possible. That'll make it obvious they're not on active duty. How about some sky-divers? Everyone likes them."

Colonel Winter jotted the points on his pad. "Coloured smoke ... sky-divers ... OK. What else?"

84

"Trestle tables. Balloons for the kids. Things to eat and drink – enough for what? Two or three hundred people, plus whoever comes from other villages to see the fun and who'll help spread the word," Courtney said.

"Fine," said the Colonel. "If you think of anything else, just let me know. I might come along to the party myself."

"I'm sure they'd welcome a kind word and a few pats on the back from you, sir. We want to be as obviously friendly and informal as possible."

Winter smiled; "Well done, Captain," he said. "That's pretty good thinking."

"Thank you, sir. Today's Tuesday. Shall we say the party on Wednesday of next week?"

Courtney and Rousseau walked out of the office, and into the mid-morning heat. Courtney said: "Let's go and see about Ndlovu." They went to the cell block and ordered the headman to be brought out into the courtyard.

He was still naked and looked in a bad way. His shoulders were slumped and he walked with difficulty. His testicles had swollen up after the electric-shock treatment, and his joints were also swollen and painful. He looked at the men with sullen hatred.

"Hello, Ndlovu," Courtney said. "Are you going to tell us who was at your village that night?"

Ndlovu made no reply.

"Never mind," said Courtney, "we don't care now. Nothing's going to happen to you any more. Do you understand? No one's going to hurt you. We're going to take you to see the doctor now. Ja, you look as if you need him."

Ndlovu was given his clothes and made to dress, wincing with pain.

They led him up to the main camp to the medical tent where he was examined, given pain-killing injections and antibiotics.

Then they took him to the cookhouse and ordered lunch. There was steak on the menu. No one knew which plate to give Ndlovu. It would cause trouble if the men knew a bantu had been eating off their own mess plates which would later be handed to them, so a private was sent down to the cell block to get a bantu plate. Then there was the question of eating utensils. Rousseau resolved the dilemma by cutting the steak into pieces with his own army knife, and letting Ndlovu eat with his fingers as he usually did. The headman sat painfully under a tree and wolfed the food, hardly pausing to chew.

Courtney watched in amazement. "Don't they feed them down there?" he asked Rousseau.

The Sergeant shrugged. "Doesn't look much like it."

"Christ."

The heaped plate was clean in two or three minutes. "Right," said Rousseau. "On your feet, Ndlovu. Back to your room."

When he was locked in again, Courtney gave instructions that, in future, the headman was to be accorded special treatment: no kicks or beatings; three meals a day, collected from the mess tent; and a walk to see the medical orderly every morning. But no visitors.

Courtney took the afternoon off and lay down in his tent. Thank God the interrogation was over. Now that the new plan was going into operation, he felt relieved, even cleansed. The bad bit was finished. He had done it – joined the club. Rousseau was right. There was no going back now, and no point giving in to feelings of shame or depression. This was the way the war was fought, and it was futile wishing it was otherwise. If he could just keep dreaming up plans to divert some of it onto different lines, to cut down the amount of routine interrogation, he would be helping to change the system from within. Maybe that would be his real contribution to the Defence Forces.

Courtney fell into a peaceful, dreamless sleep – his first for days.

THIRTEEN

On the Monday morning, a squad of men took a truck to the school near the town of Chicundu and dug up a flagpole. Then they drove to the Defence Force stores to pick up a bag of quick-drying cement, a bag of sand and a barrel of water.

The truck bumped out along the track to Lapatu village. The soldiers did not speak to the tribesmen at all, not to greet them, nor to ask for help. They dug a hole at a spot in the centre of the village – a dusty, open area with most of the mud and thatch huts circled round – and lowered the end of the flagpole into it.

While two men held it upright, the others collected small rocks to weight it in place. Then they mixed the cement and poured it into the hole.

The people of the village watched in silence, not understanding what the activity meant to them. At last the soldiers finished. They climbed back into their truck and drove off, still without a word.

The flagpole towered, high and white, over the huts.

The tribesmen waited until the truck was out of sight before they approached the flagpole. They touched it gingerly to see if there was some trick, tugged at the rope looped over pulleys, pushed the pole to see if it was set firm. There was some discussion about whether they should chop it down and burn it in their fires, but the elders cautioned against it. The white man had power and might punish them all. It would be better to leave it alone: to wait and see what happened. It was surely there for a purpose.

Wherever anyone went in the village, and for two or three miles around, the flagpole loomed up and dominated the dusty brown settlement.

On the Wednesday morning, just after daybreak, the first army trucks began arriving, heavy laden, lurching over the rough track. This time the soldiers spoke, greeting the villagers civilly, laughing and making jokes. They told them their headman was coming back later in the morning and there would be a celebration.

The people of Lapatu listened in bewilderment. But it seemed there *was* going to be a celebration. The soldiers set up long trestle tables along one side of the huts, near the flagpole, and on another side, rows and rows of chairs and metal music-stands.

The soldiers spoke to the children; gave them sweets; talked politely with the elders, asking about the crops and how many cattle they now had, and how many children. The villagers did not trust them, but did not know how to deal with them, or what to think about the sudden attention.

At ten o'clock another truck came, bringing bags of mealie meal for the village women to prepare, and the carcass of a cow to roast. The men collected firewood while the women prepared the meal.

The first trucks left to pick up new loads. They were back by noon, bringing with them crates of Coca-Cola, dozens of boxes of Lion Ale and Castle Lager, trays of buns coated with sticky white icing, packets of sweets and bags of balloons. The tribesmen watched.

By this time, word was getting around the district that the Europeans were doing strange things at Lapatu, and groups of bantu from other villages gathered two or three hundred yards off to look, not coming any closer, and not being invited to do so.

By two o'clock, everything was ready. The cow was roasting on an open fire. The sadza – thick, starchy maize meal porridge – bubbled in tins. The food and drink had been set out on the tables, and soldiers were blowing up the last of the balloons, tying them to sticks which they pushed into the thatched roofs of huts, In the middle of it all was the flagpole.

The crowd of outsiders watching from a distance grew to about six hundred.

Colonel Winter's Land Rover led the main convoy to the village. Sitting in front with him was Ndlovu. The antibiotics had brought down the swelling in his body, although there was still pain when he walked. However, before leaving camp, the army doctor had given him a powerful pain-killing injection, which would last him until the early morning. Behind Ndlovu sat Courtney and Rousseau. The second Land Rover contained other officers from the camp. Behind that came a lorry with the military band and their instruments.

The convoy stopped at the edge of the village, not with the usual skidding of tyres, but arriving as guests would.

Ndlovu stared uncomprehending at his village, with the coloured balloons, the tables laden with food and drink, the white pole in the centre, the smell of roasting meat, and then he looked out into the bush at the growing knots of people from other

88

villages standing staring, and even further on from them he saw other bantu running to join the spectators.

This time, when the people of Lapatu saw Ndlovu in the Land Rover, they did not wait silently at the edges of their huts but came to see how he was, and some women began ululating – the high-pitched call of joy. Ndlovu moved forward to tell them to stop, to say this celebration was none of his doing, to explain that he did not know what was happening but he feared it was a white man's trick: yet when he tried to speak, he found he was trembling so much that no words came.

White soldiers walked up to him quickly, clapped him on the back in mock cameraderie. One pushed a Lion Ale into his hand, white froth running over the mouth of the bottle. Ndlovu stood stricken. Then others in the village had beers in their hands, and the children had Coca-Colas, and there was loud talking beginning, and laughter.

Suddenly a white soldier shouted: "Quiet! Quiet!" and the babble died as quickly as it had begun. "Kom!" shouted the soldier. "Kom, sit!"

The villagers settled in the dust round the flagpole. Colonel Winter stepped forward and looked round at them.

"People of Lapatu," he said. "Your headman is back with you. We have brought him back with a celebration. We want to say thank you to the people of Lapatu. There is drink and meat and sadza. There is a band who will play for you. Later aeroplanes will come and perform tricks, and men with parachutes will jump from another aeroplane. This we are doing for you as friends."

Colonel Winter glanced at the flagpole and indicated it with his hand. "Now we have put this flagpole in the village, but it is ours." Rousseau moved forward with the South African flag and swiftly attached it to the rope.

Winter said: "No one must touch this flagpole. No one must pull down this flag. It must fly day and night. It must fly when the day is hot, and when it is raining. Any person who touches the flag, or takes it down, will be shot. Yes, him and his family. They will all be shot dead. Does everyone understand?"

Winter looked around. There was complete silence now. The people sat or squatted on the ground, their bottles of drink still in their hands.

"Right, Sergeant," said Winter, and Rousseau slowly raised the orange, white and blue South African flag over Lapatu, where it hung limply.

"Now," said Winter, smiling again, "that flag and the pole is ours, but the village and this celebration is yours. Your headman has returned. It is a time of joy."

Rousseau and Courtney led the soldiers in a round of applause and whistling, and the band, which had formed up behind the huts, started to play a rousing military march. The band marched round the perimeter of the village before threading through the lines of huts, and the musicians took their places in the shadow of the flagpole.

Soldiers gave the children balloons, and more beer was handed to the adults. Ndlovu stood by a hut, a few yards distant, the warm bottle of Lion Ale untouched in his hand, and watched the scene with growing apprehension.

Was this happening? Was he really awake? Perhaps his mind had gone after the torture. He wanted to shout to the people to stop, to tell them not to take the white man's drink, nor eat his meat, but to run away now into the bush and stay there until the soldiers had gone, yet he stood mesmerised and silent, unable even to let go of his own bottle.

The band swung into a selection of Afrikaans folk songs – songs from the Great Trek, when the whites colonised the land, and the Boer War, when they battled the British Empire for it. More drinks were handed out, more warm beer, more buns with the sticky white icing.

On the other side of the dusty village centre, John Courtney watched the lonely figure of Ndlovu and his untouched drink, and the sour feeling, which was now becoming familiar, grew inside him once again. You poor bastard, Courtney thought. You've no idea what we're doing to you today, have you? But we're screwing you as surely as if we had one of those crocodile clips fastened to your balls and the other to the head of your cock, and I was cranking that bloody handle as fast as I could go and listening to you scream. We're just being more devious about it, that's all.

Courtney looked at the villagers, beginning to talk again now as the beer got to their heads, beginning to laugh, while the band played "Sarie Marais" and, in the distance, hundreds of other bantu stood watching and wondering.

Suddenly there was a roar of jet engines overhead. Four Mirage F1 supersonic fighters, built under licence in South Africa, flashed overhead and did a slow roll as they disappeared over the horizon. After them came four Impala 2 jets, also locally made, South African manufactured down to their Rolls-Royce engines, and executed another slow roll. The air display lasted twenty minutes. The planes streamed coloured smoke, looped the loop, did complicated manoeuvres, and disappeared as suddenly as they had come.

They were replaced by an Air Force Dakota, rumbling overhead at 4,000 feet, banking, beginning a run-in. Then four black specks fell from the open rear door, plummeting down, coloured smoke streaming after them. The specks began to converge, now seen as men, and touched, hands gripping, then moved apart again and four parachutes mushroomed behind them.

The sky-divers manoeuvred their chutes and landed on the edge of the village, two rolling in the dust, the others not bothering, simply falling on their feet and walking off, pulling in the lower cords to collapse the billowing chutes, and rough-packing the silk as the bantu children gathered round excitedly.

More beer was handed out. The band played "Those Magnificent Men In Their Flying Machines", and then "Puppet on a String".

Courtney thought: this is too rich, even for me.

The party was really beginning now. Some men were already drunk, and women too. The noise level rose. The cow was just about roasted and the sadza had been ready for an hour.

Colonel Winter stood beside him. "Well, Captain," he said, "You've really got them going. I must say this was a bloody well-judged idea. They'll have trouble explaining it away. Look at that bunch out there."

He pointed into the veld, and Courtney saw the crowd of onlookers had grown to about a thousand.

"Shall we invite them in?" the Colonel asked.

"No, sir," said Courtney. "I don't think there's enough beer. We want the party to go on after we've pulled out. And I think we might start making a move now."

"Right," the Colonel said, "I'll give the order."

The band packed and left after playing "We Kiss In A Shadow", and most of the villagers scarcely noticed them go.

More beer was brought out. Empty bottles littered the ground. The soldiers began to drift away. The first truck moved off, then the others. Winter, Rousseau and Courtney climbed into their Land Rover, waved at those bantu who noticed, and left as unobtrusively as they could. Crates of beer, still unopened, were piled by the trestle tables to be drunk later in the evening.

Courtney looked back as they got to the ridge. It was an extraordinary sight. This dusty brown village of mud and thatch, watched from a distance by hundreds of bantu from surrounding kraals as if it were a theatre, a few coloured balloons still flying from the roofs of huts.

A late afternoon breeze had sprung up. The South African flag unfurled, and flapped lazily over Lapatu.

FOURTEEN

The terrorists came two days later. The sensor on the kopje picked them up first, and the information flashed to Silvermine for analysis. It was nine o'clock at night.

Three minutes later, the message came over the camp telex in code. Colonel Winter, Courtney and Rousseau waited impatiently for it to be written in clear.

Outside, more than a hundred men piled into trucks in anticipation, night-sights clipped to their rifles. and headed for the village. They would remain in radio contact with the signals office to find out exactly where they should be deployed, but meanwhile the vital task was to get within striking range.

On the table, Rousseau spread out the map of the area around the village and looked at the first message.

"Mountie 202059. Arms, explosives Rate Three," he said. "That's it so far, sir. They're up on the kopje behind the village and they're not moving."

Colonel Winter looked thoughtful. "I wonder if bantu from the village are going to go and meet them up there? Perhaps that's where they'll be asked for their explanations."

"Could be, sir," Rousseau said.

The signals Sergeant called across: "Another message coming in, sir."

The decoding was going faster now. "How about that," Rousseau said in surprise. "Mountie's now rated at four, at six minutes past nine. Another group's joined them. Looks like they're having a big gathering."

Courtney asked: "How many terrorists would there be on rate four?"

"You can't really tell the number," Rousseau explained. "The sniffer reacts to explosives, not people. It's telling us that there's a lot of arms and ammunition up there. If they've got a big quantity of gelignite that would account for it, or a few rockets and land mines. But if they've just got Kalashs, ammunition and hand-grenades, then it would probably be, what – twenty-five terrorists? Thirty maybe. It's only a guess."

"Another message," called the Sergeant.

The men waited. "Jesus," said Rousseau. "They're rated at five now." He turned to Winter. "Sir, I think we'd better get a move on. I'd like to take the Land Rover and catch up the others."

"Of course, Sergeant," the Colonel said. "Just bear in mind one thing: the terrorists must be left to deal with the headman and the village. Afterwards, we deal with the terrorists."

"Yes, sir."

Winter turned to Courtney: "Aren't you going along?"

"Yes, sir, if I can."

"You should. It's really your show," said Winter.

Courtney and Rousseau ran for the Land Rover and it jerked, wheels spinning, into the night, bucking and heaving over the potholes, engine roaring in four-wheel drive, headlights bright and sharp. Courtney hung onto the door with one hand and the padding of the seat with the other.

Rousseau shouted to Courtney over the noise: "Well, bloke, this is it. This is where it pays off."

Courtney nodded. "Ja," he shouted back. His voice sounded hollow. There seemed nothing more to say. He supposed he ought to feel triumphant, but he was gripped with an unease he couldn't explain.

After a while Rousseau said: "Christ, what's happening back at camp? Why no more messages from Silvermine? Bloke, can you just check that the radio's working OK?"

"What do I do?" Courtney asked.

"Just ask for signals. Our callsign is One-zero. Press that red button and say, 'One-zero, signals, over.' "

Courtney followed instructions. Immediately control replied: "One-zero, OK, over."

"What do I do now?" Courtney asked.

"Nothing," said Rousseau. "If there's a message from Silvermine, they'll pass it on to us. Just say, 'One-zero, OK, out.' "

Courtney did as he was told, and clipped the handset back onto the radio, still holding on as best he could to prevent himself being thrown about the cab of the Land Rover.

"How long till we're there?" he asked.

"We ought to be catching up the trucks soon. They can't move as fast as we can. We'll have to turn out our headlights in about ten minutes because we'll be getting near. Then it's going to be a question of getting in close enough to the kopje," Rousseau said.

The radio crackled into life. "All stations, message, over."

"Come on," said Rousseau. "We're first to answer: 'one-zero send, over.' "

Courtney picked up the handset and depressed the transmit button. "One-zero, send, over," he said.

Then the other trucks came in quickly. "One-two, send, over."

"One-three, send, over."

"One-four, send, over."

"All stations," said control, "Mountie out 202120. Magazine at 2125, Rate Five. Out 2127. Over."

"Fantastic," Rousseau said jubilantly. "They're going towards the village. Now all we've got to do is get there in time. Acknowledge the message, bloke. Say: 'One-zero, OK, out.' "

Courtney did so. Ahead they could see the tail lights of one of the other trucks. Rousseau pulled close behind it and moved to overtake. The Land Rover slammed into a mound of earth, lurched over and careered sideways, Rousseau fighting to recover, then it was back on the track in front of the rear truck and moving up to the next in line. In five hair-raising minutes, the Land Rover led the convoy.

At last Rousseau slowed his vehicle and halted it. The others stopped behind him. He got out of the cab and ran from truck to truck, jumping onto the running boards, saying urgently through the windows: "Lights off from here. Keep your distance."

Then he raced back, and the convoy started off again, lumbering in darkness, only the red rear lights flicking on when a driver touched the brakes.

The night was dark and it was difficult to make out the track, but the Sergeant seemed to know where to go.

Finally Rousseau stopped and the others pulled up beside him. "This is as far as we drive," he said to Courtney. "I just wish I knew where the hell those terrorists had got to."

"What do you mean?"

"Their last position report was at Magazine, which is a quarter-mile from the village. There hasn't been one since. They've stopped there."

"All stations, message over." The radio again.

"There it is," said Rousseau. He took the handset. "One-zero, send, over." The others answered in their turn.

"All stations," control said. "Crossroad at 2142, Rate Five. Out 2146. Zebra at 2151. Rate Five, over."

"Fine, they're in the village now," Rousseau said grimly. He depressed the transmit button. "One-zero, OK, out." He hung the handset on the radio. "Let's move, bloke. We don't want to miss the fun."

"How far is it from here?" Courtney asked.

"Not too far. Half a mile ... three quarters ... something like that. Nice brisk walk."

The men jumped out of the Land Rover. Rousseau called them to gather round him.

"OK, kêrels," he said. "They're in the village. We don't know how many. Might be thirty or forty. Could be less, could be more. We don't care what they do in the village. We leave them alone. We surround it and wait. You've all got manpack transceivers. Keep a listening watch. Headphones only, for Christ's sake. Make sure you're switched to headphones. We don't want a loudspeaker blaring out and letting them know we're here. When they leave the village, we get them. Listen for the command. At the beginning, shoot to kill. But hold off a bit at the end if you can. I want to keep a couple alive for interrogation. Any questions?"

There was silence from the men. "OK," said Rousseau. "Fan out now and let's get there. Use your night-sights. Move quietly. Let's go!"

The file of men moved out into the blackness. Courtney kept close to Rousseau, following behind him, surprised at how swiftly and soundlessly the Sergeant moved through the darkness, trying to keep in his footsteps. It was tiring work. Courtney felt his thigh muscles beginning to ache, and a light sweat broke out on his forehead and chest. They walked for ten minutes before Rousseau stopped. Courtney saw him pull the handset of his transceiver to his mouth and speak quietly into it, asking control for signals. The answer satisfied him, and he moved on.

Courtney glanced left and right. He could see only one man on either side, dimly in silhouette, about fifteen yards from him. The others were lost in the night. Courtney felt his breath shortening to a pant. They were moving uphill now. At the top of the ridge, he saw Rousseau double over and run for several yards, cutting down any silhouette there might be against the skyline. Courtney did the same.

They stopped and Rousseau looked through his night-sight. Lapatu village was ahead. The flag was still up, flapping in the light breeze.

He walked more cautiously, threading through the grass and bushes, his boots making no sound. Courtney was conscious of the scuffling around his own feet every few steps as the toe of his boot dislodged a small stone, or stubbed into an irregularity in the earth. He willed himself to concentrate on the way he walked, trying to lighten his tread. Without a night-sight, Courtney could see nothing but the white glittering stars above him and the bulky silhouette of Jan Rousseau three feet in front.

Silently the soldiers encircled the village and moved closer, reducing the distance between them, tightening the net. Then they stopped. Rousseau scanned the land immediately surrounding him through his night-sight, and chose an anthill for his firing position. He lay down behind it, head and shoulders raised above one side, and squirmed slightly, like a dog might do in a basket, to make it more comfortable, trying somehow to fit his body to the shape. Courtney lay on his stomach close by.

Rousseau studied the village through his sight. The first huts were a hundred and fifty yards away. Two fires burned somewhere inside. The flag was still up. He could see people moving around.

A hut blocked his view of the central area of the village, which seemed to be where everyone had gathered. Rousseau looked to one side and saw a second anthill. That might be better. He shook Courtney's shoulder, then moved silently to the new position, checking with the night-sight that it did give him a better view.

It took a few moments for him to realise what was happening. The bantu had gathered in the centre of the village, children too. He could see some of them standing beside their mothers, and others were strapped to backs. The terrorists were all around, thirty, perhaps thirty-five of them, Kalashs pointing at the ground, but definitely surrounding the people.

Two fires burned and some paraffin lamps had been brought out.

A group of the leaders stood at the front under the flagpole, and one of them was obviously talking, or lecturing, his arms moving emphatically to emphasise points. Then there was a noise from the crowd: a sudden wave of muttering, or protest, a sound which carried clearly to the soldiers' positions and died away.

The headman, Ndlovu, was standing up. He had been at the front of the crowd. Rousseau saw he was moving with difficulty, apparently still in pain.

Ndlovu looked up at the flag, pointed, and began to talk: some lengthy explanation. The terrorists listened but seemed unimpressed. One of them stooped in the dust, picked up an empty Lion Ale bottle and held it accusingly in front of Ndlovu.

Again Ndlovu replied, and again there was this noise, this wave of muttering from the people.

One of the leaders was shouting now, and for the first time his voice carried out into the night. Rousseau passed the night-sight across to Courtney. "Looks like it's going well," Rousseau said.

It took Courtney a minute or two to work out what was happening, and when he had, and had focused back on the activity round Ndlovu, he was in time to see the terrorist step forward and smash the Lion Ale bottle against the flagpole.

The man held the broken bottle by the neck. It was curious, Courtney thought, looking at the village through the sight, like watching a film when the sound had broken down. Action without words. It lent a sense of detachment. He saw two terrorists pinion Ndlovu's arms, and then the man with the bottle moved forward and jabbed it into the headman's face, once, twice, three times.

Still no sound. It was hard to believe that what he was seeing was happening in real life, but there was Ndlovu slumping forward, and some liquid was falling out of his face. Blood? The remains of the beer, tipped from the bottle?

The two terrorists held him up, moving closer now that his knees were buckling.

Courtney nudged Rousseau: "Look at that. They've started on Ndlovu."

Rousseau stared through the night-sight for a few seconds, then said: "Jesus Christ, what did they do to him?"

"Pushed a broken beer bottle into his face," Courtney replied.

"Poor bastard. They're taking down the flag ... there it goes." Without the sight, Courtney could see nothing.

Rousseau watched as the South African flag was torn off and wound round Ndlovu's face. One of the terrorists took a knife and cut the rope, jerking it from its pulleys. They pushed the headman against the flagpole, raised him to his feet, and tied him with the rope to the wood. Then they moved away.

Rousseau could see the leader raise his Kalashnikov and aim at the flag round Ndlovu's head. The explosion of the shot, and then the dozen that followed it, echoed through the valley.

Courtney started: "Jesus! What was that?"

"That was goodbye Ndlovu," Rousseau replied. "They've just chopped him."

Courtney said: "Oh."

He stared into the darkness, wishing he could see what was happening, but at the same time glad he had not witnessed the end of the headman.

"Oooooh," said Rousseau, a deep sound of wonder and disbelief as he watched through the sight. "Here we go!"

"What? What's going on?"

"They've all raised their rifles. Shit, they're really going to do it."

Courtney was about to say "What?" again, when the noise came, starting low, but rising – an apprehensive rumble of voices turning into individual cries, and then the explosions, the bullets from thirty or forty Kalashnikovs and the screams now, the cries of children.

Rousseau watched in silence. The terrorists fired into the crowd. People rose and tried to flee but were cut down. Children ran and fell in their tracks. The firing went on for five minutes, perhaps six. It seemed like an hour. Then the noise died away, and the terrorists examined what they had done. More shots now: someone was seen moving. The terrorists walked among their victims, a couple of hundred bodies crumpled in the dirt, prodding some with their boots, turning them over to see that they were dead.

Rousseau asked: "Do you want to have a look?"

He proffered Courtney the sight. Courtney stared into the village, at the band of armed men standing over the carnage, inspecting their work, and said: "Oh dear God." From that distance, it was difficult to make out detail, and it looked for all the world like a mound of old clothes spread over the ground, except at the edges where he could glimpse arms and legs and faces. He saw the terrorists gathering into a group.

"I think they're getting ready to move out," he told Rousseau.

"Let's have the sight," Rousseau said, putting out his hand. The terrorists were still talking, but seemed in a hurry now, anxious to leave in case the volleys of firing had reached the ears of a security forces' patrol.

In a moment, they began to move out towards the perimeter of the village.

Rousseau clipped the night-sight onto his R1, and rested the rifle on the ground, the butt under his shoulder. He slipped the headphones of the manpack transceiver over his ears and pushed the button on the handset.

He spoke quietly into it: "Wait for the command."

He squinted through the night-sight, picking up the terrorists as they reached the perimeter, lining up individuals in rehearsal for the proper moment.

They turned north, towards him, picking their way through the darkness of the grass and the small bushes, Kalashs slung over their shoulders. With his thumb, Rousseau slid the safety catch into the OFF position. It made a slight click.

The terrorists were walking diagonally from his position, a hundred yards away now.

Into the radio Rousseau said quietly: "If they're too far from you, don't waste your bullets. They'll bombshell when we open up and everyone will get a chance. Ten seconds."

He watched them through his sight and began to count. One thousand, two thousand, three thousand. They were about eighty yards away. Six thousand, seven thousand, eight thousand, nine thousand. Rousseau pressed the transmit button.

"In your own time," he said, "fire."

The front man was in his sights and he squeezed the trigger. The rifle recoiled hard into his shoulder and the explosion made his ears ring. He heard it echo round the valley. Then immediately there were other explosions, small tongues of fire in the night. Rousseau kept his eye squinting through the sight. The front man was knocked back, half turned in mid-air, and dropped onto the ground.

Rousseau picked out the next, aware that the group had frozen, heads swinging from side to side, staring into the blackness to see where the shots had come from. Rousseau squeezed the trigger again. Others were falling now, some dead, most diving for cover.

One tried to run, and made fifteen yards, ploughing blindly through the bush, stumbling and dying as the back of his head blew away.

Into the radio Rousseau said: "Hold your fire."

The silence was almost profound. He pressed the handset button again: "Resume firing when you get the chance."

Still silence. Beside him, Courtney lay on the anthill, arms over his head, pressing down, heart thumping.

There was a sudden burst of fire from in front of them and above their heads came the high-pitched angry bbzzzzzzz of bullets as the terrorists opened up in reply. Rousseau and the other soldiers held their fire.

There were no definite targets for them to aim at, and no point in loosing wild, random bursts which did nothing except give away their positions. Rousseau lowered his rifle and watched the blackness for a spurt of fire. There it was.

He studied the patch it came from through his night-sight. There was something there, something moving. Rousseau lined it up in his sight. The face was staring into the darkness, looking at an area to his right. He steadied the rifle and levelled up the sight in the centre of the face. He squeezed the trigger gently and the R1 bucked in his grasp.

Then steady again, and another look through the sight. The face was turned away, not moving. Another one down.

Silence.

Through the sights, Rousseau could see the grass move. Terrorists were crawling away now in different directions. He picked up the handset.

"They're splitting up," he said. "All directions."

The grass stirred as if giant snakes were slithering through it. Suddenly out of it some men rose up, then others, and they began to run, away from Rousseau, in other directions, some back towards the village into the range of the soldiers on the other side of the circle. The firing began again, and more men dropped, but this did not halt the remaining terrorists in their flight, dodging, stumbling over an area where they could not see but their adversaries could. They ran like trapped animals, first in one direction until they saw the rifles flash, then turning and going in another, and more flashes, and the singing of bullets, and feeling blows in the body, like mighty fists crashing down, knocking them onto the ground, tasting the warmth of blood, and then blackness.

Nothing moved. Minutes ticked by. Courtney raised his head cautiously and then looked into the night. "Is it over?" he asked in a whisper. Rousseau shook his head.

"It's not even half time," he said. "It's going to be a long night." He reached for the transceiver handset again. "Stay down," he instructed quietly. "We haven't got them all yet."

Courtney touched Rousseau's arm. "What do we do now?"

"We wait," Rousseau said. "There could be a dozen still alive. They're lying low, but they'll have to try and get away before daybreak. They don't know we've got night-sights."

"Why don't we just close in and pick them up?" Courtney asked.

"We could," Rousseau said, "but we'd risk taking casualties. I'd sooner hang on and be patient. We'll sweep them up in a few hours. You getting stiff?"

Courtney shook his head.

"Ja, well you will before we're finished. Try and stretch your arms and legs. Move your shoulders and your toes. Keep the blood circulating."

The men lay in silence. One hour passed, then another. Courtney felt he could go to sleep on the anthill. Rousseau stayed motionless, checking his night-sight regularly for signs of movement.

And there it was, in the grass, the slightest waving of the dry stalks, which could have been the wind if it had been repeated elsewhere. It was twenty yards from his position.

Shit, Rousseau thought. One of them's trying to wriggle through. He nudged Courtney and put his mouth close to the Captain's ear. "Terrorist twenty yards dead ahead. Trying to crawl out."

Courtney felt his stomach tighten and his mouth go dry. Rousseau focused on the spot. The grass moved again. The man was taking his time. They wouldn't be able to see him until he was at ten yards.

Rousseau debated what to do. Kill, or take him prisoner? With Courtney around, untrained, there was a danger in trying to capture the terrorist, but hell, it was such a gift. The bugger was coming straight towards them.

The grass stirred, and this time, Rousseau picked up its faint rustle, then silence again. The terrorist had been well trained. He was wriggling forward, a yard at a time, then stopping for three or four minutes, cutting down the chance of someone noticing him, and increasing his own opportunities of spotting the enemy.

Rousseau watched the grass through his sight. Another small movement.

Slowly, Rousseau moved his head towards Courtney's. Softly and distinctly he said: "I'm going to try take him prisoner. Might need help. OK?"

Courtney nodded, and Rousseau felt the movement of his head close to his cheek.

The direction the terrorist was taking led straight for the middle of the anthill. He would have to go left or right to get round it. If he went left, he'd be on Rousseau's side, which would be ideal. If he went right, Courtney would be between them. That would make life difficult.

The grass again, not much more than ten yards now. He should be coming into sight very soon.

There he was. A black hand. The tip of the muzzle of his Kalash. Both motionless. Rousseau watched. The terrorist searched the darkness for clues. Forward another yard, and there were his arms and head. He would soon be aware of the anthill ahead, either because he would see the silhouette, or because his skin would pick up the different, rougher texture of the earth. He would also recognise it as a natural cover for his enemies.

The man wriggled forward by degrees. Another yard towards them and his whole body was exposed. Then he lay still for a long time, looking, not moving, and Rousseau knew he had seen the anthill.

Courtney without the night-sight was as blind as the terrorist, and could not tell how close the enemy was, but neither he nor Rousseau stirred.

Ten minutes passed. The terrorist began moving again, pulling himself to Rousseau's left: Courtney's side.

Rousseau cursed under his breath. Courtney didn't even know where the man was. Jesus. Perhaps he should just shoot him now.

But they needed a prisoner, at least one. Rousseau pulled back, sliding silently down the slope of the anthill, moving as quietly as the guerrilla but faster. Courtney shifted the position of his head to watch the dark shape beside him. Rousseau edged down until his trunk was parallel with Courtney's legs, and then wriggled sideways, sliding across the backs of Courtney's thighs, lying parallel to the officer on the left-hand side, and edging back up to a commanding position.

The guerrilla had not shifted his spot. Now Rousseau was ready. He felt in his webbing belt for his bayonet, and silently slid the night-sight off his rifle. He pushed the R1 across until it touched Courtney's chest, and felt the other man grasp it. Rousseau hoped Courtney realised the safety catch was still off.

The guerrilla was three yards away. Rousseau eased himself down the slope again and felt for a firm foothold. He crouched, knees almost against his chest, bayonet in his right hand, ready to spring.

With the night-sight in his left hand, Rousseau watched the man wriggle into range, three feet from him, no more, and stop. Moving slowly, Rousseau lowered the sight and accustomed his eyes to the darkness. Gently he placed the night-sight on the ground and his grip tightened round the bayonet, muscles standing out strong and well defined in his arm. He could see the outline of the terrorist clearly now. The terrorist could see some of his outline too, but Rousseau was motionless and there was no way of identifying him among the dark shadows of the anthill.

The man moved another yard, his head and shoulders level with Rousseau, but still the soldier waited. One more movement, and just as he halted, Rousseau sprang, flying out of the darkness, landing on the man's back, left hand tearing into his short woolly hair and jerking his head back, right hand bringing the bayonet up hard under the man's chin and slightly to the side, the point piercing the taut flesh of his neck to the depth of half an inch but going in no further. The terrorist grunted as the weight crushed onto him, and felt the almost simultaneous tearing in his scalp and pain in his throat, trying to roll over but being held down, his arms splaying out.

Rousseau's voice in his ear, quiet but determined: "If you move, kaffir, I'll kill you." The man stayed motionless, frozen lest the bayonet slide deeper into his throat.

Rousseau called quietly to Courtney: "Bloke! Over here, quickly." He heard Courtney's boots stumbling on the anthill, and then his shadow was close. "Take this bastard's Kalash," he whispered.

Courtney fumbled down, feeling along the man's arms for the wood and steel of the rifle, finding it and pulling it out.

"Right," said Rousseau, "get it out of the way."

Courtney took the Kalashnikov and laid it on the side of the anthill, well out of reach.

Rousseau said: "Feel along there – a bit further back from where you are – and there's the night-sight on the ground." He could see Courtney move forward cautiously and fumble around the anthill. After two or three minutes, Courtney said: "I've got it, Jan."

"Fine," said Rousseau. "Now have a look through it. Come up and check this bastard out. See if he's got any other weapons."

"Yes, there's a bayonet."

"Get it out," said Rousseau. "OK. Now fetch me my R1." Courtney did so. Rousseau waited until he had the rifle in his hand before he eased his weight off the terrorist's back and slipped the bayonet out of the flesh of his neck, leaving the blood to well up and stream out.

He went round to the prisoner's side and kicked him hard in the ribs. "Roll over, you bastard," he said quietly. "On your back. Hands behind your head!" The man obeyed.

Rousseau glanced at Courtney. "Bloke, check him out this side: hand-grenades, ammo, that sort of thing." Courtney bent over the man, unclipped three grenades and laid them to one side, then unfastened the guerrilla's webbing pouches and pulled three magazines of bullets from them.

"There're some documents as well," Courtney said.

"Take them," Rousseau ordered. "We'll have a look later." The Captain did as he was told. "Now what are we going to do with this kaffir?" Rousseau mused aloud. "We're going to be here a little while yet. I don't suppose you've brought any handcuffs?"

"No, sorry," said Courtney.

"That's all right." Rousseau handed Courtney his R1 and told him to guard the prisoner, then went and picked up the Kalashnikov. He put the safety catch on.

"On your face, kaffir," he said softly, and the prisoner rolled over. Rousseau raised the Kalashnikov and brought the butt sharply down on the side of the man's skull. He twitched and lay still.

Rousseau rolled the man over again and felt his pulse. He

unfastened the terrorist's webbing belt and pants and pulled them down around his ankles, then took off the shirt and hung it over his head like a hood, tying it in place round his neck with the sleeves.

"That should hold him for a while," he said. "Just keep an eye on him, bloke. We'll hear if he tries to move."

Courtney nodded. They dragged the terrorist behind the ant-hill and resumed their places. Rousseau scanned the bush with his night-sight. Nothing moved. He reached for the handset of his transceiver.

"I've got one prisoner," he said quietly. "Has anyone captured any others? Reply only if the answer is yes."

There was silence.

"Right. Does anyone see any movement? Reply only if yes."

No one answered.

"OK," said Rousseau. "I'm going to call for surrender. Hold your fire." He raised himself up onto his knees, cupped his hands around his mouth and yelled into the night: "You are surrounded!" His voice echoed in the valley. "There is no escape!" ... escape ... escape. "If you want to live you must surrender!" ... render ... render. "Drop your rifles and stand up with your hands in the air!" ... air ... the air.

No one stood up. No one replied. Rousseau waited a few minutes, then dropped down and radioed to the others. "OK, we keep watch till dawn. We'll move in at first light."

The long night dragged on and became chill. Behind them, the captured terrorist groaned and rolled over. Rousseau slid to where he lay and said in a low, warning voice: "Stay where you are, kaffir, or you die."

The man stayed motionless.

It seemed as if the night would never end, but imperceptibly the sky lightened. The dark silhouette of the kopje appeared; then, gradually, the faint outlines of the huts of Lapatu village, and the dark line of the flagpole stretching up from it. Courtney shivered. His body was cold. His shoulders and neck felt stiff and ached when he moved. But he was alert and, now, only a little scared.

Rousseau picked up his transceiver handset again. "I want a volunteer who's near the kopje," he said.

There was a pause and a voice crackled back: "I'm near the kopje, Sergeant. Du Preez."

"Ja, OK, Frik. Get up there and let me know what you can see."

"Right, Jannie."

On the horizon, the sky became pink, and beyond it, a deep blue fading quickly into black. Some details of the landscape emerged. Rousseau stared into the darkness to see if he could spot du Preez as he moved to his new position, but it was still too dark for that.

Rousseau looked through his night-sight for the movement of terrorists in the grass but, apart from a rippling caused by the early morning breeze, there was nothing.

The soldiers waited. The sky became brighter, and with it the land. The edge of the scarlet sun tipped the horizon.

The radio crackled. "Du Preez here. There are lots of bodies in the veld. I don't see anyone who looks like he's still in business. Over."

"OK, Frik," Rousseau said. "Keep watching for another ten minutes. Over."

"Ja. Will do. Out."

Courtney could feel the sun's first warm rays on his back and arms. The sky was cloudless. One star still shone faintly. Ten minutes – then what?

Rousseau checked his watch and called du Preez on the radio. "Anything yet?"

"Nothing moving that I can see, Jannie."

"Stay up there and keep watch. We're going to start closing in. Warn us if you see anything. Over."

"Right, Jan."

Rousseau turned to Courtney. "You stay here and guard the prisoner, if you don't mind, sir. Use his Kalash."

Courtney nodded and picked up the terrorist's rifle.

"Blast the bastard's head off if he so much as moves," Rousseau said. "Don't speak to him. Don't go close to him, even if he's dying. Don't give him anything."

"I won't," Courtney said.

"We'll just clear this area, then I'll come back to you and we can hand him over to one of the others to take back to the camp. I expect you'll want to have a look at the village."

Rousseau did not wait for an answer. Lapatu was the last place Courtney wanted to go into, but he knew he would have to. He could not refuse.

Rousseau picked up the radio handset and pressed the transmit button. "OK," he said into it, "let's move. Take your time. We don't want to start picking up casualties now. Listen for warnings from du Preez. If shooting starts, for Christ's sake watch out for crossfire. Move now."

Rousseau stood up into a half-crouch position in the soft morning light, and looked around. Other soldiers, spaced out in a sweep around the village, also rose out of the grass and from behind rocks, rifles at the ready.

Inside the circle, nothing stirred. Rousseau began walking forward cautiously, scanning the bush right and left.

The first guerrilla was thirty yards away, lying on his face, his Kalash just out of reach of his fingers. Rousseau prodded the man's body with his boot, lifting it slightly, and seeing the dead, staring face he let it drop and moved on. There were two other corpses seven yards further on, and one sprawled over a rock.

The circle was closing now. On the far side, the first soldiers reached the perimeter of the village. Rousseau inspected more bodies in the grass: no one alive.

The shooting had been very accurate. The wounded had not survived the night.

A terrorist was spread-eagled over the ground, his hand still fastened around a grenade. Rousseau went to check that the pin was still securely in.

He squatted down and suddenly froze.

"Holy God," he said in a quiet, awed voice.

He reached down to touch the back of the terrorist's hand, running his finger along the cold skin. He leaned over and pulled at the dead man's clothes, turning him onto his back.

The bullet had blown away most of his chest. His eyes were half open and so was his mouth. Black cream had been smeared over his face and hands for the night operation.

"Ja, white man," said Rousseau softly. "What were you doing here last night?"

FIFTEEN

The only survivor was the prisoner. Rousseau radioed back to camp and alerted them about the dead European. He handed the prisoner over to a corporal then took Courtney on a tour. They inspected the body of the white guerrilla, and Rousseau went through his pockets. There were some documents in a foreign language – it looked like Russian – but no immediate identification.

Courtney had never seen death before, and found himself surprisingly unmoved by the terrorists' bodies. They could have been sacks of potatoes. He walked among them with a sense of detachment.

At last the two men stood at the perimeter of the village. Soldiers moved about inside it, and Courtney could see the civilian bodies clearly now. Christ, he thought, what a mess.

They walked up a dusty path past empty huts. A few yards from the main central area lay a group of people, shot down as they fled: two women, a man, and two small children, a boy and a girl, aged probably seven or eight.

One of the women seemed to be lying on something, her back raised at a curious angle. Courtney watched Rousseau go to give her clothes a pull and turn her over. Rousseau struggled to get a grip and Courtney stood by, not offering to help. He knew he would not be able to touch any of them. The body rolled and flopped.

Rousseau said in a resigned voice: "Shit, look at that."

A dead baby was strapped to the woman's back. The bullet which killed the mother had gone through her neck, so that her head was almost severed, but it had not touched the child. The baby died, crushed or smothered, when the impact spun the woman round and she fell on her back.

Almost all the other corpses lay around the flagpole, sprawled on top of one another: mouths open, eyes staring vacantly or in terror, clothes ripped by bullets and soaked with blood – flies already being attracted and settling on the wounds to feed.

Neither Courtney nor Rousseau spoke. They picked their way around, looking, occasionally prodding, peering into huts where sleeping-mats were laid out, seeing the bicycle propped against a mud wall, two bells on its handlebars, the cooking pots, the flat, unpainted piece of wood with the wire wheels made from a coat-hanger, which had been a child's toy. On the far edge of the village, scrawny fowls scratched around in the dirt, the only things left alive.

Courtney and Rousseau turned and walked back through the village, looking again at the bodies in the central area. There must have been two hundred of them: two hundred killed in a few minutes by their own side.

Courtney felt something under his foot. He looked down quickly, and saw he was standing on a man's hand. He moved away, rubbing and scraping the soles of his boots hard in the dust as if to get contamination off them.

Courtney felt suddenly as if he might cry. "Jesus, Jan," he said, his voice soft and shaking. "What have I done?"

Rousseau shook his head. "It's not your fault, bloke," he said. "You didn't know the terrorists were going to kill everybody."

"We knew something was going to happen. We could have guessed it would be like this," Courtney persisted.

"Don't take it personally. This is war. They were the enemy."

Courtney pointed to the ground around him. "What about the kids?"

"Ja, even the kids. Give them a couple of years and they'd have been going across the border for training. You've done good work. Colonel Winter will be over the moon."

They walked out beyond the perimeter of Lapatu.

"What're you going to do now?" Rousseau asked.

"What do you mean?"

"There are going to be a lot of questions about this. You're going to have to deal with them."

"Questions from who?" Courtney looked blank.

"Jesus," Rousseau said. "You should know. Journalists. Television. Two hundred bantu are dead, not counting thirty-seven terrorists. They're going to want to know about it."

Courtney said thoughtfully: "I suppose you're right."

"Colonel Winter's going to be after you for a plan," Rousseau said. "You'd better work one out before we get back."

Special Branch and BOSS men were beginning to arrive at the village. Courtney and Rousseau could see the Land Rovers driving up, clouds of dust rising behind them.

Courtney sat on a rock and tried to focus his thoughts. What should they do now? How should they present the massacre?

Then it occurred to him that he'd achieved exactly the opposite of what he'd set out to do. It was true that the village had been neutralised: neutralised by being wiped out. But Courtney hadn't wanted to do that. He'd tried to make an example of Lapatu, to demonstrate to bantu in the area that co-operation with the terrorists didn't pay, and that they ought to come over to the government's side. Instead, he'd shown that only a madman would help the government and risk reprisals on such a scale.

Lapatu was a terrorist village which had apparently gone over to the whites, and the terrorists had destroyed it. The unmistakable message was: help the government, and we'll kill you. Courtney's breath came out in a long sigh.

Could anything be salvaged from the mess? Well, there were positive points, he had to admit. They'd killed a lot of terrorists, and they'd taken a prisoner. They'd found their first white guerrilla. That must be worth something.

Courtney glanced up. A quarter of a mile off, Colonel Winter had arrived and was looking around. Courtney saw him deep in conversation with Rousseau, then being taken to view the body of the white, and finally into the village for a quick tour.

Afterwards, Courtney watched the Colonel consulting a group of BOSS officers, and saw them walk over to inspect the white man's body again.

Courtney waited until the Colonel had finished before he presented himself. As he approached he thought: when in doubt, brazen it out. He took a deep breath.

Winter was in good spirits. He returned Courtney's salute and grinned. "Well, Captain," he said, "how do you feel?"

"Fine, sir."

"Good. Do you have any suggestions on what we should do next?"

Courtney nodded. "I think it's important we keep the initiative," he said. "The terrorists have massacred an entire village – about two hundred bantu dead, as you've seen. There's going to be a lot of interest in this – South African and overseas. We want to make sure the story gets out quickly, and that it doesn't get twisted round so we find ourselves blamed in any way. Also, we've got the body of the white terrorist. There'll be a lot of interest in that."

Winter said quickly: "Oh no. Nothing must be said about him. That's top secret."

"Oh?" Courtney replied, surprised. "Why's that, sir?"

"We don't know who he is. He might be South African, of course, in which case it wouldn't be so serious. But it's most likely he's Russian or Cuban, and that means trouble. We don't want to cause panic, so we're saying nothing."

"What about the village itself?" Courtney asked.

"Ja, I agree we should make a big issue of that," Winter said. "We'll get some transport laid on and bring journalists up here to see for themselves. I'll contact the Information Department to help us out. But you can be responsible for showing them round and briefing them."

"How about the other terrorists?" Courtney asked. "What can I say about them?"

"Say what you like," Winter told him. "Give the journalists some people to interview. Select a few soldiers and make sure you agree a story between yourselves. Don't make it too different from what actually happened, and leave out all references to the white man."

Courtney thought for a moment. "We need an explanation for how we knew about the attack on Lapatu. What I suggest we do is clear away all the terrorist bodies from here. They're a bit close to the village at the moment. The journalists can see them back at camp, except for the white, of course. Then we just have to say a patrol was in the area and heard shooting. They went to investigate, saw the terrorists leaving so gave chase and killed them all. We don't have to say exactly where they died."

"What about the bodies in the village?" Winter asked.

"It depends on when the press can get here, sir."

"Sometime today," Winter said. "As early in the afternoon as possible, I should think."

"In that case, let's leave everything as it is, and they can see it just as we found it. It's a pretty powerful sight."

"Right," said Winter. "I'll start arrangements for the visit. You can look after everything else they'll need."

"What about the prisoner?" asked Courtney.

"What about him?"

"It might be useful if we hold off interrogation for a while," Courtney said. "Let the journalists see him, and that he's being well treated. We can keep him under guard in the camp itself for a few hours. The journalists don't have to talk to him: just see that he's all right and get photographs. It's only for today. We can move him to the prison outhouse and start interrogation as soon as they've gone. We only lose a few hours, and I think there's quite a big public relations advantage."

Winter hesitated. "I'll have to clear that with BOSS," he said. "Obviously they want to find out about the white terrorist as quickly as possible. Hold on here."

Colonel Winter went across to the group of security men for a brief conversation. He came back shaking his head: "No," he said, "they're going to start interrogation this morning. There's no hope of delaying it."

"Fair enough," said Courtney. "We've got enough other points to make. Where are they going to do it?"

"Initially at the camp. They don't want to take him too far away in case he decides to lead them to hide-outs in this area."

"Right, sir," said Courtney. "I'll make sure we keep the journalists away from the outhouses."

Courtney went off to find Rousseau. He didn't much like the idea of briefing four or five soldiers on the story they'd tell to the journalists. The more versions there were, the more likely it was there'd be a slip up. If any serious discrepancy arose, it would raise doubts about who had actually killed the villagers, and more than anything Courtney wanted to avoid that. This was why he felt it necessary to have the terrorists' bodies moved away from the village. They were so near now that the question automatically arose of how many villagers had died under security force's fire, either by soldiers' mistakes or because they had been caught in crossfire.

Rousseau was checking the pockets and webbing pouches of dead terrorists for documents, diaries and identification, which reminded Courtney that he still had the papers found on the prisoner. He approached the BOSS officers and handed them over. They'd need them for the interrogation.

Then he squatted on his haunches beside the corpse of a young guerrilla and watched Rousseau pushing his hands deep into the dead man's pockets, extracting papers, flicking through notebooks, searching for any obvious leads which should be pursued without delay. When he was finished, he replaced the documents and looked up.

Courtney said: "Jan, this is your lucky day. Today I'm going to make you a star."

For the next hour Courtney and Rousseau rehearsed what they would say, and walked through the surrounding area deciding exactly where first contact with the terrorists would have been made, according to the new version. The location they chose was beside the kopje, far enough away from the village to make it impossible for any civilian to have been killed by mistake.

Afterwards, they returned to camp – Rousseau to catch a few hours' sleep; Courtney to prepare a list of questions they would probably be asked and to make sure he had the answers, then later to the signals office to lay on telephone communications for news agency journalists, and on to the officer's mess tent to see about supplies of cold beer.

The Department of Information moved quickly, first putting out a short Press Release which said that terrorists had massacred more than two hundred bantu men, women and children in the Eastern Transvaal during the night, and that a Defence Force patrol, hearing the shooting, had gone to investigate. After a chase, the statement said, the soldiers made contact with the terrorists, killing thirty-seven of them and capturing one. There were no Defence Force casualties.

The Department of Information then issued a general invitation to local and overseas journalists to visit the area. They organised a Dakota to fly them from Johannesburg to the airfield near

114

Chicundu, and a French Super Frelon helicopter to ferry them from there to the camp.

Courtney and Rousseau waited on the edge of the landing zone to welcome the visitors and take them to the main building, where Courtney explained briefly what had happened, using a map of the area to illustrate his points. He introduced Rousseau and said the Sergeant would answer any questions they might have.

From the back of the room a mild-mannered American, middle-aged, wearing a light blue safari suit, asked: "You say the guerrillas just came into the village and murdered everybody. Have you any idea why?"

Before Rousseau could reply, Courtney stepped in: "We can only guess," he said. "It's probably because the village was friendly to us. The people were anti-communist and they weren't prepared to give terrorists food and shelter."

"So it was a reprisal?" the American asked, making notes on a small pad.

"It looks that way," Courtney said. "You'll be able to judge better for yourselves when we go to the village in a few minutes. We haven't touched anything. You'll see it as we found it."

"Exactly how many villagers were killed?" the American wanted to know.

"We don't have an exact number," Courtney replied. "Again, when we get there you'll see why. The bodies are just heaped on top of each other. But there must be more than two hundred."

Someone else asked: "What time did it all happen?"

Courtney nodded to Rousseau to answer. "We first heard the firing at around ten o'clock last night," Rousseau said. "We were on our way back from a patrol, so we went to see what was happening."

"How many of you were there?"

"It was a twelve-man patrol."

The American again: "And how many guerrillas?"

"Thirty-eight."

"One taken prisoner, the rest dead?"

"That's correct."

"Didn't any get away?" the American asked.

Rousseau shook his head. "Not as far as we know. We didn't

see any get away, but it isn't impossible there were others."

"Are you looking for others now?"

"Well, there's a general hunt round the area," Rousseau said, "but, as far as I know, we're not actually in hot pursuit of anyone."

"Can we see the prisoner?" the American wanted to know.

Courtney shook his head. "Sorry," he said. "He's been taken away for questioning." There was a pause, then Courtney said: "OK, let's go and have a look at the terrorists' bodies, and then we'll see the village."

He led the way to an open field three hundred yards away. The bodies were laid out on the ground, covered by a tarpaulin. Courtney and Rousseau pulled it back and the cameramen crowded round, shutters clicking, while the reporters watched and made notes.

After a moment the American said: "Did I get this right? There were thirty-seven guerrillas killed and one taken prisoner?"

"That's correct," Rousseau replied.

"Well, I only count thirty-six bodies. What happened to the other one?"

Rousseau looked across at Courtney. The American waited for an answer. "We decided not to show you the last one," Courtney said at last, improvising. "There wasn't much of him left. He'd just pulled the pin from a grenade when he was shot and it exploded as he fell. There's not much to see, just bits of meat."

The American was satisfied and nodded.

When they had finished viewing the terrorists' bodies, Courtney escorted the journalists back to the helicopter landing zone, and the Super Frelon flew them to Lapatu, landing on the side away from where the main action had taken place. They walked in to confront the carnage.

Courtney let them go on ahead, watched them pick their way past the corpses on the edges of the central area of the village, and then stare at the mound of bodies. Cameras whirred and clicked. One of the journalists said: "Jesus Christ."

The others were silent. They walked slowly around, staring, making notes.

It was the American who spotted the flagpole on the other side of the bodies. He squinted at it, puzzled. Courtney watched him from a distance and felt sudden apprehension. That bloody flagpole, he thought. We should have taken it out. The American walked round the bodies for a closer look, and found himself standing in front of Ndlovu, now slumped almost in a sitting position, still roped to the pole, with what looked like a bullet-ridden, blood-soaked rag around his head.

Courtney wondered whether to approach the American and try to head him off, or wait and see what he made of it. The American was obviously intrigued. He looked up at the top of the pole, shook it to see how firmly it was set in place. Then he caught Courtney's eye and beckoned him across.

"What do you make of this, Captain?" he asked.

"Looks like they executed him specially. He's the only one tied up."

"Any idea why?"

Courtney shook his head. "Can't even tell who he is."

The American peered closely at the material wound around Ndlovu's head. "What's this blindfold?"

Courtney looked at the tattered, stained South African flag and shrugged: "A bit of rag, I suppose."

The American stood up. "The thing that puzzles me, Captain," he said, "is this flagpole. Why does a village have a flagpole?"

"To fly a flag."

The American refused to be put off. "Exactly," he said. "Which flag?"

There was no point beating about the bush. "The couple of times I've been to the village," Courtney said, "they've been flying the national flag."

"The South African flag?"

"Ja, that's right."

The American scratched his head. "Isn't that peculiar?" he said. "A black village flying the South African flag? What's more, a black village in a front-line guerrilla area flying a South African flag?"

"No, not really," Courtney said. "I told you earlier they were anti-communist. They were friendly to us. I suppose this was their way of showing it. A lot of villages are friendly to us."

"A bit provocative, wouldn't you say?"

"It's their country. They can fly their national flag if they like, just like any other citizens."

The American shrugged. "Perhaps," he said, "but even accepting what you say: in this area, at this time, it just seems like asking for trouble."

"That's a matter of opinion," said Courtney.

"No, Captain, it's a matter of fact. If they were flying the South African flag in a front-line terrorist area, they were asking for trouble, and by God," he looked around – "they got it."

"It hardly warrants a massacre though, does it?" Courtney asked. "Women, kids. Look at them."

"Maybe not," the American said, "but it does provide the reason."

"Lots of other villages in this area are anti-communist," Courtney said.

"That's not what I hear," the American said with a friendly smile. "But even if I grant you that, can you tell me how many other black villages fly South African flags?"

Courtney shook his head. "Offhand I can't," he admitted.

"Do you know of a single other black village which flies the South African flag?"

"No."

"So you see my point."

Courtney said: "To an extent, of course I do. It could be the reason, but it's hardly an excuse."

"I'd go along with you there," the American agreed. He looked down at Ndlovu's body again, and the material wrapped around his head.

Courtney prayed: please God, don't let him recognise the flag under all that blood.

The American turned away and moved off. Courtney felt a wave of relief. He did not follow him.

The journalists left at about three-thirty to return to Johannesburg and file their stories. Tiredness was overcoming Courtney now and he felt emotionally drained. He remembered suddenly that he had not slept at all the night before.

He went to Colonel Winter's office to report on the visit.

"Sit down, Captain," Winter indicated a chair. "How did it go?"

"It seemed all right, sir. We had a bit of trouble with an American reporter."

"Oh?" Winter leaned back and lit a cigarette.

"He spotted the flagpole and made heavy weather of the fact that the village was flying the South African flag. I told him it was every citizen's right to fly the national flag if they wanted to."

"Absolutely," Winter grinned amiably. "What did he say to that."

"He said it was provocative. His report will make that point too, of course."

Winter shrugged: "That's not too bad," he said. "It shows the bantu are on our side."

"Ja. Otherwise it went well."

"Good. And how about you, Captain. You've had a busy few hours. How do you feel?"

"Tired, sir," Courtney said.

"I expect you do, Still, you've done a good job. First rate. Imaginative and effective."

"Thank you." Courtney wondered if he should admit that, as far as black co-operation in the area was concerned, the incident had probably been a disaster. If they'd had a ninety-per-cent fall-off in information before, there would now be a total silence from the bantu. Winter saw him hesitate, uncertain.

"What's on your mind, Captain?" he asked.

There was no point keeping it to himself. Winter would find out for himself very soon. "Well, sir, I'm a bit worried in case the whole thing backfires on us," Courtney said.

"In the press you mean?"

Courtney shook his head. "No, I don't think we have to worry about that," he said. "They came and saw for themselves. No one's going to be able to argue with them, and once their eye-witness reports are in the paper, they're committed. They're all going to write essentially the same story. But I'm worried about local bantu. Are they going to think now that it's more than their lives are worth to co-operate with the Defence Forces?"

"I don't follow you," Winter said.

"I mean, are they going to feel that the terrorists will come and wipe out *their* whole village if they don't give them one-hundred-per-cent support?"

Winter looked thoughtful. "Oh yes," he said. "I see."

"It is a danger, sir."

"Well," said Winter, stubbing out his cigarette, "what are you going to do about it?"

Courtney shook his head wearily. "I've no idea, sir."

"There must be something. If they're going to co-operate with the terrorists because they're frightened of them, we've got to make sure of a number of things. First, we must offer them some sort of security. I'm sure we could get more sensors into the area pretty quickly. In fact, I know we can. We just advance the plans we've already got in hand. But as far as the bantu are concerned, we must be more visible, and we must have a better rate of detection and capture of terrorists. Secondly, we must be more positive about providing bantu with rewards for information."

Courtney broke in: "Oh, I'd be careful about rewards, sir. We rewarded Lapatu, and look what happened to them."

Winter accepted the point. "Ja, all right," he said. "We should make sure we give rewards discreetly. And thirdly, and most important, we want the iron fist in the velvet glove. If they're scared of the terrorists, they must be more scared of us."

"It's difficult to make them more scared of us, sir," Courtney said. "A massacre is a hard act to follow."

Winter fell silent. "Ja, I see what you mean," he said at last.

"So if we're not going to go and wipe out a village ourselves, and I take it we're not, how are we going to frighten them?" Courtney asked.

Winter stared at the ceiling. Courtney looked at his boots. And then the answer came to him.

"There is a way," Courtney said quietly.

Winter looked at him encouragingly. "Ja, go on."

"It depends on us establishing certain factors," Courtney said. "We must show the world beyond doubt that the people of Lapatu were shot and killed by terrorists."

"Well, what about the journalists today? They should do that for us."

"To a point, but we need to go further. We should persuade

the government to get the International Red Cross or some really independent group to appoint their own pathologist to take part in the post mortems."

"Post mortems?' Winter was puzzled.

"Yes, sir. We ought to have a post mortem done on every one of those bantu. We ought to have every Kalashnikov bullet extracted from them and shown to the world."

"Isn't that going a bit far? Isn't it enough to have reports in all the newspapers blaming the terrorists?"

"Normally I'd agree with you. But this time it has to be proved beyond doubt," Courtney said.

"Why?" asked Winter. "I don't see the point."

"Because I think we ought to put out another story locally saying that the terrorists didn't massacre the people at Lapatu, but we did."

Winter looked at him strangely. "You're saying we should announce responsibility for killing two hundred civilians in cold blood. Including children."

"No, not announce it, sir," Courtney said. "Just let it be known. Put out a rumour, and watch it spread. Say that the soldiers did it because the people of Lapatu were co-operating with the terrorists, and that they'll do the same to any other village that doesn't give them information. The rumour will eventually get back to Johannesburg and Pretoria, of course, but no one will pay any attention if independent pathologists' reports have proved exactly the opposite. And we maintain the balance of fear."

Winter sat thoughtfully. "Ja," he said. "It might work. I'll have a word with Pretoria, see if they'll go along with the independent pathologist idea. If they do, we'll give it a try. I don't see there's much to lose. We're in a bad way here, by the look of it, so desperate measures may be needed."

"You mean the drying up of information, sir?"

"I mean, Captain, that the dead white man turns out to be a Cuban regular," Winter replied. "There was identification on his body."

"Oh I see. Christ."

"As far as we know, it's the first time a Cuban's actually come across the border. What we have to find out now is whether he was exceeding his authority and disobeying instructions, or whether there's something deeper in it."

"What sort of thing?"

Winter shrugged. "Preparations for an all-out attack," he said. "A Cuban invasion."

Courtney felt as if his breath had been taken away. "I've heard that said before, sir, but it isn't really possible, is it? It's just an empty threat."

Winter laughed wryly. "I wish it was, Captain. No, our intelligence reports say that a lot of tanks, armoured cars, SAM missiles, ammunition, that sort of thing, are being landed at Beira now, and they're *not* going to the Mozambique army. Also, there's been a build-up of Cubans in the area. Eight hundred more came in two days ago. It looks serious. Ja, I think we might have a real fight on our hands one day."

SIXTEEN

Courtney and Rousseau were walking along the dirt path between the mess tents and the main administration building the following morning when the noise began. At first it was difficult to place what it was. It carried faintly: just enough to alert them, too low for identification. They stood motionless, and tried to pinpoint it. Around them, other soldiers had stopped to listen, and some were moving in the direction of the prison outhouse.

Rousseau said: "Want to go and have a look?"

Courtney shrugged. "We'd better see what's happening."

They walked quickly towards the line of trees, and climbed down the slope to the outhouses. The noise was someone shouting, baying almost, then it stopped. Courtney and Rousseau walked into the concrete courtyard, but everything was quiet. The Sergeant in charge of the day's guard saluted.

"Anything the matter, Sergeant?" Courtney asked.

The man shook his head. "No, sir, all quiet here. I think there's a bit of fun around the interrogation room."

"Oh I see," Courtney said. They took the path which ran beside the trees.

A Land Rover was parked outside the interrogation room and a group of people stood around it. A few yards to one side soldiers were gathering to watch, although some had taken a look and immediately turned back.

Rousseau said: "It's BOSS."

"What are they doing?" Courtney asked.

Rousseau shook his head. "I don't know. Looks like they're working on the terrorist. Jesus, I'm glad I'm not him. If you think we're bad, wait till you see these buggers. They don't mess around."

"Why aren't they inside the room? It's a lot more private."

"Why should they worry? They're among friends. Anyway, they had him inside all yesterday. I suppose they've tried the tricks we've got there, and they're onto something else now."

Courtney and Rousseau were close enough now to see the guerrilla huddled naked in the dust behind the Land Rover. The BOSS men were standing around smoking, except for two who knelt beside the man shouting into his ears in Afrikaans.

Courtney and Rousseau stopped four or five yards from the group to watch. The man was hunched, almost in a foetal position, on the ground. There were no obvious marks on him. Then Courtney saw the hosepipe taped securely to the Land Rover's exhaust, the other end lying on the ground. He frowned. What the hell were they doing?

He pointed it out to Rousseau. "What do you make of that?" he asked.

Rousseau shrugged. "I've no idea." Then he said, "Oh, ja, I have. The old exhaust treatment. I've never seen it done before but I've heard about it. See that tin over there by the side?"

Courtney nodded. "The engine oil tin cut in half?"

"That's the one, well . . ." Rousseau stopped. The two BOSS officers were getting to their feet, still shouting angrily. "You can see for yourself. They're going to do it now," Rousseau said.

One of the BOSS men got into the driver's seat of the Land

Rover and waited. Four of the others went to hold the guerrilla, forcing his buttocks up off the ground, his knees under his chest. The man stayed silent but Courtney could see his face screwed up in an effort to keep control. A fifth BOSS man dipped the end of the hosepipe into the tin.

"What's in there?" Courtney asked quietly.

"Grease of some sort," Rousseau said.

The fifth man fumbled with the end of the hosepipe around the guerrilla's anus and then pushed the pipe in deep. The others held the prisoner tight so he could not move or draw away.

The fifth man raised a hand and gave a thumbs-up. The driver turned the key in the ignition and the engine burst into life. The hot exhaust gases were forced down the hosepipe and pumped into the man's bowels.

Through clenched teeth, he began to gasp and whimper. One of the BOSS men called out: "Give it a couple of revs this time, man, then cut it."

The driver pressed his foot onto the accelerator and the engine roared. The screaming started immediately, a sound of unbelievable, unbearable pain. The guerrilla's bowels and stomach filled with hot carbon dioxide, which burned the linings and membranes, and then distended, swelling out grossly. Courtney felt nausea rising, but found he could not look away.

Suddenly the engine was turned off and its noise died. The fifth man pulled the hosepipe free, and the carbon dioxide began farting out of the guerrilla's body. But the screaming went on. The man rocked on the ground in his pain, hands tearing at his hair and face. The BOSS men watched impassively.

Rousseau glanced across at Courtney and saw that his face had gone chalk white. No one moved. The noise went on for several minutes. The guerrilla's stomach was shrinking back to shape now, but Courtney and Rousseau could see dark red blood coming from the man's mouth in a dribble. If the BOSS officers noticed, they gave no sign.

The screaming gradually reduced to sobs, then the sound of vomiting and Courtney could see that most of what was coming up from his stomach was blood. The others noticed it too. There was an uneasy stirring in the group of BOSS men. One of them went down on his haunches beside the guerrilla and peered closely at his face.

He stood up and consulted his colleagues. One of them went to the Land Rover and radioed for a medical orderly.

The guerrilla was lying quietly now. He had stopped vomiting. His feet twitched. His breath was low and uneven and the trickle of blood still ran from his mouth. Suddenly he gave what sounded like a sigh, and then there was silence.

Courtney thought he had fainted. He saw that the blood had almost stopped. Courtney and Rousseau stared at the man. The BOSS officers leaning against the Land Rover watched, showing no emotion. The group of soldiers gathered fifteen yards away, two dozen of them, sat on the grass, leaned against trees, smoked, looked on.

Courtney stood transfixed. A voice in his head said: it's for the greater good.

The guerrilla lay still. The blood had stopped completely. Courtney watched his chest and stomach for the slight rise and fall of his breathing, but there was none. He stared at the man's face, turned in his direction. The eyes were half closed. He had seen that look before.

Courtney spoke, his voice loud to carry across the few yards separating him from the BOSS officers. "Did you get anything out of him?" Courtney asked.

The officers looked across. "Nee, Captain," one of them said. "Not a bloody thing."

"Ja, well you won't get anything now," Courtney said. "He's dead."

The officers moved towards the guerrilla to see if this was true, and Courtney turned away. "Come on," he said to Rousseau. "Let's get out of here."

They walked back towards the camp. The other soldiers were drifting away now. The fun was over. It was back to writing letters home, to mothers and girlfriends, saying that the food wasn't too bad, and it was quite hard work with patrols and everything, and how they hoped to get a four-day pass soon: back to lying around in the shade, waiting for the next duty to begin, playing cards, reading Mickey Spillane, waiting for lunch.

125

Courtney and Rousseau went straight to Colonel Winter's office and knocked on the door.

"Yes, Captain," said Winter, looking up from some papers on his desk.

Courtney came to the point. "Our friends from BOSS have killed the prisoner."

The Colonel raised his eyebrows. "Oh?" he said. "How did that happen?"

"They taped a hosepipe to the Land Rover exhaust, stuck the other end up his arse and started the engine. He died," Courtney said.

The Colonel clucked his tongue in disapproval. "That's bloody unfortunate," he said. "Did he tell them much?"

"Not a thing apparently."

Colonel Winter sighed and scratched his head. "That's too bad," he said. "We needed him to talk. It'll be more difficult now. Well, there's a lesson for everyone there, Captain. If they'd taken a bit more time with the terrorist, he'd have told them everything they wanted to know. More haste, less speed."

"Yes, sir."

"Well, Captain, it's done and it can't be undone. We'll just have to work with what we've got."

Courtney felt his anger rising. "Perhaps you can reprimand them, Colonel," he said, keeping his voice steady.

"Reprimand them?" Winter looked at him puzzled. "I can't reprimand the security branch. Perhaps you don't know – BOSS can do what they like. They're a law unto themselves."

Courtney felt his heart sink. There was nothing more to say. He stood in front of Winter, feeling impotent and stupid. He wanted to move but his feet seemed rooted to the spot.

Winter said: "Sit down, Captain. You too, Sergeant Rousseau." He reached into his desk drawer and pulled out some sheafs of paper. "Your pamphlets have come back," he said to Courtney. "They liked them very much in Pretoria. They did a quick print job as you can see." He handed the specimens across.

Courtney saw that an artist had redone his drawings in broad, primitive outlines, the sort one finds in a child's colouring-in book. They didn't look too bad.

Winter said: "They've sent us five thousand for a start, but

126

they're distributing a lot more than that to other areas. These things are going to be dropped right along the border. Pretoria wants you to work out some other pamphlet ideas as soon as you can. They seem to be very interested in you. The Principal Private Secretary to the Minister of Defence wants to meet you. He's in the area today with an official party, discussing our Cuban friend, and he's going to drop over here for a talk. I don't have an exact time for it, but it'll be this afternoon, probably after three."

Courtney felt surprised and gratified. "Yes, sir," he said. "I'll be in my office."

"The other thing I have to say is much more serious," Winter went on. "Have you been listening to the news?"

Courtney and Rousseau shook their heads. "Well," said Winter, "there's a big debate coming up at the United Nations tonight on whether or not to impose economic sanctions against South Africa. I must tell you there's a chance they might. This would be a retrogressive step for us, and a boost for our enemies, but it wouldn't be the end of the road. We're almost self-sufficient. The government has built up huge stockpiles in preparation for just such a day. However, we must see to it that morale stays high in the Defence Forces. Our fight is just beginning. The latest information from Silvermine tells us that an arms build-up has started in some areas on the other side of the border, including kraals and villages in a direct line from here. So we must be ready." Winter looked at the two men appraisingly. "By the way," he said to Courtney, "Pretoria has agreed to invite independent pathologists to attend post mortems on the Lapatu people. This means we can go ahead and put out the rumour."

"Fine, sir," Courtney said.

"And you, Sergeant" – Winter glanced at Rousseau – "I think it's about time you got some men and went and had a look across the border. I think Captain Courtney can get on by himself now."

Rousseau nodded. "When do you want me to go, sir?"

"First light tomorrow. Select three men and let me have their names by lunchtime. What we need is information on who's at the terrorist bases. The sensors tell us about the build-up of arms and men there, but they don't say who's white and who's black. Take care, Sergeant. The camps will be well guarded. You need to do your observing from a distance. See Major Isaacs in Intelligence for a detailed briefing on what the computer analysis has shown so far." He leaned back in his seat. "One last thing," he said. "You saw what happened to our prisoner today. I must tell you again that none of you must be captured. Their interrogation is a lot tougher than ours. I don't want any of my men to ever be in that position. There's too much at stake now." Winter stopped and smiled at Rousseau. "I don't really need to tell you that, do I? Good luck, Sergeant."

Courtney and Rousseau stood up and saluted.

The Principal Private Secretary to the M⸺ ter of Defence arrived at the camp early and angry. The news of the prisoner's death had been given to him at a meeting of senior security officers in Chicundu two hours before and he had lost his temper, something which happened only rarely. He was sharply critical of the BOSS men involved.

The captured guerrilla had the answers to crucial questions, and they had let him die before he revealed anything. Piet Bosman could still hardly believe that they had done it. The ham-handedness of it, the sheer stupid, thoughtless, wasteful inefficiency kept his anger fuelled.

Piet Bosman stepped out of the Alouette helicopter at the camp's landing zone, and automatically ducked his head until he was out of range of the still-turning rotors. Colonel Winter waited to greet him. They shook hands briefly. Bosman was a trim, dapper man in his early forties. His hair was thin on top and he had a small moustache. His eyes were light brown and shrewd. The men went to Winter's office and got straight down to business.

"I'm bloody annoyed about that terrorist dying this morning," Bosman said. "I can't imagine what the Minister's had to say about it. Or at least, I can imagine only too well what he's saying, that's the trouble. He'll have hit the roof. What happened?"

Winter shrugged: "It wasn't any of my men," he said. "It was BOSS's show. I wasn't there, but it sounds as if they were over-zealous."

"You're telling me," Bosman said. "We've got the United Nations debate tonight on sanctions. God knows what sort of information that man could have given to help us out if he'd been properly handled."

Winter nodded sympathetically. "Ja, I know what you mean. It's a big disappointment. Tomorrow I'm sending one of our best trackers across the border to see if he can come up with any new information on the arms build-up and what the Cubans are doing."

"Oh good. When can we expect a report?" Bosman asked.

"Not for about four days, I'm afraid. I've told him to go carefully. We don't want any of *our* men captured."

"Bloody hell," said Bosman. "That's all we'd need. Now, what about this man Courtney? How have you found him?"

"He's fine," Winter replied. "He settled in very quickly and has done some good work. He's got imagination and he understands psychology. It was really because of him we got that Cuban. Courtney set up Lapatu village like a fairground target, and the terrorists couldn't resist coming to have a crack at it. We were waiting. Now he wants to put round a local rumour that the army was really responsible for wiping out Lapatu because the village was helping the communists. And unless information starts coming in again, other villages might find themselves in the same position. Courtney reckons it'll help keep the balance of fear."

Bosman sat thoughtfully, pulling at his ear. "Those pamphlets he drafted were very good," he said. "Did we tell you we're distributing them right along the border area?"

"Ja. I passed it on to Courtney."

"Good." Bosman paused again. "I suppose you'll be sorry to see him go."

Winter looked at him sharply. "What exactly did you have in mind? I understood Captain Courtney was spending his twelve months in my battalion."

"Ja, that was the plan," Bosman said breezily, "but with your agreement, I think we can make even better use of his services in Pretoria. He'll still keep an eye on winning the hearts and minds of the bantu, of course, but we must start thinking about winning the hearts and minds of some of the whites."

Winter shook his head. "I'm sorry. I don't follow you."

"What I mean, Colonel, is we're approaching a crisis. White immigration is down and emigration is very high indeed. The next set of statistics will shock a lot of people, I think. There's a flight of capital. As you know, we've just tightened up on the exchange control regulations, but we're well aware we're just creating a currency black market. Businessmen will smuggle their money out somehow. Rhodesia proved that. There's black unrest in some of the townships. Agitators have been at work of course. The old rent-a-mob have been out in the streets. It all increases the uncertainty. The army call-up has been extended. As you know, we're going to have to impose a state of emergency if the UN resolution goes against us. You see how a snowball effect is created?"

Colonel Winter nodded. "Yes, of course."

"Defence is the key to all this," Bosman continued. "Strip away all the crap, and you find that most whites aren't leaving because they oppose apartheid, or because they think some of our laws are harsh. Hell, they've lived under apartheid for a long time. Many of them immigrated into it. Certainly some of the laws *are* harsh – we make no apologies for that. But they don't touch most ordinary, non-political people at all. No, Colonel, people are leaving because they don't think South Africa is going to be able to survive. They're getting out while the going's good. If they genuinely believed we'd come through in the end, they'd stay. They'd put up with the odd hardship, they wouldn't mind the military call-up, because at the end of it they'd still have the South Africa they knew, and it would be theirs permanently, to be handed on to their children, and their grand-children. So that's our task. We've got to be more aggress-ive in our approach. We've got to make people believe they're here to stay, that South Africa can't be defeated, either by sanc-tions or by armed force. That's what we want Courtney for. It's basically a marketing operation."

"What are you going to do?" Winter asked. "Put adver-tisements on television, that sort of thing?"

Bosman shook his head. "Not immediately," he said. "It's too obvious. We've got to create the confidence in other ways – by what we do officially, by the actions we take, by what we say."

Winter offered Bosman a cigarette, then went round his desk to light it. "I'd have thought," Winter observed, "that Pretoria was full of government men who'd be able to do that for you."

Bosman agreed. "Thousands of them," he said, "and all career civil servants. They lay out the options for us, and the Minister concerned chooses one of them. They've been doing it for years, and whites are leaving in their thousands. Civil servants are in touch with other civil servants. A man like Courtney's in touch with consumers and their psychology. He doesn't have a career in government to think about. We've just borrowed him from his agency for a few months. You've listened to his advice, Colonel, and you've benefited. It'll be interesting for the Minister to hear it too."

Winter shrugged: "Well, I don't have much choice. When do you want to take him?"

"He can come back with me in the helicopter," Bosman said. "He's only got his kit here. He's not in the middle of anything, is he?"

"No, not really. Do you want a word with him?"

"Please."

"He's in his office," Winter said. "I'll call him through."

"No, don't bother," said Bosman. "Show me where it is. I'll go there."

Courtney sat at his desk, staring gloomily at the pamphlet he was preparing. The drawing showed terrorist recruits in a camp somewhere in the bush, cowering on the ground, while a fat communist beat them with a whip. Something to remind them of home, he thought.

Colonel Winter opened the door without knocking, and Courtney got to his feet.

"This is Mr Bosman," Colonel Winter said. "He's the Minister's PPS. You'll be working with him from now on."

Courtney looked blankly from one to the other. "Oh," he said. "Good."

Winter left them together and closed the door. Bosman sat down in a hard-backed chair in front of Courtney's desk.

"Well, Captain," he said. "We all admire the work you've been doing."

"Thank you, sir."

"How do you like being in uniform?"

Courtney hesitated, then said: "It's certainly different."

"I suppose you're looking forward to getting back into civvies," Bosman said.

"Well," said Courtney, slightly embarrassed, "it's interesting here. I suppose the year will go pretty quickly. But yes, it will be nice to get back into civvies."

Bosman smiled at him suddenly: "How about tonight?"

"I don't follow you, sir."

"You'll be back in civvies tonight. You're coming with me to Pretoria. We're basing you there, probably for the rest of your call-up. You'll keep your rank, of course, but you'll be working in a government department, so you don't have to worry about a uniform."

"Oh fine," said Courtney, still baffled. "What'll I be doing?"

"I'll explain that to you on the way. I want to get off as soon as possible. How long will it take you to pack?"

"Half an hour?"

"OK. I'll meet you as soon as you're ready in Colonel Winter's office."

Courtney was grinning as he went to his tent. Forty-five minutes later, the Alouette helicopter lifted off the ground, and Courtney looked down for the last time on the rows of gum trees and the dry veld around them, on the white-painted prison outhouse buildings with the small figures of the soldiers standing guard; on the innocuous-seeming interrogation room, isolated a distance away. Was there anyone screaming in there now, Courtney wondered, anyone lying on the cold cement floor in pain and misery?

He remembered suddenly he hadn't seen Jan Rousseau to say goodbye. But hell, he was glad to be going.

SEVENTEEN

An army Land Rover took Rousseau and his men through part of the Kruger National Park and dropped them off five miles from the border.

They watched it drive off, back to the camp, setting up a trail of dust, and then began to march in single file. They covered four miles in an hour, and made camp to wait for night.

Inside Mozambique, they would move only during darkness. They would make the crossing before the moon rose. The hours passed and the men sat, sometimes talking quietly, but mostly in silence. They took turns dozing in the shade, resting their heads on their lumpy khaki webbing packs. The shadows lengthened and faded into the rest of the landscape.

With night came the noise of the crickets. When it was dark enough, Rousseau gave the signal and they left their hiding place in silence. They paused to look through the night-sights and get their bearings.

The land was flat, covered in long dry grass and dotted with trees. Rousseau kept to the grassy area, heading east, taking the straightest, least complicated route, picking his way slowly and cautiously, his ears straining for other sounds.

Beyond the faint rustling of grass, undetectable more than ten yards away, the soldiers moved noiselessly. It was impossible to tell exactly when they crossed the border. There was no obvious boundary. The grassland rolled on, some hills in the distance.

Three hours had passed and they were well into Mozambique. The moon had risen and the glow it cast made the march simpler and quicker, but it also made it easier for them to be spotted by the enemy.

At last Rousseau raised his hand and the others stopped and waited quietly. He looked through his night-sight at the country dead ahead, and took it slowly round in a complete circle. There was a plume of smoke about a mile away, east-south-east, obviously from a camp fire. Otherwise nothing.

Rousseau unfolded a map on the ground and studied it through the night-sight, then checked the position of the hills. They had gone too far north, and had slightly overshot their first target, Cabala village. That fire was probably the marker.

They headed off again towards the smoke. This time Rousseau charted a course which kept them close to trees and thorn scrub, cutting down the silhouettes which might be seen by anyone on guard.

The nearer they got to Cabala the closer to the trees they went, until the cover ended and ahead of them were the huts.

Cabala was surrounded by trees on three sides. Rousseau and his men lay flat on their stomachs and crawled forward a few yards to a heap of rocks. They skirted them until they had a better view.

Men were moving round the village. There were some vehicles – at least one truck, and a couple of Land Rovers. They could see only the back of one of them, protruding from behind a mud and thatch hut.

The computers at Silvermine had given this area an arms and explosives rating of nine. It was either a chemical sniffer malfunction, or those huts contained a huge arsenal. They would have to try and discover which it was.

Rousseau crawled up to each of his men in turn and whispered instructions. "Split up into twos. You and Pienaar go together. Go round as far as those trees, there behind the Land Rover. Then back here and wait. We meet back here. Look out for sentries. For Christ's sake, don't get caught."

Rousseau and his second, Roger Stuart, a British immigrant, would move in the other direction and check the south-west side of Cabala.

Immediately the pairs headed off, crawling back to the line of trees, and into cover at the perimeter, then slowly round in a pincer movement, stopping every few yards to examine the village. Most of the men inside were armed. Sentries were posted at a dirt road which led into it.

There were another two trucks, parked behind a group of huts.

Rousseau and Stuart crawled round to another vantage point.

They would not be able to go much further before they hit the road, which would mean moving away from the camp, well out of range of the sentries, and crossing there.

Headlights were coming up the dirt road, swinging round, beams hitting the trees. Rousseau and Stuart pressed themselves flat and the lights flashed above them. Another Land Rover was coming into the village. The soldiers watched through their night-sights.

The sentries waved the vehicle on. It pulled into the village and four white men got out. Rousseau and Stuart saw them being greeted by two other whites and three bantu. All were in military camouflage uniforms. They disappeared into a hut.

Rousseau began to crawl further round. Suddenly, a match flared in the darkness directly in front of him. A flash of fear pulled the skin into a grimace round his face and subsided in prickles down his back and neck. He felt his heart pound.

Six yards away, no more, a face was illuminated by the match, a black face, tilted slightly sideways as he lit a cigarette. The flame went out. The cigarette glowed red as the man inhaled, then dimmed and arced down as his hand fell beside him.

Rousseau lay frozen. How could he not have seen the man earlier? He had checked the area with his night-sight.

More to the point, how was it the man hadn't seen them or, at least, heard some noise which would arouse his suspicions?

The cigarette arced up through the blackness and glowed red again as the man pulled on it.

Slowly, his hand moving an inch at a time, Rousseau reached for his night-sight and brought it up to his face.

The man was a guerrilla, in camouflage jacket and pants, and his Kalash was slung over his shoulder. He was sideways on, looking down at the village.

Behind him and slightly further away was a bulky shape, which at first Rousseau could not recognise. He stared hard, and suddenly he knew what it was.

It was the camouflage netting which had thrown him: that and the branches cut off and propped alongside. But underneath it all was a tank. He could just make out the long muzzle of its gun covered by the netting.

He tried to identify it, but it was difficult in the circumstances.

Its silhouette was fairly low, so it wasn't a Soviet T-34. Probably a T-54. They'd used those in Angola, and it made sense they'd be here too.

Rousseau was aware of Stuart lying motionless behind him, waiting for a lead. The guerrilla's cigarette glowed again in the dark.

They obviously couldn't get past him, so somehow they'd have to go back without being noticed and then skirt round. If there was one tank, there would be others.

With great care Rousseau began to move, stretching out his elbows and forearms and pulling up the sides of his feet in slow motion, like a chameleon, testing the ground cautiously for loose stones or twigs which might snap, and only then lowering his weight. He kept as close to the ground as he could. When he had covered five or six yards he stopped and looked back. Stuart was right behind him. The guerrilla had not moved.

On they went, and turned deeper into the trees before skirting back behind the tank with its guerrilla guard.

Rousseau knew what to look out for now, and he quickly spotted the camouflage netting draped over the second tank. It was only twenty yards from the first. He could not see the guard, but presumed another was in there somewhere, probably on the other side of the tank.

Rousseau located the guerrilla at the third tank before he had gone another five feet, because the man was walking straight towards them. Rousseau and Stuart froze.

The man was coming in a direct line. They could hear his boots. The man stopped and there was silence. Rousseau dared not raise his head to look, and waited to feel the butt of the rifle come down on him, or the explosion in his body as the bullet tore through.

Suddenly they heard the sound of water, a steady stream under pressure.

Rousseau closed his eyes and grinned. He'd just come for a piss. Bloody hell.

He looked up cautiously. The guerrilla was six yards away, a dark shape facing a tree. If the tree was at midday, Rousseau and Stuart were at ten o'clock. It needed only the slightest sound or movement to attract the guerrilla's attention.

The soldiers waited. The sound of water went on. Rousseau could hardly believe any bladder could hold so much.

At last the man was finished. There was another long pause while he fastened his fly buttons. The soldiers stayed motionless.

Then the footsteps again. Rousseau wasn't sure at first whether they were coming closer, and he risked another glance up. The guerrilla was moving back to his position. The soldiers waited until he was at his post before Rousseau crawled to the west again, putting even more distance between them and Cabala with its ring of Soviet tanks.

Rousseau and Stuart crossed the dirt road just round a bend, out of sight of the sentries, and continued their recce. They counted twenty tanks. It was impossible to estimate the number of guerrillas in the village – the Silvermine computers had put the population at around five hundred – but there was no way of telling which of these were civilians.

To get an assessment they would have to keep watch during the day, and Rousseau was determined to put a couple of miles between his men and the camp before dawn.

Rousseau and Stuart turned back, making a wider sweep to avoid the tanks' guards, and crawled back to the rocks near the perimeter to wait for Pienaar and Smit. They lay in the dark for an hour before Rousseau saw through his night-sight the slight movement in the dry grass which signalled the others coming back.

No one spoke. Rousseau looked at his watch. It was four in the morning. It would start getting light in an hour and a half. He let Pienaar and Smit rest for ten minutes, and then motioned to them that it was time to get going.

The four soldiers crawled off, away from Cabala, and headed for a kopje two miles away. They reached it as the sky was lightening. First they checked the kopje with their night-sights for signs of anyone else. As dawn broke, they scoured it for the criss-cross bootprints of terrorists. When it was found to be clear, Rousseau chose a spot near the summit and they sat down resting on their packs.

"Any trouble?" Rousseau asked softly.

Pienaar and Smit shook their heads.

"Some close calls," Pienaar said, "but no one spotted us.

There are tanks around that side. Looked to me like T-54s — about thirty of them. They're under netting."

Rousseau nodded. "The same with us. We saw twenty. Anything else?"

"Sentries on them all. That's it. There are quite a few terrorists in the camp, but I couldn't see any other weapons, apart from the T-54s and the Kalashs." Pienaar turned to Smit. "How about you?"

"No, that's it. T-54s and terrs," Smit said.

"OK," Rousseau replied. "That was good work. We've got two villages to look at tonight. I reckon we'll split up to do them. Now let's get some sleep. We'll do three-hour shifts. I'll take the first one. You're next, Pienaar, then Stuart, then Smit."

The men stretched themselves on the ground among the rocks and bushes. Rousseau took his binoculars and rifle and settled down to watch.

EIGHTEEN

John Courtney looked round his new office and felt pleased. It wasn't Van Niekerk and Tessler, of course. There was no air-conditioning, and the carpet wasn't wall-to-wall. The desk was not an executive model, just an ordinary wooden desk. There were no expensive, numbered prints on the walls, just two colour photographs: one of the President looking stern; the other of the Prime Minister looking wrathful.

There was a map of the world. While he waited, Courtney cut an arrow out of a piece of plain paper, wrote "YOU ARE HERE" on it, and stuck it on the map, pointing at South Africa. But when he heard footsteps outside his door, he peeled it off quickly and crumpled it in his hand. The footsteps passed by.

Courtney tossed the ball of paper into the wastebin and sat at his desk, grinning.

What now? Mr Bosman had said there would be a meeting of the State Security Council first thing in the morning, and he would be tied up until after that. Afterwards, he would show Courtney round.

It was ten-thirty. This time yesterday he'd been watching a bantu being tortured to death. Now he was in Pretoria in his own cream and brown office, and the Prime Minister was glaring at him, with eyes that followed him all around the room. Jesus, he was glad to be away from that camp. Whatever it was he had to do in Pretoria, it would be better than that. Jan Rousseau would be starting on his patrol across the border. He'd probably be there by now, if he'd set out at dawn.

It was hard to believe – the things that happened at the camp, and Jan now across in Mozambique. There was an unreal quality about his life.

It was unreal last night, too, when he took a train to Johannesburg and a taxi to his flat. Nothing seemed to have changed there, except no one was about. Stephen, the servant, had obviously been given the night off. Moira was out, and there was no way of knowing where. She hadn't taken the car. It was still parked outside.

At first he felt disappointed. They could have had a meal, slept together; but then he remembered she'd probably be angry because he hadn't written to her, and the night would be spent explaining that away. He'd meant to write, but the first day he arrived he'd watched a man being tortured, and everything seemed to accelerate from there. He'd started two or three letters, but found there was nothing he could, or wanted to, tell her about his duties, and it seemed futile writing about the state of the camp cooking and the weather.

Courtney put a record on the stereo, and poured himself a drink. Mr Bosman had given him the key to a furnished flat in Pretoria. It was small, just one bedroom, a lounge, kitchen and bathroom, but it was his for the duration, and he could come and go as he pleased.

He thought he might wait for Moira to return and get back to Pretoria early in the morning, but he felt tiredness creeping over him and decided against it. He finished his drink and began to pack. He filled two suitcases with clothes, and then went to the bathroom to shower and change out of his uniform.

He was towelling himself dry when he saw the two toothbrushes in the glass above the basin, but the penny didn't drop for several minutes. When it did, he stood with the towel round his neck and stared at them. There was probably a simple explanation. Moira had bought a new toothbrush and forgotten to throw out the old one. He opened the medicine chest. He'd cleared most of his stuff out when he went into the army, but there it was: a man's safety razor and, next to it, a can of mentholated aerosol shaving foam of a brand he'd never used. He felt a strange emptiness in his stomach, and a wave of regret, followed by anger. Courtney went methodically through the flat now, opening Moira's drawers and cupboards. He found a freshly ironed man's shirt, size fifteen collar, and a change of socks and underpants.

Courtney poured himself another drink. What a bitch, he thought. I'm not gone a month and she's moved someone else into my flat and got my bloody houseboy to do his laundry. He wondered who the man was, but could come to no conclusion. What should he do? Stay and make a scene? Kick her out of his flat? In the end, Courtney did nothing. He left a note saying: "Sorry you were out. I've collected most of my clothes. I'm off on a mission. Not allowed to say where. Don't know when I'll be back. One night I'll just walk in. Be good. Love, John." He added a PS: "I've had to take the car. Sorry about that."

Then he left. OK, he thought, he'd stay in Pretoria. He had his own place there. He could date other girls. He had eleven months to play the field before he needed to make a decision about Moira. Let her screw whom she liked. He would, too.

He drove back to Pretoria feeling angry and hurt. The following morning he was less angry, but still regretful. Even that will pass, he told himself. I just have to sit it out.

He thought about Moira and the other man in his bed, while the Prime Minister stared angrily at him from the wall.

The phone rang at his elbow and he picked it up.

"Hello?"

"Courtney?"

"Yes, sir."

"Piet Bosman here. Are you settled in?"

"Ja, fine thanks," Courtney said.

"Well, can you come along to Room 416? I'll wait for you there."

"Four-one-six? I'll be right along."

Courtney walked down the corridor until he found the office, and knocked. Piet Bosman opened the door immediately. Beyond him Courtney could see a desk with an electric typewriter, and a middle-aged woman secretary at it.

"Thanks, Mrs Brown," Bosman said to her. "If I could have it for signature before lunchtime I'd be very glad." Then to Courtney: "Come on, let's go and see the Minister."

They walked along the corridor, and Bosman asked: "You've seen the papers?"

Courtney shook his head. "No, I'm afraid not."

"Hell," Bosman said. "I'll arrange to have them delivered to your office every morning. Overseas ones too. The thing is, the UN voted to have sanctions against South Africa. We're going to declare a state of emergency this afternoon and bring in regulations to deal with it."

"Christ," Courtney replied. "That's bad news."

"Yes, but not too bad. It had to come sometime, and it's almost a relief to get it over with. The more cards they play, the less they have hanging over our heads."

Courtney nodded: "I suppose that's true."

Bosman opened a door and they stepped inside. It was obviously the ante-room to the Minister's office. Three secretaries sat clicking away at typewriters. The oldest looked up.

"Good morning, Mr Bosman."

"Morning, Miss Rabinowitz. This is Captain Courtney. Is the Minister back yet?"

The secretary nodded at Courtney then said: "Yes, Mr Bosman. Go right through."

Bosman rapped on the double doors leading to the main office and went in. The Defence Minister, Piet de Wet, sat behind a large, highly polished oak desk. The office was quiet and luxurious, wood-panelling, heavy velvet curtains, thick pile carpet, a standard lamp in the corner.

"This is Captain Courtney, Minister," Bosman said.

De Wet came around his desk to shake hands. "I'm pleased to meet you, Captain Courtney," the Minister said. "I've been reading and hearing quite a lot about you."

He indicated some arm-chairs by the side, and the three men sat in the comfort of what could have been a rich man's private study.

The Minister leaned heavily back in his chair. "As you know," he said to Courtney, "we've got some new problems. With the latest UN move and the state of emergency this afternoon, we can expect considerable repercussions. Also as you know, the security situation across the border in Mozambique is not good. It's anybody's guess what we can expect from there. Now you may be wondering what you've got to do with any of this. I'll tell you straight out. We're after a new perspective on our problems and what we might do about them. You're an advertising man, one of the best in the country, I'm told. We want an advertising man's mind on these matters. Our civil servants are top grade. I make no complaint about them, except perhaps this one: that they sometimes lack imagination. They give me advice. Some of it I accept, some I reject. But whatever I do, whites are leaving the country in increasing numbers. We can't afford to lose whites. I could close the borders, I suppose, and stop them going. But would that improve morale? No, there must be a better way."

"What are you thinking of, Minister?" Courtney asked. "An advertising campaign of some sort?"

De Wet shook his head. "Not at the beginning," he said. "We might start one later. But I think the lead must come from the top. For example, is there something that I, as Minister, can do, to improve morale and stop people leaving? If you've read my speeches, you'll see that I never cease telling people we're not going to give in, and that we're here in South Africa to stay, and still they pack and leave. Hundreds of families emigrate each month. Each one of them is a loss to us. Each one has a snowball effect. Other families start thinking: should we leave also? This is our problem, and I'd like to hear what you recommend. You report directly either to Mr Bosman or to myself. If you feel you need briefing on any aspect, Mr Bosman can organise it for you.

But remember that ordinary South Africans don't have access to special briefings and government secrets. They need something they'll understand straight away, and believe. Now there's one last thing," the Minister said, "and it's this. As I've said, my civil servants give me advice. Sometimes I accept it, sometimes I don't. You'll of course be in the same position. Sometimes I'll say yes, and sometimes I'll say no. If I turn down an idea, I'll do my best to explain why. Do you have any questions?"

Courtney shook his head. "No, sir."

"Well then, go off and get started. Time is of the essence. The state of emergency is being declared at two o'clock, and the Prime Minister is making a statement on radio and television at seven."

"I'll do my best, sir."

They shook hands again, and Bosman escorted Courtney back to his own office. Courtney sat by himself, hands behind his head, staring at the wrathful Prime Minister.

Half an hour later there was a knock at the door and a white messenger came in, carrying a pile of South African and overseas newspapers. Courtney skimmed through them. Even reading only the main stories about the sanctions, it took him nearly two hours. Then he sat down with sheets of papers and made notes. He worked through the lunch hour without noticing the time, but by three o'clock hunger stopped him.

Courtney put on his jacket and went out of the Defence Department building to find a café. The newspaper placards were already up: STATE OF EMERGENCY DECLARED. Courtney joined a queue and bought a paper. Christ, he thought, a queue for a paper! He'd never done that in South Africa before.

The moves announced by the government included petrol rationing, new restrictions on currency transfers and allowances, and laws against passing on sanctions-busting information. Courtney bought a Cornish pastie and a pint of milk and sat down to eat at a Formica-topped table, propping the paper against bottles of sauce.

As soon as he'd finished, he went back to his office and got to work again. He screwed pieces of paper into balls and tossed them into the wastepaper bin. The ideas just weren't coming clearly. The problem was so vast.

What about myself, Courtney thought. What would keep me in South Africa? He stared at the Prime Minister for a long time. It won't be your charming manner, he thought. What would it be?

At six o'clock Courtney packed up and went home. He bought a six-pack of beers from a bottle store, and a few groceries. He was back in time to watch the Prime Minister's nationwide broadcast.

It was as he'd expected: an attack on Western double-standards and on the United Nations; a simplistic analysis of communism's grip in Africa coupled with a reprise on the theme that South Africa was the last bastion of Christianity and civilisation in Africa; an exhortation to South Africans to keep quiet about sanctions-busting, and finally an expression of determination that the country would win through.

Later there was an interview with the Prime Minister:

QUESTION: Prime Minister, many people in South Africa are probably a little worried about what sanctions will mean. Have you anything to say to them?
ANSWER: Yes, I have this to say. We expected sanctions. We have made timeous provision for them.
Q: How do you think South Africans' lives will be altered?
A: I don't expect they will be altered very much.
Q: Well, in what ways do you think there will be some change?
A: You know as well as I do that there's full petrol rationing. We've had it in small measure for years, but now it is more formal. That's one of the changes.
Q: What, in fact, is the position about our petrol supplies? Is there anything you can say about that?
A: No.
Q: But is there any assurance you can give the people that the situation is not as critical as some may think?
A: I can't help what some people think. It's not critical. I don't want to go into this at all at the moment. It would be irresponsible of me to do so.

The interview went on in this vein. Courtney listened, first with interest, then with exasperation. The Prime Minister was giving away nothing. He was dismissive. If anyone was watching and looking for reassurance, they were tuned to the wrong channel.

Courtney slept badly. The following morning he went into the office early and began working on a fresh set of ideas. He phoned Bosman's office and arranged to be given a briefing on how South Africa was combating sanctions. This was scheduled for two o'clock, and Courtney was back in his office at four. An hour later, he phoned Bosman and said he'd like to see him. Bosman listened with interest to Courtney's plan, and dialled the Minister.

At six-thirty, Courtney had a crystal whisky glass in his hand and was going through his proposals.

"Do you mind me being frank, Minister?" he asked.

The Minister shook his head. "Please do," he said.

"I think the Prime Minister's interview last night was a disaster," Courtney said bluntly. "He said nothing."

De Wet's face was impassive. "Ja, well there's a war on," de Wet said. "Sanctions is a war in just the same way as we have with the terrorists."

"With respect, Minister, that's not entirely true," Courtney replied. "There are some similarities, of course. Obviously, no one must know about sanctions-busting deals. We all accept that. Ordinary South Africans accept that. But nonetheless, there's a lot that can be said."

"Such as?" de Wet asked.

"I had a briefing this afternoon on our anti-sanctions operation. I've divided it into things which are now entirely South African run, and things which still rely to some extent on imported parts or materials. Anything that relies on imports, I've ruled out. But that still leaves a lot. Let me take one example. The Prime Minister was asked last night about our fuel situation. He flatly refused to answer. Now to a degree he was right. We're still getting a proportion of our oil from the Middle East – but Christ! it's down to forty per cent. That means that in Sasol One and Sasol Two, both major coal liquefying projects, we're producing sixty per cent of our own fuel requirements! And that's sixty per cent before sanctions. With rationing, it'll be even higher. Neither of the Sasol projects depends any more on foreign imports or investment. Deutsche Babcock sent in the last supplies for Sasol Two a couple of years back. It's running by itself now. We've got a lot of spares in stock, and we're starting to manufacture others. Why don't we say so?"

De Wet shrugged. "We keep our enemies guessing. The less they know, the better it is."

"Ja, we may keep our enemies guessing," Courtney persisted, "but we keep our friends guessing too. And they're packing up and leaving. Who gains? Not South Africa."

De Wet looked thoughtful.

"There's also the matter of our oil stockpiles," Courtney said.

"What about them?" de Wet asked.

"Simply that we're not stockpiling any more. We're starting to use the stockpile. There's three years worth in disused mine-shafts that we can bring up, and another two years' worth at Saldanha Bay. Even if both Sasol oil-from-coal plants stopped tomorrow, and not a single drop came into South Africa through the sanctions net, we can keep going for at least five years. Now why don't we tell our people that? It takes the sting right out of oil sanctions."

De Wet sipped his whisky. "I suppose we could," he said. "It's not a bad thought. What else?"

"Arms. Defence," Courtney said. "Everyone is desperately worried about security. What do sanctions mean to the Defence Force?"

De Wet smiled. "Not much," he said. "They've been in force for a long time."

"But people still think last night's UN resolution is going to make a big difference," Courtney replied. "Let's be more open about exactly what we produce locally. We're building a lot. We've got our own surface-to-air missiles, South African de-signed; we're building Mirage F1 supersonic fighters, and we've got casts of all the parts. Even if the French do withdraw co-operation, we can put the planes together from scratch by our-selves. The same with Rolls-Royce Viper turbo-jets. We make everything ourselves. We don't need the British nor the French. We make our own electronics: surveillance transmitter-receivers, manpack radios, vehicle radios, field telephones. We make our own bullets. We make our own tear gas. Our own Eland ar-

146

moured cars. And no one can stop us doing these things. Why the hell don't we spell it out to our own people?"

"You could be right, Captain," de Wet admitted.

"And I don't think we should just say this sort of thing baldly. We must show people. Take journalists round the Sasol plants. Let them see an underground oil-storage tank in a disused mine. Show them round some of our munitions factories. I'm thinking particularly about South African television. This is what people here watch and remember. The basic idea I'm trying to put across is this: there's a lot we *can* say which won't harm us. Let's try and see how *much* we can say in future, not how little."

De Wet asked: "Can you let me have all this on paper, Captain. I think it's a good plan. If I can have it first thing in the morning, I'll put it to the Prime Minister."

NINETEEN

Rousseau, standing first watch near the summit of the kopje inside Mozambique, saw the dust trails: plumes rising thickly behind the wheels of the vehicles, and then dispersing out into the clear morning air. He watched through binoculars. The lead vehicle was a Land Rover, but he couldn't make out the second immediately because it was almost completely enveloped in the brown cloud. Behind that were two trucks, and further back still, two other Land Rovers. They were coming from Cabala village, moving fast. Rousseau watched them out of sight. Gradually the dust cleared.

It was going to be a humid day. The signs were already there. Although it was not yet eight in the morning, Rousseau could feel the slight stickiness on his skin as the damp air heated under the sun. There were some clouds at about five thousand feet, but at this time of year, before the rains, they just built up tantalisingly then drifted away.

He became aware of the sound of an aircraft, a jet, coming closer. When he saw it, it was still on the South African side of the border, and he identified it as a Canberra. The aircraft banked and swept along the border. It was on an aerial photo reconnaissance, Rousseau thought. And then he realised why the vehicles had pulled out of the village.

In a photograph, South African Intelligence would be lucky to spot the ring of tanks parked under the thickness of the trees, camouflaged with branches and netting to break up their outlines. But they would immediately have picked up the Land Rovers and the trucks parked in Cabala, and the Cubans would have risked a pre-emptive strike: Mirages flashing in suddenly and low, rockets hurtling into the huts, napalm exploding in a Christmas tree of phosphorus.

The Canberra turned back to make another run, nearer in this time, certainly on the Mozambique side of the border, flying slowly and lazily at about four thousand feet, the pilot apparently confident he was unchallenged in the sky.

Suddenly Rousseau noticed the plane was being followed. Coming up quickly from behind and to one side, he saw a vapour trail, beginning in an area about five miles from the kopje. The white trail arched up into the sky behind a silver missile. Jesus, Rousseau thought, it's a SAM-7.

Rousseau watched with his heart in his mouth as the missile closed on the Canberra, homing in on the heat blasted out from its jets. The Canberra was taking no evasive action: the pilot unaware of the danger seconds away.

The gap between the missile and the plane narrowed and, at once, the SAM-7 slammed into the exhaust of the Canberra's port engine. There was a puff of white smoke, followed by a flash of orange, and the jet disintegrated in the sky.

Two large pieces plunged down: the starboard wing, almost intact, and the tailplane. Apart from that, there was just debris, some burning. Rousseau waited for a parachute to blossom out, but there was nothing. The pieces fell to the ground, scattered over more than a mile, raising small plumes of dust. Then the sky was clear.

Rousseau felt sick. Should he wake the others and tell them what had happened? He decided against it: there was no point, nothing any one of them could do.

He studied his map. The SAM-7 appeared to have been launched from near a village they would be checking that night, Igoma. The computers had given it an arms and explosives rating of six.

Rousseau stared over the dry landscape. If anyone was moving out to look at the wreckage of the Canberra, he could not see them. When his watch was up, he shook Pienaar awake and told him what had happened.

"The Air Force are going to come looking for that Canberra," Rousseau said. "As soon as you hear a plane, wake me up."

Pienaar nodded and took up position. Rousseau put his head on his webbing pack and found that he was very tired. He fell asleep at once.

It seemed almost at once, too, that Pienaar's hand was patting his face, and his voice saying urgently: "Jannie, there's a plane!"

Rousseau stumbled to his feet, looking round quickly to re-orientate himself, and followed Pienaar to the lookout point. The Air Force had sent a Mirage 111 to look for the Canberra, checking the area where radar showed it disappearing from the screen.

The Mirage was cruising, but obviously on guard. The pilot banked and ducked, watching for the enemy. The control tower would have seen the SAM close in on their radar screens, but there wouldn't have been enough time for them to have warned the Canberra pilot. The Mirage crossed and recrossed the area where the Canberra came down, but there was no way of telling whether the pilot had spotted the wreckage. Rousseau and Pienaar waited for the guerrillas to launch another SAM-7, but nothing came. At last, the Mirage turned for home, opening its throttle and accelerating through the sky, out of sight in five or six seconds.

Rousseau went back to sleep. It was getting dark when he awoke. They ate quietly, and Rousseau divided the duties. They would keep in the same pairs: himself and Stuart – Smit and Pienaar. His pair would look at Igoma village, which was where the SAM-7 seemed to have come from, while Smit and Pienaar would tackle the settlement further up towards the hills, Guba.

The computer gave Guba an arms and explosives rating of five. They would meet back at the kopje before daybreak.

The four set out together, going cautiously through the dark, pre-moon bush, and splitting up after two miles. Rousseau and Stuart headed north-east for Igoma, about three miles further on. It was a slow, silent, nerve-wracking business. Last night's recce around Cabala had shown the degree of the arms build-up. They had been very lucky not to have been spotted. Security was a lot tighter than anything they'd come across before.

Rousseau and Stuart walked for more than an hour before Igoma came into sight. It was more exposed than Cabala, although there were trees along one side. The rest was grass and thorn scrub.

Rousseau inspected the area through his night-sight. There was the usual fire in the village, and some men walking about, but they did not appear to be armed. The trees were not thick, and Rousseau could not pick out the bulky black masses of camouflaged tanks.

Yet the Silvermine computer rated Igoma at six. The arms and ammunition had to be hidden inside the huts. There was certainly a rocket-launcher somewhere there. But on the surface, nothing distinguished Igoma from thousands of innocent villages.

Rousseau led Stuart in a skirting movement round to the trees, but there was nothing special to be seen from that side either, and no sign of sentries. The men crawled forward, closer to the huts.

Rousseau never saw what hit him, or where it had come from.

There was a sudden explosion on the side of his head, a sharp shaft of pain, and he felt himself tumbling down, engulfed by blackness. As he did he heard, very close, other explosions: rifle fire, and he thought without emotion: now I'm dying. He tried to put together other thoughts, but he could not and they melted into silence.

On two or three occasions he drifted into semi-consciousness, to the state where he almost felt he was dreaming. He heard voices, but they faded. He felt himself being carried some distance, and he glimpsed a face which was gone in an instant.

Somewhere above his eyelids dawn seemed to be breaking, a globe of brightness surrounded by pink, fading off to grey and

150

finally edged by the dark. He felt his body had been pulled. There was an indefinable pain around his ankles and wrists, and an ache behind his eyes.

He tried to move. His arms and legs stayed as they were, stretched. The brightness above his eyelids increased and he screwed up his face to block it out. He twisted his body and found there was an extent to which he could move, but then he was held fast. The dream evaporated..

Where was he? Partially paralysed. Lying on something hard. An operating table? His eyes flickered, then closed again against the glare of the light. There were voices somewhere to one side of him, a language he did not recognise.

Gradually his eyes became accustomed to the brightness, and he saw it came from the filament of an electric light, pulsing slightly with the current from the generator which Rousseau could hear throbbing in the background. He turned his head and saw the thatch of the ceiling and the stout wooden beams, then the mud wall. Up to the light again, past the peak of the ceiling and down the other side to the wall.

Three white men in camouflage uniform stood at a wooden table, going through the pockets of another camouflage uniform, examining the contents of the pouches and the pack, paying no attention to him. The dull throbbing in his head made him shut his eyes.

Remembrance came gradually. Crawling through the grass. The blow on his head. The sound of shooting. He was a prisoner. These men were Cubans. He looked down at his own naked body, spread-eagled out and tied by the wrists and ankles to the table legs.

That uniform being searched was his own. His mouth had gone completely dry. He thought: God be with me. He should never have been captured. He didn't know how it had happened. Where was Stuart?

Rousseau looked across at the Cubans again. They were reading the documents in his pouches. Presumably they knew some English: did they know any Afrikaans? He wasn't carrying classified information, so it wouldn't matter. The most incriminating thing he had was the map of the area, and that would only tell them the South Africans knew the various villages and kraals they were using. The rest – what other information they obtained – was up to him.

Rousseau remembered Ndlovu, the headman. Is this what he felt as he waited for his interrogation to begin: this loneliness? This naked vulnerability? Ndlovu had said nothing despite his pain. What reserves of strength had he called on? And what about Rousseau himself? How would he take it? He wished he knew, and he fought to control the core of dread in his stomach.

The Cubans paid no attention to him. One of them glanced up and saw that Rousseau was conscious, but did not remark on the fact to his comrades, and they continued to be absorbed in the search. Then one of them squatted down on the floor. Rousseau could not turn his head sufficiently to see what he was doing but, by twisting his left shoulder up and straining against his bonds, he increased his field of vision.

The body of Stuart lay there, mouth agape as if screaming, camouflage jacket soaked with his blood, and ripped by the bullets which smashed through near his heart. If he had lived at all after being hit, it could not have been for more than a few moments. His blue eyes were wide open and staring sightlessly. The Cuban searched through his pockets and pouches, and rolled him over to check his back.

Rousseau subsided onto the hard table and lay still, his eyes closed, trying to suppress the fear, the pure funk, which was growing inside him.

He could not tell how long he lay there: perhaps ten minutes, perhaps thirty. It seemed like hours. He could hear the Cubans talking but he understood not a word, and soon gave up listening. Rousseau waited, keeping perfectly still, his chest hardly moving with his shallow breathing.

He could not tell immediately why he felt a sudden chill, what instinct told him his moment had come. Perhaps it was the silence in the room that alerted him. It was not the sound of the men's footsteps, because they made none when they walked. But he opened his eyes, and they were standing round him, like surgeons round a patient. Their eyes were incurious: their faces betrayed nothing. The three Cubans were young, probably in their early twenties, not much older than himself. One had a neat black beard, and the others were dark but clean-shaven. The bearded one seemed in command, or perhaps it was because he was the English-speaker.

"What is your name?" The bearded man's voice was calm and held a trace of an American accent. Rousseau tried to answer but the dryness in his mouth made speech difficult. His lips were sticking together, and the skin pulled as he parted them. His tongue felt porridgy thick and difficult to move. The words came out, low and disjointed.

"What is your name?" the bearded Cuban asked again, quietly.

"Rousseau."

"Your full name?"

He got it out at last. "Johannes Jacobus Rousseau." Then he forced himself to say: "Sergeant. South African army. Military number 6735091."

"What were you doing in Mozambique, Sergeant Rousseau?" the Cuban asked. Rousseau stayed silent and turned his head away. The Cuban said again: "What were you doing across the border?" Rousseau felt the man's fingers, hard and strong, gripping beneath his chin, sinking into his neck, forcing his face round.

"I only need to tell you my name, rank and Defence Force serial number," Rousseau said, trying to stop his voice shaking. "That's all. That's what's agreed."

"Is it?" The Cuban's reply was uninterested. He turned and spoke to his comrades – Rousseau could not understand a word – and one of them left the room.

The bearded Cuban looked back at him. "We require you to answer our questions. If you do not, we will torture you until you change your mind."

Rousseau did not trust himself to answer at first, but finally he said, as forcefully as he could: "I am a prisoner-of-war. I demand to be treated in terms of the Geneva Convention. Fetch your senior officer."

The Cuban's expression did not change. "There is no state of war between Mozambique and your country. How can you be a prisoner of something that doesn't exist? And we're not concerned with the Geneva Convention, any more than you are." The Cuban shrugged. "These things do not concern us."

The door opened again, and Rousseau raised his head to see what was coming. The third Cuban was back, bringing with him a black man, small-boned and thin, wearing a khaki shirt and shorts. In his right hand the black man carried a wooden paddle, shaped a little like a table tennis bat, but with four or five holes drilled through it.

Rousseau felt a shiver go through his body. Oh bloody hell, he thought in fright, a bastinado.

He badly wanted to go to the lavatory. He stared up into the light, steeling his body.

Nothing happened for several seconds, then it began. The first blows on the sole of his right foot were not painful, no more than he would feel jumping without shoes from a low wall onto a concrete surface. The blows came in a steady rhythm. His foot began to tingle and itch. He felt the shock waves from the bastinado shoot up to his ankle and calf. He tried to twist his foot, taking the brunt of the blows on different areas in turn, spreading them around. The thud of the bastinado, wood against skin, was the only sound in the room.

The pain began slowly, first little more than an irritation on the sole, building up as the flesh bruised and the holes in the wooden paddle sucked at the skin, then definite hurt pulsing with each thud, the feeling of nerve-endings becoming exposed, a sickness growing at the back of his throat as he waited for the next blow to fall, then the next, and the next, a slow, relentless rhythm: thud ... thud ... shafts of agony, Rousseau trying to shrink away from the blows but being held fast, no longer able to twist his foot, lying helplessly while the pain increased, half of his consciousness trying to cope with that, the other half tensed to control his bladder and bowels. Rousseau heard himself begin whimpering, somewhere deep in his throat, as the wood tortured the raw nerves in his foot.

The sounds in his throat became louder, a grunting now, first with the rhythm of each thud, then out of time with the blows, almost panting. Rousseau stared into the glowing filament of the light bulb above his head as if it were something to cling onto, something to help him, then his mouth opened and he just screamed, disbelief in the sound at first, later agony, thud ... thud ... his lungs gulping in air for the next scream, his eyes

154

streaming tears, hips and chest and shoulders twisting, but his foot being held fast, unable to pull away from the source of the agony. He felt warm wetness on his stomach and he knew he was pissing over himself, and that his bowels would soon empty, but the humiliation didn't matter now, just the awfulness of the pain sweeping over him, the burning heat from his foot, the thud ... thud, and the sound of himself howling like an animal, and blubbing like a child.

The blows had stopped for two or three minutes before Rousseau even became aware of the fact. The pain was self-generating, throbbing even without the bastinado, and only gradually was he conscious that his screaming was the only sound in the room. He tried to stop it, to control himself, and gradually he forced it back down to a whimper, a growling which he could contain in the back of his throat.

The filament of the naked light bulb pulsed in his brain and he held onto it, almost as a divine image. Jesus, help me. He lay on the table in his stinking mess and his pain, and Rousseau prayed, or tried to pray, trying to get a coherent line of thought to turn into a real prayer, then felt a different pain as a hand grabbed his hair and yanked his head up and round, and he was staring, his eyes wild and wet, into the face of the bearded Cuban.

"What were you doing in Mozambique?" The Cuban's voice was threatening.

Automatically Rousseau said: "Johannes Jacobus Rousseau. Sergeant. South African army. Military number 6735 ..." Oh Jesus, what was his number? Oh Jesus, what was his number? "6735091." He finished, almost gasping it out, desperation in his voice.

The Cuban let go his hair and Rousseau's head crashed back onto the table, sending a bolt of pain through his brain. The Cuban turned away and said to the African: "Start on his other foot."

Inside his brain, Rousseau could hear himself shouting: oh no, Jesus Christ, no, please, no! In his throat, he began whimpering again.

The blows came on his left foot. Thud. Thud. An itch. Thud. Foot twisting. Thud. Irritation growing. Thud. Thud. Thud. Bruising. Thud. The feeling of softness. Thud. In the sole.

Thud. Water trapped. Thud. In pads of skin. Thud. Nerves exposed. Thud. Pulsing pain. Thud. Filament of the light bulb. Thud. A shape on his retinas. Thud. A dove. Thud. An image of Jesus. Thud. Painful prickling. Thud. Back of his throat. Thud. Shafts of agony. Thud. Tortured nerves. Thud. Mouth opening. Thud. Screaming. Thud. Screaming. Thud. Hips and chest twisting. Thud. To get away. Thud.

Rousseau knew there must be a point at which he would black out. He waited for it, screaming. He could take no more. He must surely lose consciousness. But still it increased, pain like a stretched piano wire, becoming tauter and tauter, yet not snapping, the world, and time, halted, with Rousseau's mind not blocking off, enduring.

The thudding of the bastinado stopped but his cries could not. Was it over? Rousseau wanted to curl up in his misery. He wished for death. His feet were aflame with pain. He knew he couldn't take any more. He must answer the Cubans, at least tell them unimportant things, try to persuade them to stop the torture. Surely there were things he could tell them, things that would make no difference? The Cuban's hand grasped his hair again and yanked his head up.

"What were you doing in Mozambique?" the Cuban shouted.

"Recce," Rousseau mumbled. "Recce."

Still shouting: "What did you say?"

"Recce. For God's sake. Reconnaissance. We came to have a look," Rousseau gasped.

The fist still held his hair, and Rousseau could feel strands tearing out of his scalp. "What for?" the Cuban demanded.

Jesus it must be obvious. "Arms!" Rousseau shouted back in desperation. "Arms! Men!" The Cuban let his head crash onto the table and his brain exploded in pain again.

"How many of you are there?" the Cuban was still shouting.

God help me. "Two," Rousseau said. "Two of us."

"Liar!" The fist in his hair again, wrenching up his head. "Liar! How many?"

"Jesus! Two! Two!"

The Cuban yelled at the African. "More bastinado!"

"No!" Rousseau cried out, almost sobbing. "Jesus, no! It's the truth! Only two!"

Thud. Flash of pain. Thud. Pain. Thud. Sickness, nausea. Thud. His voice screaming again in unbearable agony.

"How many?" the Cuban shouted in his ear. Thud.

"Two!" Thud. "Two-o-o!" Thud. "Stop for Christ's sake! Two!" Explosions of agony, body writhing, smearing his faeces on the wooden table top. "Two!" Thud. "Bastards! Bastards!"

Silence again, except for Rousseau's moans.

Suddenly the Cuban yelled in his ear: "How many with you?"

"TWO! TWO!"

"What are their names?"

"STUART!"

"And the other one?" the Cuban demanded.

"No other one! Me! Stuart and me!"

The Cuban paused to consider this, and decided Rousseau was telling the truth.

"When did you and Stuart come across?" he asked.

Jesus, he'd got away with it. Rousseau felt a wave of relief. "Yesterday."

"What have you seen?" Without warning, the bastinado thudded down on the sole of his left foot and his body arched, the breath hissing through clenched teeth.

"What have you seen?" the Cuban shouted again.

"One other village!"

Thud. Rousseau cried out, an animal sound. "Jesus! Stop!"

"Which village?"

"Cabala! Cabala!"

"What did you see there?"

Thud. Another shaft of agony. Rousseau knew he was going to piss over himself again.

"What did you see there?" the Cuban yelled.

"Tanks! Kalashnikovs! Trucks!"

"How many tanks?"

Rousseau didn't wait for the bastinado to fall this time, and his answer was coming in panic and desperation before the bearded Cuban had finished the question. "Forty! Fifty! Around the village!"

"How many men?"

"Couldn't tell! Impossible to tell!"

"When did you report back?"

"Didn't! Didn't report back."

Thud. Rousseau roared, his body squirming, shoulders and hips thrashing about. God, he was pissing. "Didn't!" he screamed, "Didn't! Emergency radio contact only! Jesus, believe me!"

"When were you going to report?"

"Back at base," Rousseau sobbed. "No contact until then, except emergency."

"Where's your base?" the Cuban asked.

"Camp. Near Chicundu. Ten miles south-east."

The Cuban nodded. "I know it," he said quietly. "How many men are based there?"

"Six hundred," Rousseau said, his breath coming in pants, terrible pain still throbbing from his feet.

"Now the map you were carrying," the Cuban said, his voice calm. "Some of the villages were marked with a number. By Igoma there is the number six. Cabala has the number nine. What does it mean, six and nine?"

"I don't know," Rousseau said despairingly.

"I'll give you one more chance," the Cuban said. "Then the torture starts again from the beginning. What do the numbers mean?"

"I don't know!"

Thud. The bastinado crashed down again on his bruised and swollen feet and Rousseau's body leapt as if an electric current had been switched on. Thud. This time he managed not to scream. Thud. Rousseau began to howl. Thud. Jee-sus! Thud. He could stand no more. Thud. His cries turned into screams of pure, unendurable agony. Thud.

"Stop! Stop! I'll tell you! Jesus Christ, stop."

The black man with the bastinado paused. The Cuban waited for Rousseau to stop weeping, but the young commando could not. Even though he clenched his teeth and tried to control himself, the tears poured from his eyes, unstoppable: tears of pain; of humiliation and defeat.

Five minutes passed before the Cuban spoke again. "What do the numbers on the map mean?"

"Arms and explosives," Rousseau moaned. "Assessment – of how much there is."

158

"How much arms and explosives is in each village?" the Cuban asked.

"Yes." Rousseau nodded.

"Whose assessment? Yours?"

"No. Not mine."

"Whose?"

"Computer," said Rousseau. "Computer assessment!"

The Cuban turned to his colleagues, who had been watching silent and unmoved, and he grinned at them. "Tell me about the computer," he said.

Rousseau told him. The man with the bastinado went away. The pain throbbed around his feet.

Rousseau talked.

At last the Cubans were finished. They untied his wrists and ankles, and tried to make him walk. As the bleeding soles of his feet touched the floor, Rousseau screamed.

They made him crawl naked on his hands and knees the three hundred yards to the hut where he was to be held. They put a handcuff on his right wrist, and attached the other end to his left ankle. Rousseau curled into the foetal position on the hard earth floor and nursed his agony. The Cubans went away and he was alone.

Rousseau felt overcome with desolation and betrayal. Tears rolled down his face onto the ground.

At least he hadn't told them about Smit and Pienaar. At least the others still had a chance. Whatever else he'd done, he hadn't betrayed them.

It was Rousseau's last vestige of self-respect, and he clung onto it as he wept.

TWENTY

Things were accelerating quickly.

Overnight, the bantu townships round Johannesburg erupted into violence. Police opened fire and killed four blacks, one of them a twelve-year-old girl who had been running for cover. In the seaports, there were more disturbances. Durban reported gangs of stone-throwing bantu smashing offices and shops on the outskirts. In Cape Town, police fired tear gas to disperse two thousand people who tried to stage an illegal march.

In Pretoria, John Courtney was late for work, trapped inside his flat for more than an hour as, in the street downstairs, police clashed with rioting blacks. Courtney saw there was trouble as soon as he stepped into the street. Hundreds of bantu swarmed around, and the mood was ugly. He could hear the sound of breaking glass. Courtney glanced to the other end of the street and saw the police waiting, armed with rifles and pistols, Land Rovers blocking the exit. Courtney immediately turned and retreated into the building, locking himself in his flat and phoning an explanation to the Department of Defence.

He sat by the window and looked down two floors. The bantu were shouting slogans and chanting "Amandhla! Amandhla! Power! Power!" and a gang was running from shop to shop bashing in windows. He could not see what was happening to the whites inside, but he presumed they had barricaded themselves in offices.

He wondered why the police at the end of the street were just standing watching, doing nothing, as the demonstrators came towards them. Then Courtney saw the reason. More armed police appeared at the other end of the street and blocked it off. About fifteen hundred people were effectively trapped. Christ, Courtney thought, what are they going to do now? He watched the police for their next move.

Tear gas canisters hurtled through the air and exploded on

the ground in white puffs of stinging vapour. The crowd turned and began running in the opposite direction. Courtney could see some fall and be overwhelmed in the rush, lost to sight. Then the fleeing crowd noticed the second line of police stretched across the other end of the street, cutting off their exit, and Courtney could hear shouts of anger from the demonstrators. The second line of police aimed and fired more tear gas canisters, and the bantu fled back the way they'd come, into the still-drifting smoke of the first tear gas volley, handkerchiefs, aprons, shirts over their stinging faces and streaming eyes.

When Courtney saw the first line of police raise their rifles, he stared in disbelief. Surely they weren't going to shoot? A voice shouted through a megaphone: "Sit on the ground! Everyone sit on the ground! If you do not sit on the ground we will open fire and kill you!" Courtney could see some people sit immediately, but others stood shouting and yelling: "Amandhla! Amandhla!" Immediately there was a volley of shots and Courtney saw some bantu – five or six of them – go down. The others took to their heels, running towards the second line of policemen, then pulling back and stopping.

A megaphone blared from the other end. "Sit down in the street. Sit down now, or we will shoot!"

The people sat, and when they were all down, the police moved in, batons drawn. Courtney started to count the bodies. He had seen half a dozen shot, but there were seventeen in all. The others had presumably been trampled in the rush. Police started loading demonstrators into prison trucks, pushing them, shouting, batons flailing. It took half an hour to clear the street. The dead were removed last of all.

When it was over, Courtney let himself out of the flat and walked to work, skirting the shattered glass and the pools of blood. He went to Piet Bosman's office and explained what had happened.

Bosman shook his head: "It's the same all over the country," he said. "Troublemakers are at work."

"It's going to be hard to persuade people to stay in South Africa with this sort of unrest going on," Courtney said.

Bosman shrugged. "What can we do? If there's trouble, we must deal with it – crack down hard. That's the only language the bantu understand."

"Maybe," Courtney replied, "but it's unsettling for a lot of whites."

Bosman laughed shortly. "It's going to get worse before we're finished. There's another bit of bad news. Two of our soldiers are missing in Mozambique. We don't know what's happened to them. They're from your old camp."

Courtney felt a stab of apprehension. "Oh hell," he said in dismay. "Who are they?"

Bosman looked at a piece of paper on his desk. "Rousseau and Stuart," he said. "Both commandos."

"Christ," said Courtney. "Jan Rousseau. I know him. Poor guy. He's a good bloke."

"They went on a recce to a village and didn't come back. Two others who were over there with them radioed in a report this morning. Maybe they're just lying low and they'll turn up in a few hours. That's what we're hoping. Meanwhile, we've called the others back. They're going to try and make it through in daylight, just in case."

Courtney went back to his office and stared at the picture of the Prime Minister. Poor Jan. Perhaps he was already dead. He was a first-class man. Courtney sighed. Jesus, it made him feel suddenly vulnerable. One day it would be his turn.

Courtney pulled the pile of papers towards him and began reading through them. Violence. Rioting. Diplomats flying out of South Africa, closing embassies and consulates, the result of sanctions. Some residual missions remaining, with caretaker staff.

The day passed slowly, and in the evening Courtney went out and got drunk. He didn't know anyone in Pretoria, and he didn't much care for the idea of drinking by himself, but thoughts of Jan Rousseau weighed heavily on his mind, and he sat morosely in a series of bars, too depressed to strike up conversations with anyone else, not even looking out for a girl. At midnight, he went back to his flat and fell into bed.

His head was throbbing when he woke up. How much had he drunk? He tried to work it out but gave up. He swallowed four aspirins and lay in a hot bath, feeling ill. By the time he got to work in the Department of Defence building, he was a little better.

He went straight to Bosman's office. "Any news of Rousseau?"

Bosman shook his head. "Nothing. We must assume they've either been killed or captured. We hope they're dead."

Courtney looked baffled. "Why dead?" he asked.

"If they're alive, they'll be tortured," Bosman said in a matter-of-fact voice. "That's the way things go these days. They've got a lot of valuable information. Very few people can get through torture without talking. That's also a fact of life."

"I'd stake quite a lot on Rousseau," Courtney said. "He's a tough nut."

"I hope you're right," Bosman replied. "But you never know what a person's capacity for pain is until they're put to the test."

Courtney nodded. "I suppose that's true," he said. "I just can't imagine Jan Rousseau talking."

Bosman's telephone rang. "Excuse me," he said. "Hello?"

Courtney watched the Minister's PPS reach for a pad and begin writing. Bosman's face betrayed nothing.

He replaced the receiver slowly and made a wry face at Courtney. "Let's go and see the Minister," he said. "Mozambique Radio says they've just closed the borders and that a state of war exists with South Africa."

"Oh, for God's sake," said Courtney in despair.

"And they've got your friend Rousseau. He's a prisoner. They killed the other man, Stuart. Their radio says Rousseau made a full confession of South Africa's 'crimes' and our intentions towards Mozambique. That's why they've declared war."

Courtney stared at Bosman in disbelief. "Do you think he did?" Courtney asked.

"It's hard to say," Bosman replied, putting on his jacket. "If you were tortured, would you talk?"

Courtney shook his head. "I don't know," he said truthfully.

"That's just the point," Bosman said. "Nobody knows."

They walked quickly through to the Minister's office and broke the news to him. A joint emergency meeting of the State Security Council and the Defence Staff Council was arranged for eleven o'clock.

The Minister's face was impassive. "How much did Rousseau know?" de Wet asked Bosman.

The PPS opened his notepad. "I asked for a run-down last

163

night," he said. "He knows about the base camp itself, of course, and how it's defended. He's been in Mozambique before, laying battlefield sensors, so he could pinpoint where they are. And he could talk in general terms about Silvermine."

"Did he have any sensors on him?" de Wet asked.

"No. None of them did. They were simply on a recce. You've seen the report from the other two, Smit and Pienaar. The Cubans are all round there – tanks, SAM-7s, everything."

The Minister nodded: "Did Rousseau know anything about Operation Dingaan?"

Bosman shook his head emphatically. "No, Minister. I've double checked that. Dingaan is on a strict need-to-know basis, and Rousseau has never come into contact with it, not even remotely. He might have picked up one or two rumours, but I think we're safe on that one."

"So Mozambique Radio's claim about 'South African intentions' could just be a reference to the sensors and Silvermine?" de Wet asked.

"I can't think of anything else, Minister."

De Wet leaned back in his seat. "Now what?" he said, almost to himself. "Cuban tanks on the borders. A state of war. The next move?"

The Minister's red phone rang. He picked it up immediately. "Yes?" Bosman and Courtney watched his face, but it was totally without expression. "What have you done about it?" the Minister said into the receiver. There was a long pause. "I see. Very well."

He replaced the receiver.

"Well, gentlemen," he said, "the Cubans have invaded."

TWENTY-ONE

Colonel Winter heard the jets flash over, just above tree-top height, the deep thunderous boom of the sound barrier being broken, and he span round to see what they were, but they had already gone. Winter shrugged and continued walking from his tent in the camp near Chicundu.

He was worried. There was still no word of Rousseau and Stuart, and he hoped to God they were dead. He glanced across the bush, dry and dusty. It was a still, peaceful morning, and the sky was cloudless. But beyond that, what was there? Bloody Cuban tanks. A massive build-up of communist arms and men along the border. Scare tactics? Colonel Winter doubted it.

Suddenly in the bush two hundred yards away he saw eight simultaneous explosions, mushrooms of yellow flame, spaced evenly apart and in a straight line. Winter watched frozen. In front of them came another eight explosions, then another eight: blasts advancing towards the camp, quickly and inexorably. Only a hundred yards away, now fifty, and Winter was running for his life, hearing shouts from his men, seeing others flee, the concussion and heat from the explosions hitting into his back, chunks of brick smashing into the ground beside him, then the flash of flame in front, and Winter threw himself down, arms covering his head. Jesus, he thought, fucking rockets: 122mm by the look of the damage they were doing.

The Cubans were saturation bombing the camp. The line of explosions continued in front of him now, getting further away, smashing into the sleeping quarters, destroying tents in fractions of seconds. He could hear shouts and cries for help. In the distance, a man was screaming.

Winter scrambled to his feet. A rocket smashed into the armoury and a ball of flame blossomed out of the roof, accompanied by a mighty roar. "Get your rifles! Get out of the area!" Winter yelled. "From up by the road!"

He ran to where the remnants of a tent was burning, and he could see several men lying injured.

"Where the hell are the medics!" he roared. "Medics!" The men were in a bad way. One soldier had both his legs blown off, mangled, bloody stumps protruding from his shorts, pouring blood. He was deathly pale. Winter wasted no time on him: he could not be saved. Another man had lost an arm, and was holding onto the wound with his good hand, staunching the flow.

Winter pulled off his own shirt, laid it on the ground and ripped the sleeve off to use as a tourniquet. The man's mouth was trembling. Neither of them said anything.

From the corner of his eye, Winter could see people running. "Medics!" he roared. "Over here quickly! Stretcher bearers!" Winter pulled the tourniquet tight. "Lie down, son," he said. "You'll be all right."

He turned to the next. The third man was bleeding profusely. Shrapnel from the rocket had ripped a deep wound in his thigh and it was pumping blood. Winter rammed his fist into the wound and kept it there to slow the blood, while a medic knelt beside him, preparing a tourniquet. When it was on, Winter withdrew his hand, sticky and red, and smeared it on his trousers.

He got up and moved away. Jesus, what a mess. Winter ran towards the signals office. Part of it had been destroyed. He went through the door, and picked his way over the smouldering rubble. The bodies of two soldiers lay partially hidden. "Anyone around?" Winter shouted.

"Ja, sir. Over here!"

From under a table a corporal emerged, covered in concrete dust and shaken. "What's happening, sir?" he asked.

"Rockets," said Winter briefly. "Is there a radio working?"

The Corporal looked round. "God," he said. "I don't know. Let's have a look." He flicked some switches on a transceiver, checked connections and the power supply, and the radio hummed back into life. The Corporal turned to Winter: "If the aerials are still up, this might be OK," he said.

He tested it and got a reply immediately. The Corporal gave the handset to Colonel Winter. Outside the explosions continued sporadically.

The six MIG-21s which had flashed over the camp, sneaking in under the South African radar, set course for Johannesburg, but three of them peeled off east of Pretoria to rocket the Air Force base there, while the others headed for the centre of Johannesburg, their targets being high-rise civilian buildings.

South African defences had not yet woken up to the threat. During the night the most significant intelligence information had been received at Silvermine, where the computers showed a marked reduction in the arms and explosives ratings of the border villages. Cabala village had reduced during the night from a rating of nine to only two. It was a similar story for the others. At first it was assumed some sort of withdrawal was in progress. But the real reason was soon to become clear. The T-54s were advancing, rumbling through the Kruger National Park under cover of the rocket bombardment.

Near Johannesburg's prestige Carlton Centre, a twenty-year-old beautician, Sonia Venter, was on her way to work when the three jets screamed out of the sky from nowhere. She stood in the street, shading her eyes and watching them bank in a tight turn. She couldn't help feeling proud. Whatever the rest of the world might say, it was good to be South African. The Defence Forces were the best in Africa. Look at those jets, she thought. It was beautiful to see.

The MIGs lined up a block of flats and offices in their sights, and their 23mm cannons began blasting off, pulverising windows, smashing into brick and concrete. Sonia Venter watched uncomprehending, the smile fading from her face. Everyone had stopped in the street and was staring at the three MIGs, flashing off into the distance, banking for another run-in, while smoke poured from windows on the thirtieth floor of the building.

On their second run, the MIGs each released two of their four 550lb bombs, which crashed into streets and a shopping arcade, exploding in balls of yellow flame, sending shrapnel slicing into groups of fleeing shoppers. Sonia Venter and the others began to run as the MIGs, flying low, headed straight for them. The concussion from a blast knocked her sideways, and she felt the searing heat, then something hard crashed into the small of her back and she died as the breath was knocked out of her.

On their third run, the MIGs released their last bombs, sending them smashing through the roofs of a supermarket and two department stores, others landing in the streets. Palls of smoke rose over Johannesburg. A dozen people were trapped in the supermarket as fire raged around them. They huddled behind a display of canned food to keep away from the flames, and slowly, from their crouching position, toppled onto their faces, overcome by carbon monoxide.

The MIGs turned away, just enough fuel left to get home. There was still no sign of the South African Air Force. The order to scramble had just been given, and the first Mirage F1 supersonic fighters were only just lifting off the runways at bases miles away.

In the streets there was pandemonium. Traffic jammed for blocks around the attacked area. Fire engines and ambulances battled to get through to the wounded. Many of those who could, ran to get away, knocking into others, pushing and shouting. The injured lay where they had fallen; some waiting quietly, pale and shocked, others crying out in pain. Beside them, passers by knelt, some to give comfort, others to try and stop the bleeding where they could. Some prayed.

The MIGs got back to Mozambique unscathed, still flying below the level of the radar wherever they could, while the Mirages pursued them. At the border, MIG reinforcements came out of the sun, challenging the F1s, and the jets ducked and weaved for position. A K-13 Atoll anti-aircraft missile flashed from the wing of a MIG, connected with an F1's fuselage, and blew the South African fighter out of the sky.

At the camp near Chicundu, the bombardment continued without pause, and to the east, the T-54s rumbled deeper into South African territory. Most of the camp's wounded had been evacuated, and retaliatory flights of Mirages and Buccaneers streaked towards Mozambique to pound the known guerrilla camps. South African tanks, Centurions and Comets, headed into the Kruger National Park to take up positions and challenge the invading Cubans.

In Pretoria, an emergency call-up of all reserves was announced, and men scrambled into their cars and headed for the nearest military bases. By two o'clock in the afternoon there wasn't a seat to be had on any flight out of South Africa, or any boat, for the next two months. Those who had not been called up, together with women and children, were trying to flee to safety. The roads to the north were also jammed, but when the whites got to the border they were told it had been closed. Across the frontier was no longer Rhodesia, but black-ruled Zimbabwe. They no longer had friends on their borders.

The MIGs which had pounded the Air Force base at Pretoria had killed twelve men and destroyed two Mirage F1s on the ground. There was structural damage to a number of buildings.

Courtney in his office heard none of it – the base was several miles away.

The first three South African Comet tanks made contact with the advancing Cubans as they pushed forward through the Kruger National Park, up a sharp rise. Ahead they saw a solitary T-54. It immediately stopped, and they saw it begin to reverse away. The Comets pushed forward in pursuit, closing on the Cuban, but the T-54 kept reversing over the brow of the hill. Suddenly it stopped, and coming up the hill all around them were other T-54s, completely encircling the three Comets. They'd driven straight into a trap.

The South African tank commander shouted: "Oh Jesus!" An armour-piercing shell smashed into his tank, and it erupted in a ball of flame and burned out. The other Comets opened up in reply, dodging, trying to manoeuvre. They scored two hits on the Cubans and then, engines roaring, headed out of the trap for safety, firing as they went.

In Pretoria, the joint emergency meeting of the State Security Council and the Defence Staff Council broke up after two o'clock. The Prime Minister went to prepare a nationwide address and an ultimatum. The Minister of Defence came back to his office and summoned Bosman and Courtney.

De Wet outlined the military position as far as it was known. Bosman then brought him up to date about the rising civilian casualty toll. Eighty people had died in the first two hours, all but two of them whites. Two hundred others were in hospital, twelve in intensive care and unlikely to survive.

169

"After all our preparations," de Wet said sombrely, "we were caught asleep. This is a bad day. There have been serious gaps in our intelligence and our defensive plans."

"What happens now, Minister?" Bosman asked.

De Wet shrugged: "We have a choice, as you know," he said. "In the first place, we could dig in and fight. We are well equipped. We don't have the logistics problems that the Cubans do, but it would take weeks, probably months to secure victory. The Cubans don't have any misapprehensions about the task before them. They know they can't defeat us militarily – not at the moment. So they're trying to inflict other damage on us."

Courtney asked: "What sort of damage, Minister?"

"Economic," said de Wet. "Who will invest in a South Africa at war with the communists? Even with sanctions, people still find ways of investing. Also damage to morale. They want whites to think they're going to be driven out of here eventually. They want them to leave voluntarily now, as many as they can get. This is proved by the targets they went for this morning. What strategic importance is a shopping centre in Joburg? Or a department store? None at all. They're just trying to undermine confidence."

There was a long pause. De Wet studied his hands. Then he looked up at the two men. "So that's the one choice facing us – fight it out, regardless of the damage to the economy, regardless of the cost in lives and equipment. The other choice is that we say, here and now: that's enough. Go no further." He stopped again, and went across to the window, looking out through the net curtains down at the street several floors below.

"We have made our decision," de Wet said. "It has not been easy, and it is a gamble. It could have catastrophic consequences, but we are prepared to risk them."

"Operation Dingaan." Bosman's voice was unemotional.

De Wet nodded. "Dingaan," he said. "The Battle of Blood River again."

Courtney looked bewildered from one to the other. "I don't understand," he said at last. "What's Operation Dingaan?"

The Minister glanced across at him. "It's still Top Secret," he said, "but at seven o'clock tonight everybody will know, so I may as well tell you now. South Africa has developed her own nuclear

missiles. We're going to use them. If the Cubans haven't with-
drawn from our territory by midnight tonight, there'll be nuclear
war."

Courtney drew his breath in sharply and he knew the
blood had drained from his face. "Jesus Christ," he said,
awed.

"You see why it's a gamble," de Wet said. "We're challenging
the Russians with all *their* nuclear might. They could wipe out
most of South Africa if they were determined enough. They
might even do it. If we did destroy those black cities we have on
our list, what's to stop Russia coming in and wiping out ours?
Once we've dropped our bombs, we've played our last card. All
we can do then is wait and hope."

Courtney felt he was in the middle of a nightmare. "What
about America?" he asked. "Wouldn't America intervene?"

"That's what we're counting on," de Wet replied simply.
"America putting on pressure to get the Cubans out. And the
countries themselves: Mozambique and Tanzania. They're the
ones who'll be clobbered first. Mozambique in particular as the
host country for the Cubans."

The men sat in silence again. Then de Wet said: "Well, we
may as well prepare ourselves for tonight."

Bosman and Courtney stood up and left the Minister's office
without a word. In the ante-room his secretary had a radio on,
and the warnings had already begun. "Here is a special announcement. A broadcast of major national importance will be
made by the Prime Minister at seven o'clock tonight on both
radio and television. You are asked to make every effort to listen
to it, as it concerns the safety of us all. I will repeat that special
announcement . . ."

Bosman and Courtney passed into the corridor and walked
slowly down.

"What do you think?" Courtney asked.

Bosman shrugged: "As the Minister says, it's a gamble. Either
it pays off, or there's a nuclear holocaust. But if it does pay off,
then the nation will be safe from foreign invasion."

"What do you mean?"

"Just that South Africa formally becomes a member of the
nuclear club. It's been suspected for years that we've been

developing our own nuclear weapons, but we've always denied it. Now they'll know. Politics in Africa will change irreversibly. Ja, there'll be a hairy year or so, and some other nations might also get the bomb, although I'm sure the West will do what it can to limit proliferation. But just as we have with the Super Powers, there'll be the balance of terror in Africa. We'll all just have to learn to live with it, and the Cubans and others will think twice before attacking us."

"If we ever reach that point," Courtney said. "The Minister admits that if we use the bomb, the Russians might retaliate. But what about before midnight? What's to stop the Russians from launching a pre-emptive strike?"

Bosman nodded. "It's technically possible, of course. There might be nuclear missiles heading for South Africa right now, and they'd arrive before the deadline. But we don't think the Russians will do that."

"Why not?"

"Because their intelligence is too good. Or at least, we hope it's good and accurate, as far as our general computer structure is concerned. They must know that any nuclear strike we launch will be controlled from Silvermine, and even if one of their nuclear devices landed smack on the roof of Silvermine, it wouldn't make any difference to our attack capability."

"But surely we can't be sure of that?" Courtney insisted.

"Not to the extent that it's ever been put to the test, naturally," Bosman said. "But a model of a nuclear attack has been fed into computers, together with the Silvermine structure, and according to the figures the place is proof against the worst the Russians or anyone else can throw at us. So they have to work on the presumption that they can't stop the computers ordering an attack. This leaves them with one other alternative: destroy the South African devices themselves. First of all, they'd have to know exactly how many we've got and where they are. If they had that knowledge, they'd also know our missile launchers are mobile, so not only do they have to cope with breaking through the defences of our established missile sites, but they also have to track accurately all the mobile missile launchers, and hope like hell we haven't got nuclear devices fixed to any of our Air Force jets. The cards are stacked against them. The only point in launching a pre-emptive strike evaporates when you examine the problems they'd face."

"I see what you mean."

"No, Captain, our problem will come if we do drop the bombs. Then we can expect immediate retribution. But if we get through the next couple of days we'll be out of the woods. Your time will be spent persuading South Africans about our future stability and prospects."

Courtney smiled mirthlessly. "I suppose it could be done," he said, "but let's wait and see. It might all be academic."

Bosman nodded. "It certainly might," he said.

TWENTY-TWO

The Prime Minister came straight to the point.

"South Africa has suffered grievously," he said, his voice ponderous, his accent thick. Behind him hung the country's coat of arms. The television camera zoomed in on his face. "Eighty civilians are dead, the victims of cowardly attacks by the communist invaders. One hundred and seventeen of our soldiers and pilots have also died. The invasion, spearheaded by Cuban troops using MIG jet fighters and Russian tanks, was unprovoked, and it began without warning today. We intend to end it *tomorrow*."

The Prime Minister stared wrathfully into the camera: "South Africa is our country," he said. "We will not leave it. We are strong, economically and militarily. Sanctions make little difference to us, to our values, and to our way of life. But some whites *are* leaving, emigrating elsewhere, because they.fear that somehow we will not survive. It is on this fear that the communists are preying.

"Let us look at what happened today. This morning, we learned from Mozambique Radio that the government of

Mozambique had closed the borders with South Africa and declared a state of war between our two countries. We have still not been told of this officially.

"At the same time, six MIG-21 jets, Russian built, violated South Africa's airspace. Three of them attacked an air base near Pretoria, killing twelve of our men, and the other three went on to stage a cowardly attack on civilians in Johannesburg. Why civilians? The answer is simple: they want to make South Africans panic, to get them to leave. They think that if enough whites go, this country of ours will be a prize more easily attainable.

"How wrong they are! We in South Africa are going nowhere. But they – the communists, the Cubans – *are* going: they're going back home. I will explain to you how this will be done.

"Messages similar to the one I am now giving you have already been sent to the governments of the United States of America, Soviet Russia, the United Kingdom, France, West Germany, and, of course, Cuba, although we believe their troops are in fact controlled from Moscow. The messages have also gone to our African neighbours – Mozambique, Tanzania, Zimbabwe and Zambia.

"We have in the past," the Prime Minister went on, "told the world about a unique process for uranium enrichment which we have developed. As scientists elsewhere deduced, it was an adaptation of the jet nozzle method of enrichment, invented in the Federal Republic of Germany by Professor Becker. I do not propose going into too much detail, except to say that the benefits of an atomic and nuclear programme have been clear to South Africa for many years. Our first uranium plant was opened in 1952. Our first atomic reactor was built at Pelindaba in the Transvaal under the United States 'atoms for peace' programme, and in 1967 our second reactor, Safari Two, was also opened at Pelindaba. Our engineers and nuclear scientists have undergone thorough training overseas, both at Oak Ridge in the United States, and at research establishments in West Germany. We are conversant with the problems and the potential of our atomic and nuclear programmes.

"We started off with atoms for peace; and we have diversified into atoms for war. In plain language, we in South Africa have developed our own nuclear bomb. And not just one: we have many.

174

"We are members of the world's nuclear club. This may come as a surprise to many of you, but it is not a surprise to other Western nations. They have long suspected that we have this power at our command.

"And, ladies and gentlemen, it is not a power that is subject to international sanctions, that will be whittled away by the latest embargoes. No, sanctions couldn't matter less. The uranium we use is South African. Our scientists and technicians are South African. Our enrichment process, though an adaptation, has become essentially South African. We have refused to sign the non-proliferation treaty, on the grounds that we cannot rely on other nations to come to our aid in times of trouble, and that when we show the iron fist in the velvet glove, we must control both fist and glove! We now have access to our own concentrated fission material which is subject to no international control.

"This does not mean we will be irresponsible in our use of our nuclear potential. Far from it. We have no aggressive intentions towards any other country. Only defensive. I repeat – only defensive."

The Prime Minister paused and took off his glasses. He polished the lens of one on a white handkerchief and the silence grew. John Courtney, watching on a television set in the Department of Defence building, felt himself holding his breath.

"Why am I telling you this?" the Prime Minister asked. "I am giving you the background to the messages which I have sent to our aggressors, our enemies, and even – I dare to say – our friends, for we *have* friends in the international community.

"The message is an ultimatum. We in South Africa will not tolerate the presence on our soil of foreign aggressors – they're not even African aggressors, ladies and gentlemen, they're aggressors from many thousands of miles away. We will not tolerate them killing our soldiers, murdering our civilians. And we will not tolerate those who harbour them, who give them the bases from which to stage their cowardly attacks. Without these bases, there would be no attacks.

"An ultimatum, I said: and it is this. The government of the Republic of South Africa requires that all foreign aggressors withdraw from its territory, with their weapons, by midnight tonight. That is," the Prime Minister looked at his watch, "in less than five hours from now. For the purposes of the withdrawal, a ceasefire will come into effect at ten o'clock, South African time. If there is one single Cuban still on South African territory as an aggressor after midnight, then the Republic of South Africa reserves the right to use, without further notice or warning, her own nuclear devices against those countries who harbour and support the aggressors. This ultimatum is particularly – but not exclusively – aimed at Mozambique and Tanzania.

"Let me be even more blunt than this," the Prime Minister said. "Unless the Cubans withdraw before midnight, we will wipe Maputo off the map of Mozambique. We will destroy Dar-es-Salaam, and I mean destroy it totally. We will have no mercy and no pity. We will destroy other cities too. It's not just Mozambique and Tanzania who are responsible for today's ghastly events. Other countries near our borders are accomplices. They know who they are. Let them not doubt that we have the power. We are not bluffing. This is a warning, more solemn than any I have ever given. If it is not heeded, the consequences for the countries concerned will be tragic and catastrophic.

"The government of South Africa calls on all those who love peace, who want to avoid nuclear conflict in Africa – as we do – to persuade the Russians, the Cubans, the Mozambiqueans and the Tanzanians to think again: and to think quickly.

"There is not much time. Messages have to be sent out to the Cuban forces from their commanders, and the troops then have to be back inside Mozambique before midnight. If they are not, God help those who are their hosts. Their cities will be reduced to deserts. Millions of their people will be killed. The blame will lie at their own door.

"I just want to end," the Prime Minister said, "with this assurance.

"South Africa wants no more than to live with its neighbours in a spirit of friendship and co-operation. We will not interfere in the internal affairs of others, and we demand that they do not interfere in our own internal affairs. And to South Africans I say this: we will fight, and we will win. We are here to stay – all of us.

"Tonight we have become a nuclear power. Goodnight."

The effect of the Prime Minister's speech was electric. Jubilant white crowds gathered in the streets, dancing and singing, as if

176

victory had already been won, not realising that the holocaust could turn on them, too.

Orders for the ten o'clock ceasefire went out to all South African defence force personnel. Although night had fallen, fighting continued along the border area, right down to Natal. Most of the Cuban T-54s had pushed between twenty and twenty-five miles inside South Africa, and during the afternoon they were being given heavy air and rocket support. Now, with darkness, progress was slower.

Rockets and mortars fell on Colonel Winter's camp, and on the town of Chicundu – each one giving a high-pitched whistle lasting less than three seconds, enough to warn people of its approach, but not enough time for them to take cover, and then the flash, the blast, and jagged shrapnel singing through the air.

A tank burned in the Kruger National Park, setting light to the grass around, so that it was silhouetted against the skyline, with fire stretching on both sides, burning fiercely.

South African riflemen had dug in, waiting to see if Cuban infantry was to be deployed against them, but there was none. The foot soldiers were black guerrillas, already deep inside the country, and this night was the signal for them to draw their weapons from hiding places and attack.

Jan Rousseau, as he lay on the ground, still naked and in pain, in the Mozambique hut which was his prison, had forgotten about the sensors and the booby traps he had laid in the hidden place atop a kopje in Northern Natal, where a cache of arms was stored. The Silvermine computer had monitored the place day and night since he discovered it, but nothing had happened.

Tonight, however, the infra-red sensor buried in grass at the base of a boulder recorded a change, and computer analysis showed it as the presence of three or four men. The computer's emergency buzzer sounded and the duty commanders at Silvermine hurried over to see what had happened. The sensor configuration at this particular kopje would first have recorded only the presence of armed men going into the passageway where the cache was buried. But this early warning sniffer had shown nothing. The terrorists were therefore unarmed, and had presumably gone to collect weapons rather than deposit more. This would be the moment to strike.

The commanders looked at each other. "Let's do it," one said. He gave an instruction to a programmer, who typed a coded message on a computer keyboard.

He checked it and looked around. "OK to go, sir?" he asked.

"Ja, go."

The programmer pressed a key.

Nearly a thousand miles away four guerrillas were crowded into the narrow hidden space on the side of the kopje. Two of them were on their hands and knees. They had scooped the dirt out of the hole and were beginning to lift up the Kalashnikovs and hand them to their comrades, when the remote control device on the gelignite underneath the cache received the command from the computer and detonated.

The side of the kopje, rocks and all, catapulted into the air. A fiery ball roared out and lit the night. Grass and trees caught ablaze, and fire ate its way down into the dry grassland.

At Silvermine, the programmer announced: "No further readings from any of the sensors in that configuration, sir."

The commanders nodded, and turned back to monitor other readings.

A group of guerrillas crept up to a white farmhouse outside the town of Louis Trichardt. The lights were on. They waited quietly. Inside they could see the farmer moving about, and his wife too. The guerrillas went up to the front door and knocked: not the timid knock of a servant, but the assertive knock of a white man. They stood and waited. Inside they could hear a dog begin to bark. Soon there was the shadow of a man behind the opaque glass in the door and the guerrillas raised their Kalashnikovs. As it swung open, they fired, pumping round after round into the farmer, even after he'd fallen, and then they ran into the lounge where the woman was reaching desperately into a desk drawer for a weapon, and they shot her. The dog, shut in another room, barked wildly. The guerrillas left the house and ran out.

In Pretoria, Mrs Nellie du Toit, a widow, was sitting by herself watching television when the glass of her lounge window shattered and a hand-grenade crashed onto her floral carpet. Mrs du Toit picked it up and threw it back out into the garden. It did not explode. Police found later that in the excitement of the attack, the pin had not been pulled.

But the Williams family, four blocks away, were burned alive. Petrol bombs crashed into their home, the fuel erupting with a fierce whooooosh sound, curtains and bedding catching alight immediately, furniture quickly aflame. Hearing screams from the children's rooms, Mr and Mrs Williams raced in to rescue their young son and daughter, whose pyjamas were on fire. They rolled the children in their eiderdowns to put out the flames, and then tried to get out of the house. The windows were all burglar barred. Their exits were blocked by fierce flames and heat. They died with the children sobbing in their arms.

Plastic explosives toppled power pylons and railway signal boxes. A parcel bomb, left outside a Johannesburg restaurant, exploded without killing anyone. But it blew the arms off a young policeman who had gone to pick it up.

Rockets and mortars still rained down on the army camps and towns in the border area. It was half past nine. In thirty minutes, the South Africans would cease fire. But would the Cubans?

Whatever intense international diplomatic activity there was in other places of the world, the fighting in Eastern Transvaal and Northern Natal showed no sign of abating, and elsewhere, in towns and cities, guerrillas pressed their attacks.

Ten o'clock, and the order went out to cease fire. It was as if nothing had happened. The Cubans were using Stalin Organs again – the multiple rocket-launchers which sent off volleys of 122mm missiles for saturation bombing. The night erupted into balls of flame and fierce explosions. If anything, the level of aggression had increased.

In Pretoria, Courtney, Bosman and the Minister de Wet sat monitoring reports from the forward areas, their faces more and more concerned.

At ten-thirty, they learned that T-54 tanks were moving forward again, deeper into South African territory.

De Wet shook his head: "It's not working. They're calling our bluff."

Courtney asked quietly: "Is it a bluff?"

De Wet shook his head. "No, we're deadly serious. They just

don't believe us." The men sipped cups of coffee and waited. The minutes ticked slowly by.

In the Eastern Transvaal, the observer in a Centurion tank watched a T-54 edge up over the skyline, clearly visible in silhouette on this bright, moonlit night. The Centurion's gun turned and dipped, until the T-54 was a sitting duck. If there had not been a ceasefire, it would have been destroyed in seconds, but the South African, under orders, waited for it to try and press on past him, or make the first aggressive move.

Suddenly the T-54 turned around on its tracks and moved away quickly. The Centurion followed it for a few yards, but the Russian tank was heading east, and two others were going with it.

Elsewhere, similar reports came in. At last the Cubans were retreating, back towards the border. The South Africans followed them out, keeping their distance, but the Cubans did not stop.

By twenty minutes past midnight, they were all back inside Mozambique.

The mortar and rocket bombardment continued right up until midnight, and then it, too, suddenly cut out.

In the silence, the soldiers waited.

In Pretoria, John Courtney felt like weeping with relief. It had worked, dear Jesus. It was over.

News of the retreat was on the radio at half past midnight, and white jubilation in the streets was unbounded. Sounds of singing carried for blocks. People cheered and waved bottles of beer, whisky and champagne. Cars hooted as if it were New Year.

The black townships were quiet. Only armed policemen were on the streets.

TWENTY-THREE

Even the Muzak sounded good. Courtney sat in the restaurant bar waiting for André Tessler, and grinned. Above his head the tiny light-bulbs, recessed in the dark blue ceiling, shone like stars. The indoor plants – delicious monsters, trailing vines, ferns, and a palm – almost completely covered the whole of one wall, and smaller plants were scattered in tubs through the bar. Courtney sipped his Scotch. Behind the sunfilter curtains, it was a lovely day.

A voice said: "John, sorry we're late. Good to see you." Courtney swung round to greet Tessler, and saw he had brought Ron Prentice from the agency. The men shook hands and ordered drinks.

"I knew you wouldn't mind me bringing Ron along," Tessler said breezily. "He's been handling the Nu-Kreem account. I thought he could fill you in on how it's going."

"Oh Christ," said Courtney. "Of course. I'd almost forgotten. Best feed your baby. It seems like a long time ago."

"Couple of months, that's all," Prentice replied.

"How's it getting on?"

"Fine," said Prentice. "Nu-Kreem are very pleased so far. Of course it's early days. We've only really been pushing for six weeks or so, but the sales figures are very promising."

"That's great," said Courtney. "How are the nanny girl nurses doing?"

Prentice grinned. "Fine. Everyone thinks they're qualified. Some of them have mothers bringing sick piccanins along for them to treat. We've told them not to do it, but it's human nature, isn't it? I hear one of them's got a nice sideline going in herbal medicine: crushed berries, dried leaves, that sort of thing."

"Bloody hell," said Courtney. "I'm glad it's not my problem."

Tessler broke in: "You're doing very well for yourself in the army I hear. Where's your uniform?"

"Oh, I don't have to bother with that any more."

"My brother tells me you're a captain. Congratulations," Tessler said.

"Thanks," Courtney replied. "But I'm still in advertising really."

Prentice laughed: "Just what are you trying to sell, John?" he asked. "Join the army reserve for twelve months?"

Courtney shook his head. "I'm selling South Africa, I suppose. To the bantu, I'm saying: God help you if you don't help us. To the whites, I'm saying: Don't leave. You're safe here."

"Are you going to launch a campaign?" Tessler asked, interested.

"Maybe later. At the moment, I'm advising the Minister of Defence on what line he should take, the things he should say, to give whites more confidence."

"Jesus," said Tessler. "You've got your work cut out, John. Admit it, man, we're in a whole new ball game, and I don't mind telling you, I'm very worried."

"What about? The bomb?" asked Courtney.

Tessler shook his head. "No, the bomb's a good thing, I suppose. It'll keep the Cubans out, although I don't suppose it will stop terrorism. The thing I'm worried about is the economy and sanctions. The agency feels these things immediately, long before the rest of the country, and even with the Nu-Kreem account, we're in a bad way. It's just going to get worse and worse. I think the time has come for political change. A lot of people are feeling that apartheid just isn't working now, and we're going to have to start sharing things out a bit more fairly. Simple economics tells us that. We can't defy sanctions indefinitely. I know the government says they won't make any difference, but do you believe that? I don't. I think the economy is very rocky, and if we're not careful, it's going to collapse. What we have to do is make the changes necessary so that the rest of the world can let us back in, and forget about sanctions. And that means at least some political change."

Courtney shook his head. "I disagree entirely," he said. "Do you want another whisky, by the way?" Courtney ordered a round. "Ja, sanctions *are* going to make a difference. Things will get tighter, as you say, and the agency is going to feel it as badly as everyone else. And all right, I agree people are going to have to pull in their belts a bit, but let's get it into perspective. What do we mean when we talk about a white man pulling in his belt? I'll tell you. We mean his waist used to be thirty-eight inches, and it's going down to thirty-seven, or thirty-six. Big deal. If anyone suffers from sanctions, it's going to be the blacks, but our problem isn't blacks leaving the country, it's them coming in – migrant labour. What real difference are sanctions going to make to us? Petrol rationing, ja. But hell, we've got a five-year stockpile right now, totally ignoring what we're producing at Sasol One and Two. Look at Rhodesia!"

"Rhodesia's black now," Tessler reminded him.

"Sure it is," Courtney agreed, "but how long did that take? A decade and a half? Let's look at Rhodesia and sanctions. Who were these people, standing out against the United Nations? I'll tell you who. There were eighty thousand whites in Salisbury. You could fit them into a good sized football stadium, and a lot of them would get in at half price because they were kids. Eighty thousand. About the same number as the staff of Ford in Britain. And in the whole country? A quarter of a million, that's all. The size of the staff of ICI world-wide. And Jesus, what were the odds against them? They had six million blacks – they were outnumbered twenty-five to one. They didn't even have a seaport. And they held out for years and years. Sure their economy contracted, but it didn't crumble. If that's the case, what are we to think about South Africa? What's the black-white ratio here? Six to one? Look, man, we're virtually self-sufficient. We've got the world's largest gold reserves, more coal than we know what to do with, uranium, our own bloody nuclear bomb, and half of the world's production of diamonds. That's before we even start thinking about chrome and things like that. We've got four major seaports and a lot of others that are being developed quickly. And we've got our security laws: if the blacks get too far out of hand, we can order them all into the bantu areas and cordon them off: let them kill themselves in there." Courtney took a drink of his whisky. "Is South Africa going to change?" he asked. "Ja, of course, but not in the way you're talking about. We're going to change by battening down the hatches, by getting tougher, not softer, by becoming more self-confident and assertive."

Tessler sighed. "I don't think I like the sound of that."

"Why not?" Courtney demanded. "It's not going to make a lot of difference to your life. If a new law comes in putting suspected terrorist sympathisers in solitary confinement for a year at a time without trial and without seeing their lawyers, how many people do you know personally who are going to be picked up? Not one. Your life will go on pretty much as it always did."

Ron Prentice was watching Courtney closely. He shook his head and grinned. "I'd never have believed it," Prentice said. "What the army's done for you. The way you've changed in the past few weeks. What happened to the agency liberal?"

Courtney gave a short, half-embarrassed laugh. "I suppose he's still down there somewhere," he said.

"Pretty well hidden," Prentice said. "You sound like one of us."

"What does that make me?" Tessler asked. "Who do I sound like?"

Prentice rounded on his boss, still grinning. "André, you sound like John did before he went into the army. The liberal conscience of Van Niekerk and Tessler."

"Not very liberal," Courtney said.

"No," Prentice agreed. "But as liberal as we like people to be in South Africa. A soft-line liberal. A bit wishy-washy."

"That's not very flattering," Tessler said.

"Oh I don't know," said Prentice, amiably. "There's a lot to be said for it. People like you can have it both ways: you keep your conscience but you also keep your way of life. You look for change, but you stay out of trouble. When elections come, you either vote for a liberal who doesn't stand a chance, or if you think he does have a chance, you'll be too busy to get to the polling booth that day. You'll live comfortably to a ripe old age, and you'll die with your morals intact. Men like John and me will fight the good fight for you."

Tessler's face was flushed and angry. "I think that's bloody rude, Ron," he said. "Let's go and eat."

They stood up and Prentice said easily: "Oh hell, André, don't take it so personally. I was only kidding." Then in an aside to Courtney, Prentice added quietly: "But not much."

They walked through to the dining-room. Luigi shepherded

them to their table and handed round the leather-bound menus. Courtney said to him: "Luigi, this is a special occasion. It calls for champagne."

"Certainly, Mr Courtney," Luigi said. "French or South African?"

"Do you still have any French?"

"Oh yes, Mr Courtney. Moët et Chandon? Bollinger? What would you like?"

"We'll have the Bollinger. Using up your old stocks, I suppose?"

"Oh no, sir," Luigi said. He lowered his voice conspiratorially. "Between ourselves, gentlemen, it's a new consignment. Our first since sanctions. I'm sorry it's more expensive, but now we have to pay a middle-man."

Courtney laughed. "There, André," he said, "what did I tell you? Sanctions are going to be a joke."

Tessler shrugged. "I hope you're right, John."

The champagne helped restore Tessler's temper and the lunch ended cheerfully.

Afterwards, Courtney walked the few blocks back to his flat. Moira would be at work. He still hadn't contacted her. Maybe he'd just leave another note, and get back to Pretoria before dark. He'd got the phone number of a girl at the Department of Defence: he might give her a try this evening. Courtney whistled tunelessly to himself.

It was a beautiful afternoon: a bright, cloudless sky and a breeze. Courtney felt on top of the world.